RECKLESS
Secrets

Gina Robinson

Gina Robinson
SEATTLE, WASHINGTON

For my college sweetheart

CHAPTER ONE

＼

My bitch of a mother has kept a secret for nineteen years. A secret from me that I should have known from the very beginning, even before I was conscious of what it meant. A secret from my father. From my grandparents. From everyone. A secret that had blossomed over the years to such epic proportions that it now threatened my very happiness. Everything good in my life was hanging on one delicate silver strand of a web of deception. While I dangled helplessly at the end of it like a spider in the wind. At the mercy of fate and the truth.

If I had known the truth, my life would have been different. Would it have been better? There was no way to know. In any case, I wouldn't have been here, fighting for the love of my life against increasingly mounting odds.

I balled my fist and pounded the concrete step I sat on in front of my dorm, huddling against not just the cold air, but raw, cold, staggering emotion. My selfish, ultra-competitive mom had kept me from joy and a happy childhood. And dragged me through her three miserable marriages and countless other horrid relationships. Through three mostly bastards of stepdads and no real dad. Certainly no loving dad. I was no one's little princess.

All the while Mom played the evil queen to my Snow White, always striving to prove she was the fairest of them all. Fairer than I was, in any case. But then, I hadn't tried. I had never wanted to compete with her. So I made myself plain and invisible.

But a one-sided competition didn't stop her. She went after my boyfriend. Slept with him. Destroyed the best of her three marriages when my latest stepdad and I walked in on Mom and Austin making the sign of the two-humped whale on Mom's living room sofa. That was a sight I still couldn't fully get out of my mind.

Her ultimate betrayal sent me running to unravel her secret—who was my biological father? Why had she refused, all these years, to tell me, or anyone, who he was?

I had been hoping I had at least one biological parent who wasn't a complete skank. I just hadn't known tearing apart the deception would be like unleashing the evils of Pandora's box. Now, like Pandora, all I had left was a sense of hope, and even that was ebbing.

I wondered—without her lie, would I have ended up in this same spot, here at the same university? Would I be the person I am? Would I have met Logan? And fallen in love with him?

I blinked back tears, wiping them away with the back of my hand as I sat alone on the steps to the courtyard that conjoined my dorm with its twin. In the cold of a clear November morning, I held my cell phone in front of me.

After spending the night with Logan, I should have been ecstatic and glowing, not scared out of my mind that I would lose him. I touched my lips, still feeling the tingle of his kiss on them, longing for the heat of his body next to mine again.

I love you, El. I pictured the way he'd looked last night when he told me and my heart broke and the phone trembled in my hand.

Would I sacrifice his love, put it at risk, for a chance to get to know my father? Being fresh from Logan's bed clouded my judgment. But I was in too deep now. I couldn't back out, not even if I wanted to. My only salvation would be if Jason didn't want any relationship with me now that we knew he was really my dad. Then maybe we could sweep this all away and no one would ever be the wiser. But that would break my heart, too. And prove that I had two horrible parents. Biologically, I'd be doomed.

I'd tracked Jason Front, the only suspect in my paternity, to this university. Transferred here from a perfectly good college across the state. Gotten a student job that I really needed to stay in school working for him in the university IT department so I could study him and decide whether I wanted to reveal myself as his potential daughter.

Logan had simply fallen into the equation, another victim of fate. I met him the week before class at a Week of Welcome event in the most adorable way possible—when he played my support person while I got my bellybutton pierced. I tried not to fall for him. I tried not to ever see him again after that first night. Was it my fault that he worked for Jason, too? That he was Jason's favorite? I'd been as surprised as anyone when Logan strolled into the IT office on my first day of work and sent my heart beating out of control.

What was I supposed to do then, when I'd only just met Logan and all there was between us was a spark of something wonderful—walk away from the job I desperately needed to stay in school? Leave the chance for the dad I'd been longing for my whole life?

I hadn't meant to use Logan. I *hadn't* used Logan, not on purpose. He'd known all semester I was keeping a secret from him. I had told him I was and he was fine with it. But would he be when he found out what that secret was? Or would he feel like I'd used him all along?

My deceit was all so accidental. The situation just evolved until I was in too deep to tell him the truth. And now when Logan was so vulnerable and just starting to heal from his ordeal and when he loved me, now I was standing on a life-changing precipice where everything could go terribly wrong.

I glanced at the text I'd gotten from Jason last night while I was still in Logan's bed.

I got the results. Looks like I'm the one. Don't share this with anyone. We need to talk.

Would Logan resent my new relationship with Jason, my blood bond? Or would there be no relationship? Jason could just as well tell me to get the hell out of his life for good. He could reject me like all my mom's other men. I could lose Logan and my father.

A chill wind kicked up. I held the collar of my cute wool coat, the Kate Middleton knock-off, closed to block the wind, but shivered anyway. My legs were bare. I had refused Logan's offer of a shacker shirt and loaner sweats. I wore my short black and white polka-dot dress and cute strappy heels from going out to dinner with Logan and his dad the night before. My hair was tousled and my makeup smudged. I looked every bit the mess I was.

After Mom slept with Austin, I did something desperate. I tore up the house, looking for her private diary, the one she had supposedly kept when I was conceived and born. I hadn't even known if it still—or ever had—existed. My grandma had mentioned it once casually in passing. I had looked for it several times over the years with no success. But after her betrayal, I was a woman possessed. And I got lucky.

I found it and a single clue—a name in her diary. *Ellie's father must be Jason Front.*

That was all the ink she dedicated to him. All the information she revealed, even to her private self. You can see why I was leery about him—why couldn't my mess of a mother say more? What if he was even worse than my stepdads?

I was crazed. I left home and searched relentlessly for him, scouring the internet and tracking down leads. Finally I found him working as director of information technology at this university. He had no idea I even existed. No idea he was quite probably my daddy.

I was trying to assess what kind of a man he was and whether I wanted to reveal myself to him. If he was a douchebag like Mom, there really was no point. My life was messed up enough as it was. But as I got to know him, I quickly found out that everyone loved Jason. I did, too. He was a great guy with a pretty wife, a beautiful baby daughter, and a perfect life. Just when I decided I didn't want to screw it up for him and would continue to keep my existence a secret from him, he pulled a Mom on me. He caught me on a nanny cam while I was babysitting his daughter and telling her she was my sister.

He accused me of having some kind of daughter fantasy about him. So I confronted him with the truth and forced him to take a paternity test from a drugstore DNA kit. And now here I was on the Saturday of Dad's Weekend, surrounded by dads, in love with Logan, and the results were in.

Appropriate, really. Dad's Weekend of all times. I had just met Logan's dad. He was a complete ass in the fullest sense. But that's a big step, right? Being introduced to the dad.

And now I had a dad, too.

I stared at my cell phone. All I had to do was open the email from the DNA testing company, click on the link they'd sent, and read the results so I could see the irrefutable proof for myself. My hands trembled. I felt like I was made of ice and ready to shatter.

I steeled myself, brought up the email, took a deep breath, and clicked on the link provided, entering my password. I closed my eyes and prayed, though I wasn't sure for what. When I opened my eyes again, my hands were shaking so badly, I could barely read the results.

I was minoring in biology. I knew all about how paternity was figured, matching alleles in sixteen different DNA markers. I stared at the report. My DNA profile swam before my eyes.

Combined paternity index, CPI, which matched genetic markers, alleles—1,448,977. My heart stopped. *Probability of paternity—99.9999 percent.*

The alleged father, Jason Front, cannot be excluded as the biological father of the child, Ellie Martin. This paternity test excluded over 99.99% of the male population from the possibility of being the biological father of the child tested.

I dropped my phone into the folds of my coat in my lap, covered my face with my hands, and cried.

I sat there, crying, broken with emotion, as the morning wore into afternoon and people appeared on the sidewalk, stumbling out of the dorms and laughing. Enjoying their day. Going to lunch and pregame activities with their dads. *Their dads.* I had a dad. I'd always dreamed of having a dad. If I'd known from the beginning...

But now, knowing messed up our lives—his with his new wife and baby, mine with Logan.

Girls and their dads walked by and shot me anxious, sympathetic looks.

I heard the whispers: "Bad breakup, has to be. Poor thing. And on Dad's Weekend."

And maybe it was the beginning of one. After all he'd been through, Logan was so vulnerable. This was no time to add more doubt and emotional trauma to his plate. I had to pull myself together before the game. I'd promised Logan and his dad I'd go with them. His dad had bought us tickets on the fifty-yard line of the alumni side. We were supposed to tailgate at some big campus tailgate event before that. But first I had to meet Jason, *Dad*. We needed a plan to deal with this.

I replied to the text he'd sent me, saying we needed to meet. *When? Where?*

He replied immediately, like he'd been hovering with the phone in his hand waiting for my reply. *My office. In an hour?*

The clock tower chimed the hour. Noon. I texted back. *Give me an hour and a half.*

I needed time to shower and pull myself together.

Done. See you then.

The hour and a half both flew by and dragged on at the same time. I showered and dressed for the game in jeans and university logoed everything—football jersey, cap, sweatshirt, even down to my thong underwear. As I blow-dried my hair, it felt like I was moving in slow motion. Yet I was rushed as I applied my makeup.

My cell phone rang. I jumped. Logan was calling. I felt guilty already as I grabbed it.

"Hey." His voice had a sultry quality.

"Hi. Miss me already?" I asked, sounding way too happy just because the sound of his voice did that to me, yet at the same time trying to hide my nerves and my guilt.

"Yeah, that too." He had a grin in his voice that made my heart constrict and my lips curl into a smile almost against their will. "And calling with a slight change of plans. Dad wants to meet at the south entrance of the field house for the tailgate function at two instead of two thirty. Think you can swing arriving a half an hour early?"

I glanced at the alarm clock on my nightstand. That was cutting it close. Two only gave me half an hour with Jason. And there was so much to say...

Logan sensed my hesitation. "El?"

"Sorry. Just running behind and feeling rushed. That's cutting it close for me." I slid into my coat as I talked, grabbed my purse, and locked the door of my door room after me as I left.

"The old man has something up his sleeve, El, otherwise he wouldn't request an earlier audience."

I bit my lip as I let myself out of the dorm. The last thing I needed in my delicate emotional state was a run-in with Harlan Walker. "I'll give it my best shot. I'll try to be there. I have a few errands to run first."

"Okay. Fair enough. It's short notice. Text me if you're going to be late."

"Will do. Are you and Harlan going to any of the dad events while you wait?"

Logan laughed. "You mean like playing rec basketball or building a birdhouse together? My old man? Are you kidding?

"Collin, Zave, and I are tailgating in classic style—drinking heavily. I need the fortification if I'm going to be hanging with Dad the rest of the day."

The thought of Logan getting hammered before the game scared me just a little. Before I met him his drinking had gotten out of control after a labrum injury ended his college baseball career and dreams of the major leagues. His dad had been pissed about both. I pushed the worry aside. Logan could handle himself.

"A word of warning," Logan said, "keep your guard up. Dad will be itching for a fight with you today. You may have bested him last night, but he doesn't take losing lying down. You have his grudging respect, but that won't stop him. Dad plays dirty. Watch for a sucker punch."

"Thanks for the warning. Isn't that why I have you around, to protect me?"

He laughed again. "Yeah, El, I'll have your backside. But after twenty-one years Dad knows all my weak points. He's the king of the surprise attack."

My pulse raced as I rounded the corner to the open, pedestrian-only avenue we called the mall and the SUB came into view. "I'll be on guard. Gotta go." I slid my phone into my pocket, trying to compose myself.

Jason's office was in the computer science building, which was sandwiched on a hill between the student union building and the alumni entrance to the football stadium. People had already begun milling into the stadium for the afternoon game as I ducked into the quiet comp sci building like I was a spy off to a clandestine meeting.

As my heart raced, I hoped no one had seen me. Though I didn't know why I was so worried. Paranoia. I could have been one of the many computer geeks who would rather program than watch a football game. Must have been my guilty conscience. I felt almost nauseous.

Jason's text had given no indication how he felt about becoming a daddy twice in such a short amount of time. There was no *ha ha* in it to indicate joy or playfulness. I tried to console myself that people over thirty were weird about texts. They didn't know how to indicate emotion like they should. Everything came out serious, almost like a scolding.

Jason's baby Mia, my now confirmed half-sister, was only six months old. And here he was suddenly the dad of a bouncing nineteen-year-old, girl, too. For just a second, I wondered whether I should have brought a cigar with a pink band. Maybe that was too much. A pink balloon?

The IT department office was nearly dark and ominously silent as I approached it. The door was slightly ajar. Odd, because it was usually locked on the weekends. Jason had obviously opened it for me. Karen's desk was dark and so was mine. Jason's walled office was behind Karen's desk. His door was open and his light on. I slid into the main part of the IT office and closed the door behind me even though I felt like running in the opposite direction.

I hardly knew how I felt about this turn of events. I couldn't blame Jason if he was confused or angry, too. But that didn't mean I wanted to face him.

"Ellie?"

I jumped at the sound of his voice. "Yeah. It's me."

"Lock the door," he said. His voice was neutral and controlled.

Only he and Karen had keys. That secretive feeling washed over me again as I did what he asked, then went to his office. He was sitting in his desk chair staring at his computer screen. When I walked in, he looked awful, like he hadn't slept at all. There were bags under his eyes. If this had been a normal day in the office, I would have joked with him about Mia having a bad night. Instead, I stood hesitantly just inside the door.

"Come on in," he said, just like the first time I had met him—only he sounded a lot more tired than he'd been on that hectic first day of class. "I don't bite." He smiled, but it was obviously forced and tight at the corners. He looked uncertain as he studied me intently. "You know what my biggest fear as a parent is?"

I shook my head as I slid into the chair across the desk from him.

"Parenting a teenager." He tried to laugh, but it came out as more of a snort. "I thought I'd have years to gain experience and grow into the role."

"Don't sweat it. In another four months I'll be twenty." I forced myself to smile and sound jokey.

He smiled for real then, and there was admiration shining in his eyes, like he liked that I could joke about this sudden upheaval in our lives. "I don't even know when your birthday is."

"February twenty-fifth. You look awful," I said.

"As it turns out, mulling over the implications of a paternity test was worse than standing by helplessly while Lyssa gave birth." He made that snorting sound again. "February twenty-fifth." He sounded almost wondrous. He nodded, but it was like he was thinking and making a mental note of it. Or maybe he was counting backwards to the day, the one time he'd done it with my mom.

Yeah, that much I knew. He'd told me they'd only done it once.

I had a million questions I wanted to ask. I started with the most basic, phrasing it without accusing. "Does Lyssa know?"

He took a deep breath. "No. You and I made a deal. Until we decided together what to do..."

I nodded, but I felt sick. He didn't sound like he wanted Lyssa to know or that he cared to acknowledge me. Ignoring the whole situation was definitely one way of dealing with it. But it still hurt.

I took a deep breath, bit my lip, and nodded. "I don't want anything from you. That suing for college expenses, that was just to scare you into taking the paternity test." I had threatened him with a lawsuit to get him to take the damn test.

He looked sad. He nodded. "No, I know. I didn't think you were serious." He took another deep breath. "It's not that, Ellie. We promised each other to keep this just between us until we decided what to do." He

sighed and ran his hand through his hair. "It's complicated with Lyssa."

I nodded. I had known it would be. What woman
wanted to hear her baby was not the special first child
of her husband like she thought? Or that she was not
the woman who made her husband a daddy? And if she
ever met my mom, she'd really go crazy and wonder
what kind of a man she'd married. Like I said, Mom is
no prize. And I was willing to bet if Mom ever found
out about Lyssa, she'd make her life miserable.

"I want to help you, Ellie. I do. But we have to think
this through carefully. For one thing, there's your job."
Suddenly, Jason was all business. Maybe that was his
coping mechanism. "If the university finds out you're
my daughter, you can't work for me. It's their policy.
I've never heard of anyone getting around it." He
paused.

I knew that already. It was part of the risk. And
since Mom had frozen my college funds, I needed my
job.

"I have plenty of connections in other departments,
but mid-semester it will be difficult to find you something. All the positions are filled. It would be better, in
that regard, to wait until the new semester, or even
next fall for the new academic year."

What he said made sense, and was nothing I hadn't
thought of before when I was trying to decide whether
to reveal myself to him or not. But I sensed there was
more to it. "Will you be in trouble because of me?"

He hesitated. "I don't think so. I shouldn't be. Not
when the truth comes out."

"But you'll be embarrassed?"

He stared at me, obviously assessing me, looking like he didn't want to hurt me. "By the beautiful young woman you've become? No."

He was trying to be kind. I admired him for that. He really was a nice guy. But I knew all too well what kind of damage was possible for him. I didn't want to destroy either his career or his reputation.

"But?" I knew from his tone there had to be a but.

As he studied me I could tell he was trying to decide whether he could trust me. "It will be an issue with Lyssa."

My opinion of Lyssa involuntary plummeted. Me being an issue with her was natural. A shock. But I wasn't as much of a threat as I would have been even just a few years ago. I was grown, not a little kid she had to raise or share him with. I frowned. I liked her and had hoped she would be a good stepmom. Now it suddenly looked like she might be of the "wicked stepmother of fairytales" variety.

Jason rushed to her defense. "Don't get the wrong idea. Lyssa likes you. When she finds out you're my daughter, I know she'll love you. It's..." He sighed, looking like he was up against it. "Can I trust you with a secret?"

I snorted, like *You have to ask?* "Isn't that what this is?"

He grinned back at me like he was embarrassed. "You got me there." His Adam's apple bobbed. "Lyssa was engaged before she married me. To another professor here. Of computer science of all things." He paused again.

I imagined an eggheady PhD would probably lord his degree over Jason. "It must be awkward."

He nodded. "He doesn't like me, to put it mildly. Lyssa broke off the engagement when she found out her fiancé had a four-year-old son he'd 'forgotten' to mention. With a former grad student of his who wasn't so former when the boy was born."

I made a sympathetic sound. "That's rough."

"Yeah. It wasn't so much the child, but the lie. He was more of a player than she realized. And a liar. She couldn't live with that."

I wasn't so sure about it being just about the lie. Maybe it *was* about the child. Maybe she didn't want any competition for Mia. "You haven't lied to her. You didn't know about me when you married her."

"No, but I'm not sure she'll see it that way. I've kept my suspicions from her. I haven't shared what we're going through. She'll see that as a betrayal. And after the scandal of her broken engagement...

"Let's just say the university may seem large, but it's really a very small community. I don't want to hurt her or make it worse for her here, professionally or otherwise." He took a deep breath. "She's barely gotten over her postpartum depression from having Mia. I can't risk upsetting her now, just at the point when she's becoming herself again."

Postpartum depression, that was new. I hadn't even heard any rumors of it around the office. I didn't know whether to be impressed with his secret-keeping ability, or worried.

"I need some time to figure out how to tell her. To think everything through. To know exactly what you and I want of each other first."

His behavior was typical of analytical types. I had some of those tendencies myself. "Won't it be worse the longer you keep it from her?"

He gave me another of his sad, but impressed smiles. "You're very mature."

"For someone my age." I smiled. "I've had to be. Mom sure isn't." I could have kicked myself. I hadn't meant to bring her up. Jason got a funny look on his face when I mentioned her. I had to divert his attention. "So you're asking me to keep this a secret?"

Jason nodded, looking guilty. "It's selfish—"

"Forever?" I stared him directly in the eye, willing him to come clean and tell me the truth—did he want me to leave without Lyssa ever knowing?

"No." He shook his head, emphasizing the point. "Just until the time is right."

But who knew when that would be?

"And if Lyssa finds out before you tell her?"

"She won't." He sounded confident. Overly positive.

Which worried me. "Secrets have a way of finding the light." That was something my grandma used to say to me.

He arched an eyebrow and pointed to me. "You were a secret for a long time."

"Yeah. What's your point? Mom's the queen of deceit, as tightlipped as they come. It took nineteen years, but here I am." I shrugged. "See what I mean?"

"It won't be forever. Not even for nineteen years." Then he laughed. "Maybe eighteen." He winked.

I bit back what I wanted to say about wanting to have a father in my life and hoping he'd be there to walk me down the aisle someday, hopefully before eighteen years were up.

"Maybe this is best," I said, trying to find the bright side of being kept secret for a while longer. "Logan will be upset when he finds out I've been hiding my search for you from him since I met him. It would be natural for him to think I've been using him to get close to you. As you know better than almost anyone, he's really vulnerable right now. Relieved that Dr. Rogers has been arrested. But he has a lot to deal with. I don't want to lose him." I paused. "So we're both doing this to save our love lives?"

"Yeah. Like father like daughter." He choked on the word "father" and his eyes misted up. "The apple doesn't fall far from the tree."

My eyes misted, too. "Where do we go from here?" I hesitated again. "I'd like to get to know you better. As a person. Or as a dad." I choked up on the word "dad" like he had on "daughter."

In a flash, Jason was out of his chair. He came around to my side of his desk and pulled me into his arms. He was tall, over six feet, and strong and firm and warm. He smelled clean, like pleasant soap and cologne. I rested my head on his chest as he wrapped me in his arms. A sense of wellbeing washed over me as I was cradled in my father's firm embrace for the very first time. Unlike my baby sister Mia, I'd always remember the first time our dad hugged me.

"It sounds crazy, and you may not believe it," he said, "but I'm glad to have another daughter. I always wanted girls."

I sniffed a little, trying to hold back my emotions. "I bet you'll have a son, too. I'd like a brother."

"I love you, Ellie."

Someone gasped loudly. We started and turned in unison toward the sound. Our office administrator Karen stood in the doorway to Jason's office, staring at us with her mouth open and a look of horror on her face.

Caught already.

CHAPTER TWO

Jason's first reaction was to jump apart, which would look guilty as sin. But I'd learned everything about lying effectively from the mistress of deceit—my mother. If there was one woman who could talk herself out of being caught red-handed in a clench with a lover, it was dear old Mom. The key was to disarm, charm, distract, and whatever you do, act innocent. So I hung on to Jason, made my eyes wide, and scrunched my face against his shirt like he was holding me too tight and I was being comical.

I fixed my face into a smile and laughed as I looked at Karen and pushed away from Jason. "Okay, enough, thanks." I managed to blush. "Some people are overly grateful. Do one small favor for this guy and he tells you he loves you." I laughed again as I pulled away from him and stared at my feet for a second.

Jason cleared his throat. "Thanks again, Ellie. You saved my life."

I shrugged and gave Karen a conspiratorial look, like *See what I mean?*

"What are you doing here?" I asked her. That's another thing I learned from Mom—go on the offensive. Make the other person explain their actions. In war, they call this evasive action.

"*Oh.*" Karen looked embarrassed. "I forgot my work laptop. I wanted to get some work done this weekend. I just dropped by to get it."

"What? You're not doing the Dad's Weekend thing?" I asked, ribbing her.

She laughed. "Do you know how many years I've lived in this town and worked for the university? It's old hat. I think I can pass. My dad's not here."

"And here I thought you were a football fan," Jason said, joining in.

"High school football. Go Panthers!" She punched the air. "What are you doing this weekend, Ellie? You don't have a dad here, do you? Going to the game with friends?"

She knew very well I didn't. Well, not that she knew about. "Sort of." I grinned. "I'm going to the game with Logan and his dad."

At the start of the semester when I first showed up at the office, Karen had warned me off Logan, saying he was a player who had broken more than his fair share of hearts. I had ignored her advice.

She frowned subtly, but I knew she wasn't pleased. "Meeting his dad—that sounds serious."

No, finding out Jason was my dad was serious. I shrugged. "Met. I had dinner with them last night. Logan and I are just friends." We were a lot more, but I didn't feel like sharing with Karen. "It's no big deal." I made a point of looking at the clock on the wall of Jason's office. "Speaking of dads and football, I have to be going. We're going to the all-campus tailgate party before the game."

The all-campus tailgate party wasn't the traditional grilling burgers on a hibachi on the tailgate of a pickup or camper in an RV park. In fact, most tailgating at my new alma mater wasn't traditional at all. Tailgating here consisted of getting up at noon, staggering to the shower, dressing for the game, eating a bare-minimum breakfast, and then consuming as much alcohol of your choice as possible before getting in line for the game. Preferably at least three hours pregame if you wanted a seat in the student section, particularly a good seat. Some people camped out overnight for the most popular games. Thanks to Logan's dad, I didn't have to worry about getting in line. We had prime reserved seats on the fifty-yard line of the alumni side. Hooray us.

The all-campus party was held in the field house across from the practice football field adjacent to the stadium. Dozens of vendors set up booths and served food and beverages. It was supposed to be family friendly. But this was Dad's Weekend, so, hey, right. The drinking would be a little less.

I raced from Jason's office to meet Logan and his dad, Harlan, at the south entrance of the field house like Logan had asked. I tried to pull myself together as I hurried down the concrete steps from the backside of the comp sci building down the hill to the practice field and across to the field house. The wind had kicked up and, although the day was still mostly clear, clouds had begun rolling ominously in. I huddled in my coat against the cold, hoping I wouldn't give myself away as being upset.

Logan and Harlan were waiting for me. Harlan looked antsy, glancing at his watch like he could hardly be bothered to wait for me. But my heart caught at the sight of Logan. He was breathtaking, sexy, hot in a way that wasn't put on, but simply was. Tall, athletic, brown hair, built, and full of charisma.

"There she is. Hey, Ellie, Elizabeth, Martin." Logan's eyes danced as I approached. "Right on time."

"She's five minutes late," Harlan said.

"Give her a break, Dad. We changed the plans at the last minute."

I pushed the encounter with my dad from my mind and tried to concentrate on the here and now. The sound of Logan's voice made my heart race. The way he said my name was a joke between us. When we first met I refused to tell him my last name. So now he liked to use it from time to time to remind me I couldn't fight fate.

"Logan Walker." I smiled and gave him a deep, lingering kiss, like I didn't want to let him go. Beside us Harlan made a grunt of disgust. Logan tasted like beer—a deep, earthy ale that was totally hot. Although he'd obviously been drinking, to my relief, he wasn't smashed. I reluctantly broke away and smiled at his dad. "Harlan."

Harlan stared at me, assessing me again, probably wondering how far I would go to defend Logan. "Ellie."

Logan took my hand. "Ready for the big game?"

"I'm ready for anything." I hardly cared about the game, just about being with Logan.

"Let's go." Logan held the field-house door open for me.

Inside, the field house was crowded with people, vendor booths, and the smell of hotdogs, barbecue, and beer. The school colors decorated everything from people to furniture and even the food in the form of giant sheet cakes decorated with the mascot. I expected Logan and Harlan to head to food row. But they walked past it, winding through the crowd toward the far end.

"Wait!" I dragged my feet and tried to pull Logan toward a barbecue stand where the food smelled delicious. "Where are we going? You promised to feed me."

Logan leaned in and whispered in my ear. "Dad has something more exclusive in mind. Don't worry, El. There will be plenty of food. The university always puts on an impressive spread."

Which was when it hit me—Harlan had a pass to an exclusive private party for donors who gave generously to the university. A man of his wealth, power, and connections? I should have known this would be the case. I had fixed my makeup and hair to impress Logan, but if

I'd known I was going to be among the VIPs of the university, I would have dressed differently.

Harlan led the way behind a roped-off area to a private room. We checked our coats at the door. Glen Lawrence, the university president, greeted us as we came in. "Harlan Walker!"

Harlan smiled at him, shook his hand, and slapped him on the back. "Glen!"

President Lawrence's gaze shifted to Logan. "Logan. Good to see you."

"Good to see you, too, sir."

Oh, shit! Logan knew President Lawrence personally?

Harlan gave Logan a one-armed hug, acting like he was all proud of his boy.

The president shook Logan's hand. "How's the shoulder?"

Logan paled slightly, and spoke with a smile frozen on his face. "As good as it's going to get."

"Sorry about that, son. Tragic accident." The president shook his head. "The baseball team lost a rising star. Glad you stuck it out here. Your dad is quite the booster. We would have hated to lose you and him." There was an awkward pause while President Lawrence assessed Logan and Harlan remained silent.

Logan had torn his labrum while pitching a game his freshman year. A torn labrum was a career-ending injury for over ninety percent of players, including Logan.

"I hear you're a star in the IT department. Your boss Jason brags about you every time I see him."

I jumped at the sound of my dad's name while President Lawrence smiled largely like a politician and Harlan remained stony. Logan was stiff beside me, obviously uncomfortable and nervous. I squeezed his hand reassuringly, finally getting what was going on. This was a CYA move by President Lawrence. Lawsuit avoidance.

The president lowered his voice. "We appreciate your help in the incident."

The incident? I wanted to scream. Was that what they were calling the arrest of my evil Chem 202 professor for manufacturing and selling illegal date-rape drugs? For using them on handsome, unsuspecting male students, including Logan? Why had the university been so blissfully ignorant? Because Dr. Rogers had been a fantastic fundraiser? Had they suffered from fundraising blindness while she raped students and failed ninety percent of her class out of spite? The woman was sick.

This was definitely a CYA move. President Lawrence would be lucky if none of the victims sued the university.

Logan and Jason had helped the police with the investigation that led to her arrest just before Dad's Weekend. But it was really my friend Dex who brought her down when we pranked her and Dex discovered her drug-manufacturing equipment.

Harlan stared President Lawrence directly in the eye with one of those shark-to-men stares of his, the kind I imagined he used in business to scare weaker competitors. "Logan has done his part. Keep his name

out of this." His threat was implicit, but totally obvious—keep Logan's name off the victim list or Harlan
pulled his generous donations, influenced his powerful
friends to halt theirs, and dragged out his legal team to
make President Lawrence's life hell.

"Dad—"

Harlan held up his hand to silence Logan. "I want
this killed. I want it clean."

So this was the point of arriving earlier than previ-
ously planned. Harlan wanted to voice his demands in
person.

"Campus police have more than enough evidence
without involving Logan further." Despite the threat,
President Lawrence's voice was so smooth and unruf-
fled, I was impressed. "I give you my word." He used a
classic liar's diversionary technique and smiled at me,
though up to that point I'd been invisible. "Who is this
lovely young lady?"

I stuck out my hand before anyone else could comment. "Ellie Martin."

"Nice to meet you, Ellie." His gaze ran over me as he
smiled. "A big fan, I see. You must be a student."

"Yes, sir. I'm here on a regents' scholarship. I work
in the IT department with Logan."

"Excellent. I'm always happy to meet one of our best
and brightest." President Lawrence's tone made it
clear he was done with us. He smiled at someone in line
behind us and slapped Harlan on the back. "Enjoy the
game. It's going to be a good one."

A brief scowl crossed Harlan's face. He wasn't the
kind of man who liked being dismissed. It was quickly

replaced with his smooth, almost slimy, politician's smile. A look of victory shone in his eyes. "We will. Thanks, Glen. Ah, there's the buffet table. Let's eat."

Logan was right. The university had put out a fabulous spread for this event. As we made our way through the buffet line I loaded up on barbecued pulled pork, fries, baked beans, and salads. The beer flowed freely. Because I was still underage and now in the midst of the very people who could expel me for underage drinking, I grabbed a glass of lemonade. Logan and Harlan each went to the open bar and got beers, a special university ale made for the event by an alum's Seattle micro brewery.

After the incident with President Lawrence, there was a definite tension between Logan and Harlan. Logan was stiff and nervous. By the time we found a table in the thick of things, in a strategic place where Harlan could hold court, Logan had downed his beer and was ready for another.

"Well, Ellie, what do you think?" Harlan asked as we took a seat. "Is this the way to tailgate? No cold. No wind."

He was bragging, digging at me. His attitude and the look in his eyes said he didn't think I was classy enough to appreciate rubbing elbows with the university elite. And he was obviously proud of the show of power he'd just put on.

"Yeah. It's really nice," I murmured. Yeah, that was an inane comment, but I was trying to be polite. I actually preferred a good cookout in the open air around a real tailgate.

Logan rolled his eyes at his dad's bragging and shook his head subtly. I had to fight not to laugh, relieved that Logan was lightening up.

"You look well rested. Did you have a good night's sleep?" Damned by faint praise. Harlan's innocuous question was obviously barbed and there was the taint of innuendo about it, like did I have fun sleeping with his son?

I caught the quick look he flashed Logan, shining with pride at his son for scoring, while warning him I was good enough to sleep with, but merely a low-class plaything. Nothing serious.

"The best." Fear of embarrassing Logan made me hold back what I really wanted to say. Let Harlan think what he would.

I wondered if after our dinner last night, Harlan had done more digging on me. That the business he'd begged off after dinner to do had everything to do with me and nothing to do with actual business. Had he uncovered more dirt he didn't like? Found out about the restraining order my mom had against my nearly ex-stepdad? Or the nasty divorce details?

The thought made me cold with dread and fear. I hadn't told Logan the story of Austin and Mom. And I didn't want to, not yet. I had come to terms with Austin, but the events were still too ugly, embarrassing, and raw. I didn't talk about my mom. Had Harlan seen that Logan and I were really into each other, not passing flings, not friends with benefits?

He couldn't know that I had slept with Logan, but not had actual sex with him. That the thought of an accidental pregnancy and becoming like my mom had kept me virginal. But that I was wholly tempted by Logan. I just needed a little more time.

"Good. Good," Harlan said, all nasty, smug smiles. "I can't believe it's November already. Hard to believe the holidays will be here soon. Any big plans for Thanksgiving, Ellie? Are you looking forward to going home for break?"

My mouth went dry. *He knew.* From anyone else this would just be stupid, polite small talk. But I could tell from the triumphant look in his eyes he knew I wouldn't be going home. I had the feeling this was the prelude to the sucker punch Logan had warned me about.

I swallowed hard, trying not to give my fear away. But I cursed myself for "fixing" things between Logan and Harlan. Because what I'd really done, I realized, was put myself and my relationship with Logan directly in his crosshairs.

"Yeah, what *are* you doing for Thanksgiving, El?" Logan smiled at me and squeezed my hand playfully. "Mom always throws a big party—"

"Logan Walker." A gorgeous blonde approached our table seemingly from out of nowhere, cutting off the rest of Logan's thought. Or maybe my attention had been so diverted by Harlan and Logan I'd blocked out the rest of the room, allowing her to sneak up on me. Though how could I have missed her?

Now that she stood before us, I noticed the effect she had on the men around us. Though probably approaching thirty, the woman standing at our table was hot and classy. She made the V-neck university T-shirt she wore look like it was pricey designer gear. Her hair, breasts, and makeup were perfect. Her waist tiny. Her voice was sultry, yet friendly. And she wore a white gold sorority lavaliere necklace with the Double Deltsie letters and a big-ass diamond around her neck.

I felt sick to my stomach. The Double Deltsie house was *the* top house on campus. "Top" defined as best-looking, hardest partying, richest girls. This woman screamed confident, moneyed sorority girl. She had the look. She had the attitude. And anyone could see she had the money.

Logan popped out of his chair like an enthusiastic jack-in-the-box on a tightly wound spring. "Amber!" His face lit up as she laughed and they hugged. "What are you doing here?"

"Logan!" She laughed back. "Do you have to ask? *All* the regents are here. How could I miss it?"

What? This woman, Amber, was a regent? Regents were supposed to be stuffy old businessmen with gray hair. Not freshly minted sorority alums.

"I thought you were in London this week?"

My tongue felt thick in my mouth and my heart raced at the intimacy of the conversation. Why would Logan know she was supposed to be in London?

Her laugh was like the gentle tinkle of a highly feminine bell. "Oh, I got out of that early. I couldn't miss a game."

A fleeting look of worry crossed Logan's face. Then, almost as an afterthought, he remembered me. He grabbed my hand and pulled me to my feet. "Amber, I'd like you to meet Ellie Martin."

Small things rankled when I was upset, like the fact he called me Ellie, not El like he usually did. Like he didn't call me his girlfriend. I know, it wasn't official. But last night he told me he loved me. And, long story, to get Harlan off his back, I had agreed before the weekend, because I literally owed Logan my life, to be Logan's fake girlfriend for the weekend. He could have had the decency to use the title now. The fact that he didn't made me worried and more insecure than I already was.

Amber's cool gaze swept over me, making me feel just a little bit inferior in the way the girls at the snooty house had of intentionally doing just that while outwardly being pleasant. I thought it was probably a skill passed down from big to little sister year after year. She looked at me in the way people with money look down on those who don't. Her smile was fixed on her face, but it was totally fake. Her tone was genial and cool only to those who had the knack for noticing. "Nice to meet you, Ellie. I've known Logan and Harlan"—she winked at his dad—"forever. Hey, Harlan. Our families are old friends. So close, we're practically related."

"Hey, join us?" Logan was reaching for an extra chair before she could even answer.

Amber put a beautiful, well-manicured hand on Logan's arm, stopping him. "I'd love to, you know that. But it's part of the job to mingle." She gave that tinkling laugh again and shrugged delicately. "The university needs cash, always."

Logan nodded.

She leaned in to him and cooed, "We'll catch up later." She smiled at Harlan again and pointed at him playfully. "With you, too." She strutted off with hips swaying to con the other VIPs into parting with their money for the good of the university.

"Now that's a fine girl," Harlan said, as if he were still a frat boy lusting after her. "I've always liked Amber."

I was understandably peeved. "You might have mentioned I'm a regents' scholar. I have to write those guys a thank-you every year. It would be good to have an in with one."

Logan wasn't listening to me. He was staring after Amber with an expression I couldn't place, except to say I didn't like it.

Hurt by Logan's sudden lapse and inattention toward me, I excused myself to go the ladies' room to collect and compose myself. Get my insecurities under control before I did something stupid again. And give myself a much-needed pep talk. Amber had had exactly the effect on me she desired—I was an emotional basket case. She reminded me too much of my mom—a man-eater. Mom would have been a Double Deltsie if she'd gone to college here. Even her lack of money wouldn't have kept her out. Her other skills more than made up for it. But I wasn't like her. Didn't want to be like her. Seeing Logan mesmerized by the kind of feminine charms Amber put on made me sick. I had hoped he was different.

I stared in the mirror in the ladies' room. A wreck looked back at me, someone trying desperately to hold it all together. All things considered, I should have been proud I looked as good as I did. I touched up my mascara and lipstick, fiddled with my hair, and took a deep breath, steeling myself to go back into the room of vipers and do battle.

When I came out of the bathroom, Logan stood at the bar with a fresh drink in his hand, bent in an intimate pose over Amber. There were talking softly and animatedly. Smiling. Laughing.

I swallowed hard. Amber was the kind of woman who brought out every one of my insecurities. On top of the conversation with Jason, nearly being caught and found out by Karen, and being baited by Harlan, I wasn't sure I could survive the afternoon.

I debated my options, like whether I should sidle up to the bar and claim my territory. Or was it better to watch and learn? What was Logan up to? The minute I turned my back, he went after Amber? Something felt off. Maybe it was me. Maybe I simply didn't belong here.

In desperate need of consoling in cookie form, I headed to the buffet. A cobblestone bar would have been better. But do you think the university had sprung for any? A cookie would have to do. Even though I was thin, almost gaunt, I felt a momentary stab of guilt. A woman like Amber would never let a cookie cross her lips. Screw her and a society that judges a girl because she enjoys comfort food.

I grabbed a small plate and a napkin, and was just about to step around a stocky guy student with his back to me so I could get to the cookies when he suddenly turned around and faced me.

"Ellie? Is that you? Funny seeing you here."

I froze. My stomach clenched. I could not believe my bad, stupid luck. This day was going from bad to worse to total disaster. "Schwartz. Didn't know you had the credentials to get into a party like this."

"Funny, Ellie. Ha, ha." His breath stank of beer and garlic. He swayed slightly, like he'd already been pre-gaming a little too hard. "I'm here with my roommate and his dad who's loaded."

I nodded and reached for the cookie tongs. "Good to see you." Not. But it was the best I could do to dismiss him.

"Heard you saw my man Austin during Halloweekend."

I stared at him and gave him a narrow-eyed glare meant to warn him to back off. "Yeah." I shrugged.

"You gave him shit for too long, Ellie. Don't know why he took it." His gaze slid over me, appraising me with an insult in his look, like I was beneath him. Not worth doing.

"Back off, Schwartz. That's my private business. I don't want to talk about it."

He swayed again and bumped into the table, rattling the serving dishes.

"Someone should give you a breathalyzer test before they let you walk home. Bet you blow a two."

"Very funny."

He sneered. Schwartz had held a grudge against me since I refused to sleep with him when he came onto me at a party shortly before Austin and I had started dating. "You really think you're hot shit, don't you?" He raised his voice with every word.

"Stop it, Schwartz. Leave the past alone. Austin and I are good now. Keep your nose out of it." I turned to go before things got uglier. When Schwartz was hammered, there was no reasoning with him. I had never told him my side of the story. I doubted he wanted to hear it anyway. I certainly didn't want to tell it. And if I knew Austin, he'd told a tale that made himself look good.

But Schwartz wouldn't let it drop. He grabbed me by the elbow. "You think you're so high and mighty. Regents' scholar. Dating a rich boy. You're nothing. Just a little cock tease.

"Austin said your mom was a much better lay than you. Hotter, too. He should have done your old lady again and forgotten about you." His voice had risen to a yell, an angry bellow.

The crowd of people around us went silent. My face flamed. At the bar, which wasn't more than fifteen feet away, Logan turned to stare at us. From his expression, I knew he'd heard every word. Everyone had. His was jaw set. His eyes were hard.

He stormed over. Without saying a word, he slammed Schwartz with a right hook that sent him staggering back into the buffet table. Dishes rattled. He landed on his ass in the plate of cookies, crushing them to crumbs. The coffeepot at the end of the table tipped over, soaking the white tablecloth.

I screamed. "Stop! Stop it."

Schwartz let out a roar and hurled profanities at Logan as he struggled to his feet to fight back, knocking over more dishes. Sending the pitcher of cream next to the coffeepot tipping over.

The scar on my left cheek pounded as if it were a fresh wound again. I grabbed Logan's arm as he cocked it to swing again. "Logan, don't. No! Please."

CHAPTER THREE

The crowded room around me disappeared, replaced with images of coming home from college to do my laundry. Walking in on Mom and Austin. The images flashed before me again with exactly the same horrifying power, in exactly the same sequence as they always did. So fresh it felt like it was happening again. I trembled uncontrollably. As I grabbed Logan's arm, it was like I was trying to pull Doug off Austin again. Trying to save him.

I couldn't get rid of the images. Parking in front of Mom and my third stepdad Doug's house. Doug's car pulling into the driveway right behind me. Getting out of my car. Waving to him as I grabbed my laundry basket from the backseat. Doug waiting in the driveway, holding his briefcase.

Doug asking, "What are you doing here?" as I walked up the front walk.

Holding up my laundry basket. "I'm out of clean clothes. What are you doing here? I thought you were out of town."

"Caught an earlier flight home so I could surprise Melissa."

His key in the front door. The two of us joking with each other. Freezing in the entryway as we heard the distinctive thumping and moaning of sex. Turning toward the living room. Looking directly at Mom and Austin having sex on the couch. So shocked neither of us could process it. As obvious as it was, it just didn't make sense.

Doug dropping his briefcase. The roar that came out of him as he charged them and pulled Austin, naked from the waist down, off Mom. The sickening thud of his fists hammering Austin again and again while Mom screamed at him to stop. The blood from Austin's nose and lip spattering the cream sofa and the carpet, the wall behind them. Mom reaching for her clothes and phone.

Not thinking, just grabbing Doug's arm, trying to pull him away from Austin before he killed him. Flailing and failing miserably, a mere gnat toying with a raging bull. Wedging myself between them. The searing blow to my head that was meant for Austin. Staggering back into the end table. A lamp crashing to the floor. My ears ringing so loudly I couldn't hear anything but the sound of consciousness fleeing. Someone catching me before I went down.

Doug's bloody fist. His prized class ring gleaming through a coating of blood. Something sticky running down my cheek. Touching my face. My fingers coming away bloody. Stunned, confused, barely hanging on. My lip swelling. The taste of blood and violence.

Logan turned to stare at me, concern and confusion etched on his face, like he couldn't understand what I was so afraid of. Like he thought I should be happy he was defending my honor, playing my white knight.

Schwartz got his feet beneath him again. With Logan distracted and restrained, however feebly, by me, he slammed Logan with a fist to his left eye. Logan's head whipped back.

I screamed again, a banshee wail, and wedged myself between them as Schwartz wound up again, bracing myself for the blow that was coming.

Two dads who were standing nearby grabbed Schwartz and restrained him before he could deliver his next punch. Several servers appeared at Logan's side, ready to hold him back. Logan dropped his punching arm and waved them off as he wrapped his free arm around me. "I'm done."

They backed off, hovering anxiously nearby like they didn't quite believe him.

Amber crossed the room, stopping at Logan's side. She put her hand on his shoulder and surveyed the damage. A tiny smile played at the corners of her mouth as she grabbed several pieces of ice from a bucket on the table, wrapped them in a napkin, and held them gently against his eye. "That eye could get nasty." A look of admiration shone in hers.

President Lawrence, his face an angry red, finally broke through from the back of the crowd to see what the commotion was. Frowning slightly, and obviously trying to maintain his presidential composure, he turned his gaze to Amber in question just as Harlan appeared at the front of the crowd, too.

"It's nothing." She gave a delicate shrug of her shoulders and laughed. "Too much pregame exuberance. A little horseplay that got out of hand. A *boy* took a tumble." The way she used the word "boy" was a final insult to Schwartz. She spotted Harlan at the edge of the crowd. "I'm sure Harlan will make this good."

Even though she was saving Logan's butt, her purring voice sent a shiver down my spine.

"Absolutely," Harlan said. He was staring at Logan and me, still held tightly by the arm Logan had wrapped around my waist. His expression was hard to read, but I knew it meant trouble for me. He didn't like the way Logan held me so possessively. He would put a stop to it if he could.

I felt like I barely knew Logan. I freaked. I had to get out of that room so I could breathe. The way Harlan stared at me. The faces of the crowd. The cool, sexy confidence of Amber. The violence.

I slid out of Logan's grip, turned, and ran out of the room without stopping to get my coat. I ran through the main body of the field house, threading my way through the crowd. Past the boisterous beer garden filled with laughing people. Past the balloons in school colors. Past the streamers. And the band playing the fight song. Past the booth selling game-day sweatshirts. Out into the bracing cold of the November afternoon where my breath made puffs of white in the air.

I paused with tears in my eyes on the path up the hill toward the main body of campus away from the stadium, trying to catch my breath. In real danger of hyperventilating. I was still shaking.

"El! El!" Logan chased after me.

I heard him pounding after me, gaining on me. I should have started running again. But I couldn't make myself.

He caught me and wrapped his arms around me from behind, curling around me like he wanted to protect me from the world. "You're freezing." He pressed his head to mine and kissed the top of my head. "I'm sorry. The things that douchebag was saying...I couldn't just stand by."

A sob stuck in my throat. He sounded so contrite. He deserved to know why I was acting like I was.

"I couldn't let him get away with it, El."

"It's—"

"Logan!" Harlan strode up the hill toward us, carrying our coats. "There you are." He shoved a jacket and an instant ice pack at Logan and gave me a hard stare as he held my coat out to me.

I took my coat from Harlan reluctantly and caught my first glimpse of Logan's eye. Schwartz had decked him a good one. His eye was swelling. But it wasn't as bad as the shiner he'd had when I first met him.

Logan helped me into my coat before shrugging into his own and putting the ice on his eye.

"I've taken care of things," Harlan said to his son. "That asshole will be feeling the beating you gave him for a while. That's what I always say—if you're going to strike, strike hard." He sounded proud of Logan, rather than upset.

Once his coat was on, Logan wrapped his arms around me again.

"Good thing Amber stepped in when she did." Harlan turned his gaze on me again, studying me in his son's embrace.

I knew from the look on his face I'd lost some respect in his eyes. Not that I cared, except for Logan's sake. If he admired striking hard, I was certain running displeased him. But I wasn't going to explain myself to him.

His gaze flitted briefly to Logan's arms around me again and his eyes narrowed. "Spend Thanksgiving with us," he said out of the blue, like he was just continuing a conversation that had been momentarily disrupted. It was less an invitation and more of a command. "Logan's mom will want to meet you."

I should have been pleased, but I didn't trust his motives. I looked up at Logan for confirmation he wanted me with him for Thanksgiving. Truthfully, the prospect scared me.

Logan hesitated. His arms felt stiff around me.

I opened my mouth to refuse just as Logan spoke up.

"Say yes. Please, El." It wasn't his usual tone of voice, the one that made me weak in the knees. He was trying to mask it, but I got the feeling he really didn't *want* me to go home with him for the holidays.

Maybe my emotions were just too raw from all that had happened. After all, we weren't even really official-ly dating, so why should I expect him to want me with him during a family holiday? But I was hurt all the same.

"Thank you, but no. I really can't—"

"Come on, El," Logan said, snapping out of whatev-er had made him waver in the first place. "You have to come. You can't say no." He turned on the charm and was back to himself.

Even as upset as I was, there was no way I could say no now.

"Okay," I said, looking up into his eyes. Then I turned to Harlan. "Thank you. I accept."

He nodded, but rather than looking embarrassed the way lots of men do when they're caught in a senti-mental gesture, he looked smug. And that scared me.

Harlan smiled broadly. "Let's get to the game. We don't want to miss the kickoff."

Logan let me go and grabbed my hand, leaving so much unsaid and hanging in the air between us. We made our way to our seats on the fifty-yard line, avoid-ing the major issues, either lapsing into silence or mak-ing small talk. I was quieter than usual, still trying to get control of myself. Trying not to be angry and upset with Logan for defending me. How could he know he'd hit a trigger?

When I got to my seat, my two good friends Taylor and Nicole Snapchatted me a picture of them with their dads on the student side. They looked so happy I envied them. The student side looked way more fun than the alum side.

Having fun? Nic texted.

I snapped a picture of Logan with the instant ice on his eye during the national anthem. *Tell you the story later.*

"Hey," he said, trying to stop me from sending it.

I pulled my phone out of his reach. "It's a great conversation piece."

We lapsed into uncomfortable silence. Halfway through the first quarter, Logan grabbed my hand. "Let's go. I need something to drink."

I didn't resist. I followed him to the top of the stands and out into the food-court area, where he tossed his used instant ice away. He found a spot away from the bulk of the crowds.

"You're still pissed. It's killing me, El. I hate it when you're upset with me." He tipped my chin up. "What's wrong?"

"Nothing. I'm being a bitch." I hesitated. "Most girls would love being white-knighted like that."

"But?"

I took a deep breath. "It's true—Austin, my ex, slept with my mom. My stepdad and I walked in on them." I stared at the ground, letting my hair fall over my face so Logan couldn't see my expression. "Oh, shit, Logan. You won't love me when you hear the truth. Your parents really won't want me anywhere near you—my mom's a slut. She set out to seduce Austin. She has always wanted what I have. She wanted Austin, so she took him to show she could."

I told Logan everything, all the gory details. Why hold anything back now? He listened quietly. I couldn't look at him, but I heard his breathing speed up like he was getting angry. When I got to the part about taking the blow Doug had meant for Austin, Logan pulled my hand away from my face and kissed it. I hadn't even realized I was touching my scar.

His gentle gesture sent me over the edge. I broke into sobs.

Logan pulled me into his arms. "It's okay, El. Fuck, I'm such a douche. I had no idea."

I laid my head against his shoulder. "It's okay. How could you?"

"You saved that fucker's life?"

"Yes." I clutched his sweatshirt.

He swore some more and paused like something had suddenly dawned on him. "No wonder you're so cautious around guys and didn't want a relationship." He paused. "Is this the secret you've been keeping from me since we met? Is this why you thought we couldn't have a relationship?"

In that moment I became a really bad person—I told another lie, even knowing it could come back to bite me big time. "Yes."

"Fuck, El." As he held me, his voice was fiercely protective. "I understand why you didn't want to tell me. But I'm glad I know. Damn, I wish I could beat the shit out your ex and that jerk inside the field house for doing this to you."

His voice became soft and tender. "We can fix this, El. You can trust me." He tipped my chin up again so I had to look him in his one good eye and his one puffy, getting-black eye.

He sounded and looked so much like the night I first met him that I couldn't help smiling through my tears. He really was adorable. "Has anyone ever told you that you look hot with a black eye?"

He grinned. "At least I have a good story to go with this one." He hesitated again. "If you want me to tell it."

"No one is going to believe a second pool ball jumped off the table and smacked you in the eye," I said. "That story was hard enough to swallow the first time around." I bit my lip. "I think we're going to have to go with you saving me from a bully. Schwartz is a mean drunk. He's so not over himself. He'll never forgive me for rejecting him when he hit on me."

"Is that why he wanted to hurt you?"

I nodded. "How bad was it in there? What do all the regents and VIPs think of me now?"

Logan shrugged. "Who the hell cares?"

I looked away.

He realized that I did. "Anyone who saw what happened was on your side, El. He was the one who came off looking bad, not you. No one's going to pull your scholarship over this."

"What if Schwartz files assault charges?"

"I'll counter-file." Logan hugged me. "Don't worry. Dad took care of it." He paused again. "But how are we, El? Are we good?"

I hesitated. "Almost." I was still thinking of Thanksgiving. "I don't have to go home with you for

Thanksgiving. Not if you don't want me to. I know your dad put you on the spot earlier, but I can still get out of it gracefully. Or even ungracefully. I'm really good at suddenly coming down with fake illnesses. And very convincing, too."

"What are you talking about, El?" His voice was soft and sincere. "Why wouldn't I want you to spend the holidays with me?"

I studied him. "But...you seemed hesitant earlier."

"Did I?" He shook his head. "I'm sorry. Maybe that was because I'd just been smacked a good one in the head. I was dazed." He wore a teasing smile and his voice was happy, but I still got the feeling he was covering. "I want you to come. Don't make me beg. Would you turn down a guy with a black eye?" He tried to make a sad, pathetic face and winced. "See? No hesitation at all." He paused. "Now are we good?"

I smiled back at him, trying to push my fears away. Maybe I'd been mistaken. "We're good."

For now. Until he found out I was keeping another secret from him.

He smiled back, winced again in the process, and hugged me tighter. "Have I told you how happy I am you're coming home with me for Thanksgiving?"

"Have you? Tell me again."

"Thrilled. Ecstatic."

I grabbed the collar of his coat and leaned up for a kiss. "Show me and then we'll get more ice for that eye."

When we went back to our seats, Amber was sitting in mine, bending Harlan's ear. It took her a minute to realize I was standing there, waiting to get my seat back. Or maybe she did it on purpose.

"Sorry!" She looked up at me and laughed. "Networking." She popped up and put a hand on Logan's shoulder. "See you at Thanksgiving." Her gaze turned to me. "Nice to meet you." Like she didn't remember my name.

Then she made her way past a sea of knees toward the aisle. Thanksgiving? I looked at Logan with the question in my eyes.

"You're missing a helluva game." Harlan's eyes were triumphant in a way I didn't understand. "We scored. We're up by seven."

Later, when we won the game, the crowd streamed onto the field. For a second, I worried some exuberant fans would tear down the goalposts and toss them in the nearby river. But they didn't. That was tradition when we beat our cross-state rivals in our annual matchup. Instead, dads and students streamed out to hit the bars and restaurants before attending the big comedy show later at the coliseum.

Logan and Harlan had tickets for the sold-out show. As we streamed out of the stadium, Logan was apologetic for not including me.

"No problem. You two need some guy time." I kissed him. "And I have stuff to do." In reality, I needed time to think.

"Come to dinner with us," Logan said.

But I had had enough of Harlan and I guessed he felt the same about me, at least judging from the look he gave me. I politely declined. We walked together to the top of the hill as part of the streaming mass leaving the stadium. Down past the library toward my dorm and the edge of Greek Row, where we parted company. I headed to my dorm and Logan and Harlan broke off toward the bars.

The dorm was buzzing, full of girls and dads returning from the game and getting ready to go back out. On the way in, I ran into my roommate Bre and her dad on their way out.

"We're going to dinner with Dan and his dad before the comedy show—want to join us?" Bre's cheeks were pink with pleasure. She was flying high, one of those girls whose dads adored her. Plus she was on her way to meet her boyfriend and his dad.

"You're sweet to invite me," I said. "But I have homework to do."

"Boring! Always studying makes for a dull girl." Bre laughed. "Chem?"

I nodded. I hoped chem would be a lot easier now that Dr. Rogers had been arrested. Almost anyone would be a better instructor than she'd been. Students were already lobbying the university to assign our favorite substitute prof to the job fulltime. But I was lying. I needed time to think.

"Okay, then. Don't wait up for me. I might spend the night with Dad at his hotel."

I smiled and watched them walk off. I was luckier than a lot of girls in that at least her dad had gotten a hotel room and wasn't staying in our room like many dads were doing. Using the bathrooms was treacherous enough with so many men around.

After the initial flurry from the game, the dorm quieted down as people headed out. My phone vibrated. I had an email coming in.

From Mom.

My heart stopped. What did she want now? Her timing had always been impeccable—impeccably bad.

Sweetie. Yeah, right. *You're avoiding me. I get it. You need your space. So I have good news—I'm going on a cruise over Thanksgiving with a new guy I've been seeing. You can come stay at the house while I'm gone if you like.*

As if. I rolled my eyes. Did she really believe I thought she was considering my feelings like she was pretending to? No way. She was just trying to justify choosing a guy over me for the holidays. Like always. Not even divorced yet and seeing someone else. Not that I had any intention of spending Thanksgiving with her.

And I wasn't really holding my breath about that empty house, either. Thanksgiving was still almost three weeks away. She could easily break up with whoever this new guy was well before then.

I replied with a simple "have fun" just to get her off my back and let her know I'd seen her email, wishing there was some way to infuse it with a snarky tone. I didn't want another message from her.

I tossed the phone on my bed. As I reached for my laptop, my phone buzzed again. "What now?"

I grabbed it. A text from Jason. *Write this down. Keep it in a secure place then delete this text.* The text was followed by a string of numbers and letters that looked like a password of some sort. Crazy.

I grabbed a pad and jotted the "password" down just as my phone buzzed again. This time an email from Jason with a link and nothing more, like those phishing schemes or emails that launch horrible viruses. But Jason was a computer geek. I had to trust him.

I looked at my notepad. At my phone. Shrugged and clicked. A secure email service website popped up and prompted me for a password. I entered the password Jason had just texted me.

From now on this is how we communicate when we're in our father-daughter mode. This email will automatically destruct one hour after being opened. For both of our safety, there will be no record of our communications. Store that password where no one else will find it and don't lose it.

If anyone ever asks why I texted you, tell them work stuff.

Sorry Karen interrupted at the office. You're right. We have a lot to talk about. Your lifetime to catch up on. Let's meet soon. Does Tuesday morning work for you? Say ten at The College Grind? I could "bump" into my student worker and buy her a cup of coffee. Pretty innocuous.

Sorry, too, that I couldn't act like a real dad and go to the game with my oldest daughter. Great game, though, huh?

Dad

Suddenly I had a catch in my throat and my eyes started to tear up. *Dad.* I had a dad and he was acting like James Bond.

At the bottom of the email was a picture of Jason holding Mia, who was smiling and waving at the camera.

I had a family. A real family. If only a clandestine one. Seeing the picture and reading Jason's message made me feel marginally better about all the lies we were about to tell and the secrets we were keeping. Maybe I had one decent parent. Maybe there was a chance we could have it all.

CHAPTER FOUR

I texted Jason back that Tuesday was good for me. I was having a hard time thinking of him as "Dad." Maybe that would come. Or maybe it was better, easier to keep up our cover, if I just kept thinking of him as Jason for now.

My stomach growled. Since I didn't have anything better to do, I grabbed my laptop and headed to the dining hall to get something to eat and read my lecture notes. My friend Taylor worked in the dining hall. But she'd gotten the weekend off to spend it with her dad. Her dining-hall crush guy was working the burrito line.

I wasn't in the mood for a burrito so I went to the sandwich shop and ordered a grilled cheese. Reading the note from Jason had made me so inexplicably happy that I flirted with the guy who waited on me in hopes of scoring a heart-shaped grilled cheese, even though he wasn't all that attractive. It was a game Taylor, Nicole, Bre, and I played. If the dining hall guys thought you were hot, or if they were just in a generous mood, they flipped the two cut halves of your sandwich on the plate so it made a heart. Given the ups and downs of my day, I could have used a heart.

I had to wait while he grilled it. When he handed my sandwich to me, he was smiling flirtatiously. He'd cut and flipped it to make a heart. Yes! Success. I wanted to do a happy dance. Scoring a heart-shaped sandwich was so rare it was a treasure.

"No dad here, either, huh?" he asked.

Little did he know I had a dad here *every* day.

"Yeah." I glanced at my plate and back at him, beaming. "You just made my day." I gave him an air kiss as thanks, and went through the line to pay for my sandwich and pop. I found a quiet booth and settled in to study so I didn't make an even bigger liar of myself.

But I was easily distracted, and as I munched my heart-shaped sandwich, I found myself on the university website staring at pictures and bios of the regents. There was Amber, smiling and gorgeous, looking like she should have been in a fashion magazine, not a university webpage. Amber Ranklin, to be exact. Her bio said she was an executive in a Seattle-based financial management firm. Yes, well, of course she was, wasn't she? Probably had family money to begin with. And now on top of beauty, she had the Midas touch with money.

I had not missed my guess. She was, indeed, a Double Deltsie. In fact, she'd been chapter president of Delta Delta Psi during her time as a student. Other than that, there was nothing incriminating in her bio. But there was *something* between her and Logan. I knew there was. And I didn't like it. Not one bit.

Which got me thinking about Thanksgiving again—what was Logan hiding from me? Was he having second thoughts about us? I tried to tell myself I was just being paranoid. He was probably right—he'd been dazed.

Then, just for fun, I looked up the staff of the university college of computer science and scoped out all the profs, trying to determine which one was Lyssa's former fiancé. None of them were as handsome as Jason. Most of them were either old or nerdy, which made me wonder about Lyssa's tastes, particularly in men. Though I played the guessing game with myself for a good twenty minutes, reading about and doing a little more snooping on each one, I couldn't make up my mind. Lyssa was pretty, funny, and smart. Maybe I was missing something, like one of these guys had a great personality, but I couldn't see her with any of them.

Bored with that, I browsed the Facebook university missed-connections page, looking for something sweet and romantic. Maybe a mention of me or one of my friends. Hey, I was on a roll. I'd gotten a heart-shaped grilled cheese, hadn't I? Maybe I'd get the prestige and thrill of being mentioned on missed connections, too.

Among all the typical kinds of messages, like the girl looking to meet the hot guy she sees every Friday studying at the corner table at the SUB cafeteria, I found this:

Gorgeous chem student—you come to me for chem help every Tuesday and bring me cookies. You're sweet and nice. I'm really into you. But outside of chem lab, I don't think you know I exist. Now that the threat is over, will you still come?

Oh, I thought. And felt like the world's biggest jerk. Every Tuesday since the start of the semester I'd gone to Byron, my chem TA, for help with the evil Dr. Rogers' class. Now that she'd been arrested, would I need to go? Would I forget Byron and all the help he'd given me?

I baked him cookies and even spent the semester bringing him my failures as I tried to replicate the dining hall's prized cobblestone bars. At first, I was bribing him with baked goods in exchange for preferential chemistry help. But eventually I had seen him as a friend. *Just* a friend. Maybe I was wrong. Maybe this missed connection wasn't about me. Or maybe I was simply fooling myself. Again.

I was studying in my room when the comedy show got out and the bars closed and the girls in my dorm came stumbling home with their dads, disrupting the normal late-night din. My room was directly above the front door. I heard all the fights and lovers' quarrels, all the passion, all the gossip. Anything that was spoken loudly enough to get past the single-pane glass in my window.

After a few minutes, I became immune to the sounds of the dorm front door opening and closing. Then I heard yelling.

"You drunken bastard! I hate you! Hate, hate, hate you! Why did you come here? Just to embarrass me in front of my friends?"

I froze, recognizing the voice as Kay's, the girl from across the hall.

"You little bitch! I'm paying for your college. Shut up! Shut the fuck up." Her dad's voice was deep and slurred from too much imbibing.

"I will not shut up. I do hate you! You were hitting on my sorority sister. You cheated on Mom. I hate you."

I didn't like Kay, but in that moment I sympathized with her. Until she hurled the next stream of insults at her dad. Then I felt kind of sorry for him, too. They were both hammered.

Their voices were muffled as they came inside. A moment later they echoed up the stairwell toward the second floor. And then they were on my floor in the hall right in front of my room, screaming and lobbing accusations and insults like they were waging nuclear war—nuclear family war.

"Say that one more time and I'm not paying another dime for your schooling. Not one. You can go to your bitch of a mother and make her pay."

"I hate you!" Kay strung the last word out for emphasis.

A door slammed. I heard a lock turn. And then pounding.

"That's it. I'm cutting you off. I'm done. Hear me? Done."

The pounding went on for another few minutes, sounding like he was going to break the door down. Just as I was about to call the RA or security or something because I was actually worried about Kay's safety if he decided to kick the door down, he cursed and quieted down. I closed my laptop and got ready for bed. I had a sink in my room. I brushed my teeth and washed my face, but I had to go down the hall to use the bathroom.

When I opened my door, Kay's dad was passed out in front of her door. As I stared at him, my RA came down the hall.

"Not another one," she said, shaking her head like she was the parent. "I'll be glad when this weekend is over. It's madness. Dads gone wild." Still shaking her head, she called campus security.

In that moment, I was glad for the secret dad I had. Things could be a lot worse.

When I got up on Sunday, Kay's dad was gone and the hall smelled like stale beer and male sweat. Like they'd coordinated it, at noon the dads got up. They hogged the showers and clogged the halls. I trundled downstairs to the dining hall, which was filled to capacity with brunching dads who looked hung over and were drinking coffee by the gallon. Tay was working, overworking. She looked stressed and tired. Her face was pink from the heat behind the counter where she worked as a barista, making coffee drinks and handing out pastries.

I shot her a sympathetic look as I came through her line. "Is your dad gone?"

"I had to work so he left early. He pulled out of town around eight."

"Smart man."

"I heard rumors of Logan and a fight. I want to hear everything."

That was a faint hope. I couldn't tell her much. "We'll catch up later. My usual?"

"Extra whip?" she asked, and made my drink.

By two the dads drove out of town in a steady stream like a trail of ants leaving a picnic. I needed to talk to Logan. I kept waiting for him to text me. Finally, insecure, I texted him *Has your dad left?*

Yeah. Finally.

I felt a sense of relief—Harlan was gone. I almost swore he left town in a puff of smoke. I thought I could still smell the sulfur.

Want to get together? I really needed, wanted, to see him. We had a lot to talk about.

My phone rang with the ringtone I'd set up for Logan. "Hi."

"Hey, El," he said. He sounded sleepy, hung over. "I never noticed before. Say 'hey, El' fast and you get 'hell.'" He laughed. "Ouch."

"Real funny. Thanks for that."

"Thought you'd appreciate it," Logan said. "My eye and my head feel like shit."

"That bad?"

"Worse."

I could hear the wince in his voice. "So—want me to come over and nurse you back to health? I'll find Nic and ask her to drop me by. I'll bring coffee." I put an enticing singsong in my voice, like coffee was simply irresistible.

There was a pause on his end. "Sorry, El. I want to, but I'm wasted. Dead tired. I need to get some sleep, get rid of this damn headache, and then hit the homework. I'm up to my black eyeball in homework and projects. I didn't get a thing done while my old man was here. A word to the wise: getting hammered on top of getting smacked in the head—not wise."

"Oh." I swallowed hard. I tried to cover my disappointment. "I see how it goes. The weekend's over so now you drop your fake girlfriend just like that?" I tried to sound teasing, hoping my hurt feelings didn't show through.

"Yeah, I'm dropping the fake girlfriend for the real thing. Come on, El. You know I wouldn't turn down the chance to spend time with you unless I *absolutely* had to."

My heart skipped a beat—was I now really his girlfriend?

"I'd never pick homework or headaches over anything, especially you."

Even though I found myself smiling, I was still feeling insecure, too. Leave it to me to be self-doubting and happy at the same time. "Okay, you're off the hook. Put some ice on that eye."

"The eye doesn't look that bad," he said. "Your friend doesn't pack as much power as that vicious pool ball did."

I laughed, slightly mollified and relieved. "Good. No offense, but you're hotter without the black eye. Less dangerous looking, but hotter."

"I'm hot, am I?"

"Don't get too full of yourself. Go get some sleep."

"I'll see you tomorrow, El. Dinner after work?"

"Sure." We worked the same shift for Jason in the IT department on Mondays, Wednesdays, and Fridays. It had become our habit to grab a bite to eat together afterward at the SUB when we had the opportunity. Logan was a field tech, so he was often out of the office and it didn't always work out.

Bre was still out with her dad. He must have been the last dad to leave town. Nic was like Logan, needing sleep after partying with her dad. Taylor was on shift at the dining hall until after dinner. Payback for having the rest of the weekend off. I had no one to talk to and nothing to do but homework.

I headed to the science library just for a change of scenery. On the way there, I had to wind through a game of Zombies. Particularly since Halloween, you'd be walking around campus and suddenly you'd see someone sprinting, trying to get away from a crowd of people who were trying to tag and zombify them. In this case, a stocky guy was running up the hill from the library with half a dozen other guys after him. A couple of them looked like they'd been on the track team in high school. They were gaining on him fast. Zombies

do have superhuman strength. I felt sorry for the guy
who was being pursued.

"Go! Go!" I yelled at the runner, who was quite possibly the last human standing in his dorm. I tried to
protect the human race and play defense by blocking
some of the zombies.

As the crowd of zombies parted to go around me,
one of them paused and catcalled at me. "Hey, you're
cute. Can I have your number?"

"Sorry. I don't date the undead."

"I won't be undead forever." He winked at me.

He wasn't bad looking. If not for Logan, I might
have been tempted. I turned and yelled at the stocky
guy. "I have your back. Run!"

I was smiling as I walked down the hill to the library
and ran into my friend and chem study buddy and lab
partner, Dex.

"Dex!" I jogged to catch up to him at the door to the
library.

He waited and held it open for me. "Nothing better
to do on a Sunday afternoon than study?" He was smiling.

"Me? What are you talking about? Just now I was
saving humanity from the zombie apocalypse."

Dex rolled his eyes. "That game has gotten out of
hand. You can't go anywhere without running into a
horde of zombies."

"Says the man who's his dorm champion." I paused
to catch my breath. "One of them asked for my number."

"That doesn't surprise me. The undead are amazingly horny."

I shook my head. "What about you? Why aren't you sleeping off a hangover after partying with your dad like practically everyone else on this campus? You'd think the campus was full of undead." I slid in the door out of the cold November air and into the foyer area in between the next set of double doors.

Dex grinned. "Some people know how to party responsibly." He winked. "Hey, Dad really liked you. That's high praise. Dad's very discriminating."

"Did he?" I smiled, pleased. Dex had one of the good dads. "I thought he was awesome, too." Dex's dad had helped bring down our evil chem prof. "How come you never told me you have such a cool dad?"

"You never asked."

I grinned back and followed him into the library. "I owe him."

"We all owe him." Dex led the way up to the second floor where the study tables were.

"The question is—will we even need to study for chem now that the witch is in jail?" I couldn't help smiling.

"Don't get cocky, kid." Dex dropped his backpack onto a prime study table. "We don't know what a new prof will do about the test grades and scores we already have. The semester's more than half over. We may still have to work like hell to bring those grades up."

The whole class was basically failing because of the way Dr. Rogers taught and graded.

I shrugged. "Maybe. But not if we get a cool replacement like Professor Kim. He was awesome when he filled in for Dr. Rogers—funny. Easy to understand. He actually made chemistry seem almost easy. I know he'd be fair. He all but told us how unjust he thought Dr. Rogers was being and how she was a horrible teacher."

I set my backpack on the table across from Dex and pulled out my laptop. "Speaking of chemistry, I need your opinion." I brought up the missed-connections page. "I hope I'm wrong, but I think Byron has a crush on me."

Dex shook his head and gave me a "well duh" look. "Of course he has a crush on you, Ellie. That was the whole point of buttering him up and flirting with him. That was why we got all the extra help from him."

I made a face at Dex, feeling guilty again. "You're supposed to make me feel better, not worse. It was your plan that got me into this mess." I quickly brought up the post I'd read earlier, the one written by the guy who'd been helping a secret crush with her chem. I swung my laptop around so Dex could read it, watching as he did.

"Definitely Byron." He shrugged again, like *What can you do?* "Sorry. Want me to tag you? Or Byron? Or both?"

"Do and I'll kill you."

He laughed.

"I'm serious. Don't you dare." I stared him down. "What do I do now?"

"Continue stringing him along until the semester is over and final grades are posted. Shouldn't be too tough."

"Shut up. I'm not going to keep giving him false hope."

"It's just another month and a half."

"No."

Dex pursed his lips, then shrugged. "What's the alternative? Stop going to your standing Tuesday chem help session? I'm warning you, if you don't go, you're taking a chance with our grades."

"Am not. Byron isn't vindictive."

Dex looked skeptical and shook his head. "You have no idea how the male mind works. You know what they say about a nerd scorned."

"No. I don't. You're just making that up."

Dex glanced back at my laptop screen and frowned as he read something. "Logan has a black eye again, doesn't he?"

"Yeah," I said, unconcerned. Of course Dex would be careful about bringing that subject up. I couldn't understand, though, why he wasn't teasing me about it. "Why? How do you know? I didn't see you at that little pregame bash. I thought you and your dad would be there."

Dex was still frowning slightly. "We stopped by after the action." Dex paused. "Dad hates those kinds of events. He really hates making small talk. It was purely a duty call. I will say Logan's antics spiced things up and made the party worth the stop and the small talk easy. They were still cleaning up the mess when we left.

Nice that you have a boyfriend to play white knight for you. I heard what that Schwartz guy said was pretty vile."

I blushed. "Yeah." I bit my lip. "And true—my ex did sleep with my mom."

"Shit, that's awful. I'm sorry." Dex looked really uncomfortable.

I shrugged. "Everyone's sorry but her. And she's the only one who should be. Even the ex apologized." I took a deep breath and stared at my hands on the table. "Let's not talk about it again, okay?"

"Sounds good to me." Dex paused. "Ellie, take a look at this." He spun my laptop around to face me.

I looked at him, puzzled.

"Someone else has a thing for Logan." Dex grinned like he was trying to joke and take the sting away. But he didn't fool me. He was still uncomfortable. "The downsides of being a hunk."

I frowned just slightly. "Do you want me to write a missed connection about you to up your prestige around campus? *Cute, slightly nerdy guy studying on the second floor of the sci library at the table in the corner. Smart guys turn me on. HMU, the admiring brunette sitting across from you.*"

"Shut up and read." But he was trying not to laugh at my antics.

Hot guy at The College Grind, a black eye again? I like fighters. I see you everywhere I go like we were meant to be. But you never notice me. I was the blonde sitting by the window with a navy pea coat slung over my chair when you arrived just after three. You got coffee with an attractive woman who looked like she was almost thirty. I can be more fun than she is. Promise. HMU—a blonde who's worshipping you from afar.

My mouth went dry and my pulse raced. I froze. The post was time stamped just minutes ago. *Amber.* The older woman had to be Amber. Logan had lied to me. Ditched me for Amber.

"Ellie?"

I glanced up at Dex, stunned.

"You okay? You look like you just saw a ghost."

I nodded. "I'm fine. Post-traumatic shock after seeing that zombie horde."

"Don't worry," Dex said. "Don't be one of those insecure, clingy girls. The blonde says he never notices her. A guy has to like a girl a whole lot to take a swing at another guy for her like Logan did for you. Logan likes *you.*"

Did he? It looked an awful lot to me like he'd just lied to me and gone out with Amber.

CHAPTER FIVE

"Logan said 'I love you'? Wow." Nic sat on her bed in
the room she shared with Taylor.

Taylor sat on her bed and I sat in her disc chair. It
was already almost eleven on Sunday night and this
was the first time we'd had to catch up since Friday
morning. They'd heard about the Dr. Rogers scandal.
Everyone on campus had. But I had so much more to
tell them.

"Like *I love you* I love you. Not like *This is the best
chicken potpie I ever ate. Thanks for making it for me,
I love you?*"

"Like *I love you* I love you," I said.

"Look, I get his dad is an ass. You don't like violence
and are unhappy Logan got in a fight, even though it
was to protect you, which I think is really sweet of him,

chivalry is not dead, but why aren't you happier?" Tay sat up straighter, looking like she really didn't understand. "The whole thing sounds pretty romantic to me. If I had a guy as hot as Logan tell me he loved me, my friends would not be in any doubt that I was delirious with joy. Over the moon."

I pulled my phone out and brought up the missed-connections page. "I think my chem TA has a thing for me, too." I spoke almost mindlessly as I handed the phone to Tay, who read it and handed it to Nic.

"That's random and off topic," Tay said. "Though probably true. So you have two guys after you—a hot guy every girl wants and a nerdy lab TA?" She shrugged. "Lucky you. I don't see the problem. Don't let the nerd liking you bring you down."

"Read down a few posts," I said. "And you'll see why I'm worried."

Nic was still holding my phone. She frowned as she skimmed the posts, looking confused. "Oh."

I knew she'd found the right one. She paused and looked up at me. "Who are you worried about? The blond chick he never notices or the older woman?" She handed the phone to Tay to read.

Just the phrase "older woman" sent a chill through me. And reminded me of Mom and Austin. I bit my lip. "Look at the time and date stamp."

Nic jumped up and plopped next to Tay so she could read over her shoulder.

"I had *just* talked to Logan after his dad left this afternoon. He told me he couldn't see me. He was too tired and had too much to do. He was going to take a nap and then study. And then..." I took a deep breath.

Nic gave me a sympathetic look. "Maybe it isn't him? Maybe you're getting too full of yourself thinking all of these missed connections are about you." The way she said it, I knew she was gently ribbing me, trying to make me feel better, even though she was contradicting what she'd said earlier.

But I didn't feel better at all. I was miserable. "I love him. I don't want to lose him. What am I going to do?"

"Fight for him," Tay said.

I fought back a wave of anxiety. "How can I compete against *her*? Have you seen what she looks like?" I grabbed my phone from Tay, brought up Amber's picture, and shoved the phone back at her.

Nic looked at Amber and then at me and shrugged. "She's got nothing on you, girl. Except age."

Tay handed my phone back to me. "And that isn't in her favor."

I loved Nic and Tay at that moment for being such true friends. But I shook my head. "And experience. She's just like my mom—confident and sexy. Competitive." I left the next part unsaid: *knows how to seduce men and wrap them around her finger.*

"Look, don't go all massively depressed on us," Nic said. "Logan says he loves you. Then the next day he goes for this Amber? That doesn't make any sense. Either he's a lying douchebag, in which case, dump him. You're better off without him. Or there's some logical explanation. Just talk to him, Ellie." She smiled at me. "Talk to him. What can it hurt? One way or another, you'll find out where you stand. Better to find that out now than later."

It was sound advice. But if the news was bad, a huge part of me didn't want to find out. *Ever.*

On Monday mornings I had chem at nine. If there had been any other section available, I would *never* have signed up for Chem 202 at that ungodly hour. As usual, I dragged myself to the dining hall and got a cup of coffee in an attempt to wake up. Dressed in yoga pants and an oversized sweatshirt, I approached the lecture hall and chemistry with a certain amount of happy anticipation—goodbye, Dr. Rogers. Hello, funny, happy Professor Kim. Hopefully.

Dex waited for me in our usual seats. I loved my seat—it had a speaker in the row in front of it that I used as a table for my coffee. The lecture hall buzzed with anticipation and the mood was almost festive as we waited for our new prof to show up.

"I'm betting on Professor Kim," I said to Dex.

"Me too," he said as I settled in.

The bell rang and the lectern was still empty. People were looking at each other, puzzled. We'd all looked on our university accounts to see who the new prof would be. The university had not announced it ahead of time, but the administration had made it clear that class was not canceled. No one really knew what to do. I looked at Dex. He gave me a quizzical look back. And then the door to the lower level opened and a skinny, nerdy guy with an acne problem came out carrying a laptop and a chemistry book.

I looked at Dex again and frowned. "What's Byron doing down there?"

Dex held his hands up palms up like he had no idea. "Introducing the new prof?"

Byron approached the lectern and set his laptop and chem book down on it. "Morning." Byron's voice unfortunately cracked just as the mic squealed with feedback. He turned bright red.

"Sorry!" He cleared his throat. "As you know, uh, Dr. Rogers has, is, unfortunately unable to finish out the semester." Pause. "Yeah. Soooo." Pause. "I'm going to be taking her place and filling in as your instructor for the rest of the semester. Uh, yeah.

"For those of you who have me as your lab TA, you'll be reassigned another grad student, Bhat. He's very good. Yeah. You'll like him."

I felt the blood leave my face. "No," I whispered to Dex. Things had just gone from bad to worse.

"Looks like you're going to be going to that standing study session of yours after all," Dex said. "Or his new office hours."

"Shut up." I was in deep trouble now—my new professor had a crush on me. Ouch. Dr. Rogers having a thing for Logan had nearly ruined him.

GPA warrior that he was, Dex turned to me. "You need to step up our game. How are you going to top cobblestone bars now?" He leaned in and whispered directly in my ear, "Maybe you should reconsider my suggestion to sleep with him." Dex's voice was teasing.

"No. Way."

"Okay," Dex said. "But you're going to have to start flirting all over with Bhat."

"Byron is your new chem professor?" Nic looked at me, just as aghast as I was.

I nodded as I got ready for work.

"This is bad," she said, sitting on Bre's bed and leaning against the wall.

"Byron's a good guy," I said, trying to be optimistic about something. "He won't sabotage me."

She looked skeptical.

I blew out a long breath. "I wish I'd never looked at missed connections. Then I'd never know...about any of this stuff."

"Ignorance is bliss for a reason," Nic said. "But you're forgetting one thing—Byron doesn't know you saw the post or have any suspicions about him. So ignore it."

"That's true," I said, thinking the same thing was true of Logan. What if I just ignored it?

"Uh-oh," Nic said. "Don't go there. I see what you're thinking—that you can ignore the post you think is about Logan. That's not the same thing and you know it. That post could eat up your relationship. You don't have a relationship with Byron. They aren't equivalent. Talk to Logan at dinner tonight."

"I'm so looking forward to going to work now."

"Hey, work's work. You should be excited about having dinner with a guy who loves you."

"Maybe. Maybe he loves me."

Nic shook her head. "Insecurity is not sexy. Just remember that, Ellie."

My phone buzzed in my pocket. I grabbed it. When I saw who it was from, my heart plopped right into my stomach. "Uh-oh. How does he even have my number?"

"What?" Nic slid over next to me and read over my shoulder. "Byron. You never gave it to him?"

I shook my head.

"Then he abused his power and got it from university records. That's my guess." Nic frowned and read it out loud. "*What do you think of my new position? Exciting, isn't it? Stop by my office tomorrow and we'll talk about how to bring your grade up.*" Nic stared at me. "Sounds innocuous enough."

"If you don't know the situation," I said.

"What do you think he's going to suggest?"

I shrugged.

"What are you going to do?"

"Nothing." I slid the phone back into my jeans pocket. "I have to run."

I grabbed my purse and left for work. I couldn't tell Nic the other reason I was nervous about work—now that I knew for sure Jason was my dad, I wasn't sure how I'd deal with it.

As it turned out, I shouldn't have worried. Jason was his friendly, boss-ly self. But now there was a secret between us that bound us and gave our relationship a new depth. Now that I knew he was really my dad, I was proud of him in a way that made me beam when I looked at him. He was a good guy. A really good guy.

We were swamped with emergency calls for tech support from almost the minute I sat down at my desk. The calls kept Logan and the other techs out in the field. Just before five, Logan texted me to meet him at the SUB. I was waiting for him when he came walking up the hill in the dark, the streetlights lighting his puffs of breath in the cold, tiny silver clouds of life.

He looked like a dark angel as he walked up the hill with his dark hair haloed by the light. A beautiful, darkly driven angel.

"El!" His eyes lit up when he saw me. He pulled me into a kiss—his mouth was warm. His cheeks were cold. I was totally hot for him, wishing the moment would last forever. "How was your day?" he asked as he broke the kiss and held the door to the SUB open for me.

I stepped inside. "Awful."

"Awful? Worse than mine?" He cocked one eyebrow, trying to make me laugh.

"Yours was bad?" I took his arm and leaned my head against his shoulder as we walked. "I'm sorry."

"It's better now that I'm with you."

I laughed, but I was nervous. "Do you practice lines like that to use on the girls?"

He winked at me. "What do you think?"

"Your eye looks better." I touched it gently.

He smiled and shrugged. Neither of us wanted to talk about what caused it.

"Do you want to tell me about your day?" I said.

"You know my motto—never divulge bad shit on an empty stomach. Let's get our food first."

"That's your motto?"

He grinned. "One of my mottos."

"Is it like on your family crest or something. If it is-n't, it should be."

He grinned. "I'll suggest that to Dad."

I protested, but Logan insisted on buying dinner. We decided on pizza. I got one slice. He got three. We got our usual table by the windows, but it was already dark outside so there wasn't much to see.

"You go first," he said, picking up a slice of pizza. "Tell me about your crappy day."

"Byron is my new chem prof." I just blurted it out.

"No way." He laughed. "Your lab TA? The one you've spent the entire semester baking cookies for and flirting with?"

"I wasn't flirting with him."

"Sure you were." He wiped his mouth with a paper napkin.

"Was not."

"What's so bad about that?"

"I think he has a thing for me."

Logan laughed. "Really."

"You aren't jealous?"

He laughed again and his smile was infectious. Logan's moods were mercurial. He was having a crappy day one minute and laughing the next. It was part of what made him mysterious and sexy. "Do you want me to be? I can play the jealous boyfriend. Do you want me to take a swing at him?" He pointed to his healing black eye. "I can take another one for you."

"Shut up." I smiled at him. "You know how much I just love fighting and seeing you get hurt." But at that moment I loved him even more. I grabbed his hand where it rested on the table and squeezed it.

He squeezed back. "Don't think I can take him?"

"Don't think I want you in jail for assault."

He turned suddenly serious. "A prof having the hots for you is serious shit, El. What makes you think he does?"

We were on dangerous, delicate ground now. It was like walking on frost—so easy to crush it. I had to proceed carefully. A professor being infatuated with Logan had led to her using date-rape drugs on him. Yeah, guys can be raped, too, using drugs like GHB. Logan had been particularly vulnerable when it happened—he'd been addicted to prescription painkillers after his baseball injury, the one that ended his career.

I froze, caught in my own trap. I couldn't reveal why I suspected without revealing my suspicions about Logan from missed connections. "You mean besides the flustered way he acts around me?" I paused, wondering whether I should tell Logan about Byron's text. Finally, I gave in, thinking I was keeping too many secrets from him as it was. "He texted me. He wants me to come to his office and discuss how to bring my grade up."

"That sounds innocent enough..." He saw my face and then it hit him. "He texted you? He has your number? El, did you give it to him?" His brow furrowed like he was worried.

"No," I said softly.

"Shit!" He squeezed my hand tighter. "He's crossing a line. What are you going to do?"

"I don't know."

"Don't go. A grade isn't worth it. I should know."

My heart broke for Logan. If I could have taken his pain away, I would have.

"El?"

I shrugged.

"If you decide to go, I'm going with you."

"I should go. Make it clear I'm not interested in him that way. It's just his office. In broad daylight. Maybe I'm reading too much into this. Maybe it doesn't mean anything." But I only said that to put Logan at ease. I was pretty sure Byron was infatuated with me. I changed the subject. "Tell me about your day."

Logan stared at me and sighed, like he knew I was using a diversion. And like his day had been really bad. "I had a long phone conversation with my dad's lawyers." He held my gaze.

"Not about the fight?"

"No, El. About...*her.*"

"Her" was Dr. Rogers. We never mentioned her by name. It was too embarrassing and painful for Logan.

"Okay," I said, not wanting to push him for details.

"I don't remember anything about what she did to me, only what happened after, but I want to testify." He took a deep breath and released my hand, balling his fist. "Against Dad's wishes. He's going to be so pissed. You know, I'll be bringing down the family name and all. But it's ridiculous. I can't be a coward. I wasn't the only victim. I can't let her get away with what she did. I have to make sure she's punished."

"President Lawrence said they have plenty of evidence against her without—"

"This is something I have to do, El." Logan pounded the table gently to emphasize his point. The look he gave me was a challenge—was I on his side or was I against him? Would I support him, or be embarrassed like his dad? Would I walk away?

I swallowed hard and nodded. "I'm here for you, Logan, whatever you decide to do." I paused, trying to get a grip on my emotions. It was hard to explain how I felt. "You're the bravest guy I know. A total hero."

Relief washed over his face and he gave me a small smile. "When Dad finds out, Thanksgiving is going to be real fun. Sure you still want to come?"

"Absolutely. I love fireworks."

He laughed softly.

And then, I did a bad thing and struck while he was vulnerable, making it look like I was just changing the subject to something innocent for his sake, while I was really fishing for the truth. "How did your studies go last night?"

He looked relieved and happily surprised by the new topic. But I wondered if I sounded too suspicious.

"Great. Got a lot done." Suddenly he looked sheepish. "But I have a confession to make—I didn't nap. I realized I had too much work to do. So I made a coffee run to The College Grind. I ran into Amber and chatted with her for a few. She was on her way out of town and needed a caffeine buzz, too."

It was like he had read my mind. I felt so relieved. How could I have doubted him?

"Why are you smiling?" he asked.

"Am I?" I hadn't meant to be so obvious. But now I had to explain myself. I grabbed his phone from where it rested on the table next to his tray. "So it *was* you."

"What was me?"

"Have you seen missed connections lately? You have a secret admirer." I brought it up for him and watched him read it.

He frowned as he read it, then turned a serious look on me. "You thought I ran out on you to see Amber?"

I shrugged.

"El, you have nothing to worry about. You're the only girl for me."

"That's not what the blonde thinks."

He laughed. "Well, she's dead wrong. But thanks for letting me know. Now every blonde I see, I'll think they're lusting after me."

I shook my head. "You're awful."

He leaned across the table and kissed me. "Always talk to me," he said. "If you ever see anything like this again that makes you doubt me, just ask. We have to be able to talk to each other. No more secrets."

I swallowed hard and nodded. No more secrets. *Right.*

"Hey, did you see there's an Up All Night event on Friday? The theme is magic—free food, a hypnotist, magic acts. You want to go?"

We had met at the first Up All Night event of the fall semester. "Are you asking me out on an official date that doesn't involve dads or being your fake girl-friend?"

He grinned. "Yeah. This will be kind of like our anniversary."

"We haven't been together all this time."

"But I wanted you the whole time."

He could be just so darn adorable. He made my heart melt.

His eyes danced. He knew he had me. "Some people have a song. This is our thing. We have an event. Pick you about at eight thirty?"

"Yeah," I said.

CHAPTER SIX

Nic caught me in the hall when I returned from work. "See! I told you there was a logical explanation." Nic was insufferable about being right about Logan. "All you had to do was talk to him." Her eyes sparkled. "Must be something in the air—I got asked to Up All Night today, too."

"No? Are you going?"

"Yeah."

The way she said "yeah," I knew the guy was someone special. "This isn't the guy from your English class is it?"

"Kurt. Yeah." Her face lit up. Kurt was some kind of poet or artist or something. She'd been trying to get his attention all semester.

"All right—dish!"

She pulled me into her room to tell me the details. As she talked, I found myself wishing my life were as uncomplicated as Nic's. Wouldn't it be nice to just like a guy with no secrets involved?

Tuesday morning was cold and frosty. There were rumors that it was supposed to snow later. I got up, showered, and dressed with care, making sure I looked extra cute to meet Jason. He saw me in the office all the time. But when I was working, I was generally dressed with the dual purpose of looking professional and im- pressing Logan as much as possible. This was different. There was something about having an official coffee date with my dad that made me want to impress *him*. I didn't want to disappoint him. Or have him reject me. I was so insecure about all of it. So I applied my makeup carefully, using all the tricks Mom had taught me, and dressed accordingly—dark-wash jeans with rhine- stones on the butt, cute pink sweater, knee-high boots. Frankly, I was as nervous as I was excited.

I bundled up in my cute wool coat and sweet hot- pink hat and left early so I could arrive early and be waiting for him. Eager-looking, maybe. But that was okay. By the time I left, it was already snowing and sticking to the grass and trees.

When I walked into The College Grind, I was still early and too late. Jason waved to me from a table in the corner. "Ellie! Fancy meeting you here." There was a twinkle in his eyes at our inside joke, and he looked only the slightest bit nervous, not upset.

Like father, like daughter. We shared the early gene and were both in the same frame of mind. I was touched he was trying to put me at ease and relieved—after having a couple of days to come to terms with it, he looked like he was dealing with it.

"Hey, boss." I walked over to his table, hopeful we could get off to a good start now. "What are you doing here? Need your morning jolt to make it through the day?"

"Hey, Ellie! Have a seat and let me buy my favorite dispatcher a drink," he said.

I laughed as I took my coat off and hung over the back of the chair. "Careful! Someone might get the wrong idea." I sat and stuffed my gloves in my coat pocket.

"What am I supposed to say?" He looked amused.

"How about: 'Would you like a hot beverage, my treat'? But the 'favorite dispatcher' was a nice touch, even if there are only like five of us to choose from. Still an honor."

He laughed. "Ah, I see. Much better. Much less suggestive." He paused to study me.

It was weird for both of us, this new shift in our relationship going from boss and stranger to father and daughter.

"So, would you like a hot beverage?" he said. "On the boss for being a stellar worker."

I nodded. "The perks of doing a good job." I laughed at my pun. "Grande mocha with whip."

"You got it." He jumped up and ordered while I saved our table.

My dad was buying me a coffee. It was almost impossible for me to really comprehend, surreal.

He returned to wait for the barista to call out our order. "How was your Dad's Weekend?" he asked.

I couldn't tell whether his question was barbed or not. I didn't know him well enough to recognize the subtleties of his personality.

I was certain Jason had heard about Logan punching Schwartz. He'd seen Logan yesterday at work and I was certain Logan would have told him how he got his black eye. Maybe Logan had even called him after it happened. They were that close. But had Logan told him exactly *why* he'd gotten into the fight? Or that I'd been with him when he'd punched Schwartz? Or that I'd tried to stop him? I knew Logan and Jason talked, but I didn't know how much they talked about Logan's love life and relationship with me, if at all. And suddenly it struck me—I hoped they didn't talk about it at all. It was bad enough thinking Logan might confide personal things to my boss, but to my dad? Can you imagine? I was horrified. I made a note to ask Logan not to talk about me to Jason.

I stared at Jason, trying to hide my thoughts. "It was good," I said, noncommittally. "I had dinner with Logan and his dad Friday night. I went to the game with them on Saturday."

I couldn't read the look in Jason's eyes, but if I had to guess, I would have said it wasn't exactly pleased. *He knows everything*, I thought.

Before either of us could react, the barista called our order. Jason jumped up to get it before I could.

When he returned to the table and set my drink in front of me, his expression was masked. "Logan's dad is a hard man, a real piece of work."

Since we were in public, it was understood between us that we couldn't say anything confidential that would give me away as his daughter. We had to be subtle and imply things.

"Yeah," I said. "I know."

"What did you think of him?" Jason took a sip of coffee while keeping his gaze level on me over his cup. He had piercing eyes, beautiful eyes. But he was dancing around the main issue.

For just a sec I had the unsettling thought of my mom looking into those eyes and falling in love with them and him. That was crazy—Jason and Mom had a one-night stand that resulted in me. Nothing more, as far as I knew. Someday, when we knew each other better and were on firmer ground, someday when we were alone, I was going to ask him about his relationship with Mom and demand answers. I wanted to know my story. But now was not the time. Now I had to tread cautiously, hoping to build a real relationship with him. Right now that long-ago past wasn't as important as building a future.

"He's just like you say—a hard man and an ass."

"I don't remember calling him an ass."

I smiled at him. "But you wanted to."

He smiled back. It was obvious he didn't like or respect Harlan. We were in complete agreement. Jason took another sip of coffee. His expression turned serious. "How serious are you and Logan?"

Again, I wondered how much Logan had confided in Jason since we met—had he been telling Jason all along how into me he was? How impossible it was for us to be together while Dr. Rogers was my chem prof?

I masked my own expression, trying to keep my true feelings from showing, and went on the offensive rather than answering. I leaned close and whispered so no one else could hear: "Fatherly interest?"

He didn't smile. "Maybe. Maybe it's just my way of getting to know you."

I shrugged. "What has Logan told you?"

"Don't be insecure, Ellie. Don't fish for information out of me or try to throw me off. Whatever Logan has told me is confidential. I can't divulge it. I'm certainly not repeating it to you. You're hedging."

"Is this conversation confidential, too?" I held Jason's gaze.

"Absolutely."

I nodded. "Good to know."

"So?"

I shrugged again. "Not that it's any of your business, but I like him *a lot*. You know that." It was a non-answer and we both knew it.

Jason sighed. "He has a temper, Ellie. Be careful."

I shook my head. I could not believe this. "You mean because he punched out Schwartz? That's what you're talking about, isn't it?" I grabbed my napkin and balled it in my fist as I leaned toward Jason. "He was defending *me*. Did he tell you what Schwartz said about my ex-boyfriend sleeping with Mom?"

Jason nodded and set his jaw. "Yes." He looked pained, like he was sorry again for sticking me with a mom like Melissa. And like he couldn't believe the person Mom was or had become since he'd known her. "I'm sorry Melissa hurt you like that. Schwartz was a jerk for throwing it at you. If I'd been there..."

He sighed again. "I admire Logan for defending you. I'm grateful for it. It's what a man should do. But violence is not the answer. Logan should have maintained control and handled it differently. Asked Schwartz to leave. Gotten security. Not taken the first swing in a blind rage."

Jason was definitely different than the rest of Mom's men. All of them would have reacted exactly like Logan—swung first and asked questions later. I suppressed a shudder. *Logan isn't like them*, I told myself.

"You weren't there," I said, defending Logan.

Jason didn't back down. "I didn't have to be." He paused. "How much do you know about Logan?"

"Everything." I blurted it out like I was defending him, and accidentally giving away how serious I was about him.

"Everything?" Jason raised one eyebrow.

"I know about his career-ending baseball injury, and what happened with Dr. Rogers. And how he was out of control for a while and you saved him."

Jason nodded almost imperceptibly. "I don't know that I *saved* him."

"Don't be modest. He told me you did. He said without you..."

Jason set his cup down, but kept his hand wrapped around it, still studying me.

I blushed for real now.

He hesitated a second, then looked like he came to a decision about something. "I'd be surprised if you know *everything*, Ellie."

I didn't answer. I didn't believe him. Of course I knew everything—everything important.

Jason sighed. "Look, Logan is one of my favorite students *ever*. He has more potential..." He took a deep breath. "He could be a great man *someday*. I'll do everything I can to help him be the man I know he can be. But right now..."

He paused again, looking tormented or conflicted or something. "I have to say this and it's going to sound bad. I don't mean it to, but as your—" He cut himself off and held his hands out in front of him, palms up, in that gesture that meant "fill in the blank."

"I have to warn you. Logan has issues, serious issues. I don't want to see you get hurt. *Either* of you."

I couldn't believe what I was hearing. I simply stared at him. "What are you saying? That I shouldn't see him?" I couldn't keep the anger from my voice.

Jason looked tortured, but resolved. "I realize I don't have the right to say anything. But, yes, it would be better, I think, if you didn't become too attached to him."

I didn't know what to say. This was so unexpected. I was stunned.

Jason grabbed my hand. "See? Remember what I told you about teenagers? I'm messing this up. I care about *both* of you." He squeezed my hand. "I want the best for each of you. But you and I have a special bond. You're my priority. I have to look out for you and warn and advise you when I can. I haven't been there to do that while you were growing up like I should have been. I'm furious at Melissa for that and trying to deal with it." His eyes got a hard look in them that made me believe him.

"Even though I didn't know about you, I feel guilty as hell for that. I'm trying to do my best now, from here on out.

"What you ultimately do is up to you. I'll be here for you. Either way. *Know* that."

I looked at him, nodded, and swallowed a lump in my throat. He spoke so forcefully and with such emotion, I knew he meant it. I was upset with him and angry because he was going all dad on me. But touched at the same time because he cared enough about me, however misguidedly, that he was willing to risk our relationship and warn me about Logan. Even if he was dead wrong. I squeezed his hand in return. I let go and reached for my coffee.

"Promise me you'll think about what I said? And proceed cautiously? Don't move too fast or lose your heart too completely?"

It was too late for that. But I nodded anyway, suddenly feeling like I couldn't breathe. My worst fear was coming true—without meaning to, I was driving a wedge between Jason and Logan. And unknowingly, Logan was coming between me and my dad.

Jason looked at me tentatively. "You okay? Are we okay?" His voice was touchingly tender and concerned.

"Yeah," I said. How could I be mad at him?

"I just found you. I don't want to lose you." He gave me a lopsided grin.

"No. Me either." It was so true, I spoke without hesitation. "Promise me something?"

"Yes?"

"That you won't talk to Logan about me. It's not fair to him, or me. He doesn't know he's talking to my..." I trailed off, leaving the blank for him to fill in. "He might tell you things he ordinarily wouldn't tell, you know, my boss."

Jason smiled very slightly. "I can't promise that, Ellie. If he brings you up—"

"Just don't bring it up on your own. And if he veers into personal territory, you veer him right back out of it." I looked at Jason for confirmation. "That's fair."

"All right. You make a good point. I promise."

"And—"

"There's an and, too?" His tone was teasing.

I had to fight not to smile. This was serious. "Promise you won't discourage him from seeing me."

Jason stared at me as he considered my request. "Okay. On one condition."

"What? You get a condition, too?"

He nodded. "Oh, yeah. Fair's fair. You have to trust me and listen if I find it necessary to warn you about him again." He held out his hand like he wanted to shake. "What do you say? Deal?"

I hesitated only a second before shaking his hand. "Deal."

"Good." He glanced at his watch. "I have to run. We don't want to linger so long we start tongues wagging." He smiled. "Can we make this a standing weekly date?"

I smiled back. "Yeah. Sure."

"Great."

"Good. Now before I go, tell me something I don't know about you. I'm dying to know everything."

I smiled. "That's easy—you don't know much."

"Did you just insult my intelligence?"

I shook my head and grinned. "My favorite color is blue." I grabbed my coat from the back of my chair and pulled my gloves from my pocket.

He laughed. "Be prepared with something more personal next week."

When we left, it was snowing even harder. I got a text from Byron telling me he had an actual office now in the chem department administration suite on the third floor, office number 323. He told me to meet him there for our appointment.

During the semester I had sort of bonded with Byron. He was nerdy and awkward, but he knew chemistry and had been a huge help to me in it and with my quest to bake the perfect cobblestone bar. He'd been really sweet to me that time I'd been upset about Logan and had broken down and cried in his old office, a small, partitioned-off space in the back of the chem lab. But none of that made me any more eager to see him.

At our regularly appointed time after chem lab, I made my way to the chem building through an ever-intensifying flurry of snow. The ground was covered with several inches. It showed no thought of slowing. In the chem department offices, the admin pointed me to Byron's new space—a dank little office with a window that once again looked out on the parking garage next door and the garbage dumpsters below, like his old office in the lab had, only from a few floors above. Better view of the garbage. His door was open. I knocked on it anyway.

"Ellie! Come in." Byron was sitting at his desk. His face lit up when he saw me and went blotchy in red patches, like it did when he was nervous or excited. He studied me. "You look gorgeous today."

Damn! Bad planning on my part. I should have taken off my makeup, and even the snow hadn't managed to ruin my hair. I'd fixed up for my dad, but now Byron was getting the completely wrong idea.

It was warm in his office. As I unbuttoned my coat, I thought again how hard it was for a guy like Byron to be a romantic figure when he blushed so unevenly like that. I felt sorry for him, but there had to be a girl out there for him somewhere. I took a step in and made a show of scanning his tiny, dark office with its cast-off furniture. It looked like it had recently been used for storage. Was that a broom in the corner? I could imagine the other professors complaining about having to give up their storeroom.

"Wow!" I said, trying to sound awed, but really being awed by how crappy it was and how much it

smelled like cheap grocery-store-variety cologne. I
didn't want to think what *that* meant.

"Close the door," he said, beaming. "What do you
think? I haven't finished moving in yet, obviously."

I shut the door and thought it wasn't obvious at all.
His old space in the lab had looked pretty much the
same. "I'm sure it will be great when you do."

"Are you impressed?" He popped up and stood behind his desk, trying, I assumed, to look professorial.

"Yeah. Like I said, wow."

He shook his head and came around his desk. "I
don't mean the office. I mean—we did it!"

I froze, cold as the snow outside, and my heart nearly stopped. *We did it? What did that mean?*

I panicked, thinking he'd somehow discovered I'd
been part of the group who pranked Dr. Rogers, which
had led to Dex discovering her illegal drug lab. Not
that anyone besides our group knew Dex had been the
one to find it. I couldn't think how Byron could include
himself in that, though. Unless he'd realized I'd duped
him when I'd gone to his office hours and unlatched his
window so the gang could get into the chem building
the night of the prank.

I paled. Guilty consciences suck.

Byron put his arm around me. My first instinct
should have been to shake his arm off, but I was too
stunned to move.

"I got the job and we found away to make sure you
get a good grade, maybe even an A. A win for both of
us." He smelled like that cheap cologne and an over-
powering breath mint. "Now that I'm the professor..."

He smiled, creepily staring at me. "It's going to be okay now." He brushed my cheek.

I suppressed a shudder.

"No more tears." He did remember and was obviously, ineptly, trying to play hero. "No more worries."

I smiled weakly back at him and stepped out of his embrace. "Yeah, congrats. It was a real surprise when you were the guy who stepped out of the wings to lecture. We were all placing bets on Dr. Kim replacing Dr. Rogers."

"Probably next semester." Byron sighed like he was unhappy at the thought of being demoted back to TA. "He was too busy finishing up his research project this semester."

"Enjoy it while you can. It's still an honor for you to be chosen from all the lab TAs. And it will look fantastic on your résumé." I paused, realizing I was doing it again without meaning to. It was so easy to lead Byron on without trying. "Why don't you give me the tour?"

He beamed. "Can I take your coat?"

"No. Thanks, I'm fine." I wasn't planning to stay long, not a moment longer than necessary to secure my A.

He nodded. "There's not much to see—my bookshelves, file cabinet, desk. Some of the profs have tables and chairs and coffee machines in their offices."

I glanced at the far corner. And some of the profs still had a boatload of junk in Byron's. I hadn't imagined that broom. The janitor had been using it, too. Hmmm, Byron's office really was a broom closet.

"Ignore that," Byron said. "Some of the profs haven't gotten all their stuff out of here yet."

Yep, storage room.

"You can always bring in your own coffee machine." I tried to reclaim my personal space by stepping to the window, facing it, and looking out at snow falling on dumpsters. "You have pretty much the same view, I see."

"What? Oh, yes." He laughed nervously. "I'm just above the lab." He paused. "What did you think of my lecture?"

Touchy subject. I kept looking out the window at the falling snow, hoping he couldn't see my expression reflected in the window as I tried to be gentle. "It was great, for your first one. Just be yourself. You're a really good teacher when you're relaxed." I looked over my shoulder at him. "Back to my grades—what are you going to do about the grade mess Dr. Rogers left?"

Byron came up and stood right behind me. Like right behind me, so close I could feel his body heat. "I was going to ask your advice—what do you think is the best thing to do?"

I didn't have to think twice on that one. "Curve the grades, generously. Throw out the outliers like the one person who got an A on a test, if there is one." I snorted. Dr. Rogers only gave one A per semester and that was usually to her pet, the guy she had the hots for. "Then give extra credit to make up for all the injustices of her grading."

"That's exactly what I was thinking." He put his hand on my shoulder. "You still seem tense. You can

relax now, Ellie. I'm going to take care of you. Chemistry won't be a problem."

I froze again. Byron had the misguided notion that
all my emotional upheavals of the semester resulted
from thinking I was going to flunk chemistry. Probably
because he'd seen how unhappy I was and I'd cried on
his shoulder once, like literally. And let him think
chemistry was the problem because I really couldn't
talk about what I was going through. He had no idea
my problems really revolved around Logan and my dad.
And after talking to Jason, they still did.

"Thanks, I appreciate that," I said.

"How was Bhat in lab today?" he asked, too casually
to be uninterested.

I was growing more uncomfortable by the minute.
"Great. Good. Helpful. Knowledgeable." There was no
way I was going to rat on Bhat and give him some kind
of job performance review to his now boss.

"Good. Still come to me for help. Bhat will be busy
enough learning the job," Byron whispered in my ear.
"Everything will go on like before."

I froze. "Um, thanks." I paused. "I'm sure you're
busy. I'd better be going." I was hoping he'd get the
message and move out of my personal space. But when
I turned around to leave, he was right there.

"I think I love you, Ellie." He leaned toward me.

CHAPTER SEVEN

My mouth opened and closed, but no words came out. As I stared at him, stunned, he tried to kiss me. I side-stepped and ducked out of the way, trying to think of a way to let him down easy, which was purely a grade-preserving tactic, and cursing myself for being so naïve. I was only being nice to Byron. Why did he have to misinterpret it?

"Byron, that's all very sweet of you. I'm flattered. But you're my professor now. And the university frowns on professors and students..." I took a deep breath. "We can't... You could get in trouble. I don't want you to lose your job. And I—"

I was cut off just then by a quick knock on the door, followed by Dr. Homer, another chem prof, sticking his head in the door. "Byron? Do you have a minute?" He frowned. "Oh, sorry to interrupt. Didn't realize you were with a student."

"No problem," I said. "I was just leaving." I brushed past Byron and Dr. Homer and walked as fast as I could to the stairs. I just wanted to escape. When I finally reached the doors to outside and stepped into the bracing air, I took a deep breath and buttoned my coat. What was I going to do about Byron and chem now? Running out on a guy who'd just told me he loved me wasn't the best plan, maybe, but it was all I had.

I grabbed my cell phone, ready to text Logan and tell him what had happened. Remembering Jason's warning stopped me cold. I didn't believe, not for a minute, that Logan would threaten Byron or punch him or anything. But why look for trouble?

I made a snap decision to keep this to myself and not share it with Logan. The semester would end before Christmas break and then this problem would disappear. There were no more chem classes required for my minor. I just had to hang in there, act like nothing had happened, and avoid Byron as much as possible.

When I got back to the dorm, Tay and Nic were in their room. I told them about Byron's awkward pass.

Nic shook her head. "That's a stupid, crazy-ass plan. You should tell him to fuck off."

Tay laughed. "I think that's what he's looking for."

I laughed with her.

Tay frowned like she was thinking and considering. "You need a good grade and you have an uphill battle after what Dr. Rogers did. I'm for appealing to a higher authority—letting him think there might be hope, but blaming university policy for your reluctance to get involved. Once you have your final grade—bam! Run! Sever all ties."

Tay was taking psychology. She liked to spout things she'd learned.

"I tried that," I said.

"Yeah, but you ran out before you saw the effect," Tay said.

I frowned, doubtful.

"Give it another try and keep working it until the end of the semester." Tay nodded. "Bake him more cookies and go on, business as usual."

Nic shook her head. "You're a cruel woman, Tay. That's much harsher than my plan." Nic looked to me. "You're going to listen to her, I can see it on your face. At least take this piece of advice: keep the office door open at all times. See what I'm saying?"

It snowed and snowed and snowed. By nine that night there was a good six inches or more on the ground and excitement ran high—the first real snow of the season!

Logan texted me while I was studying in Nic and Tay's room. *Steal a tray from the dining hall. I'll be by to pick you up in fifteen minutes.*

"Logan wants me to steal a tray," I said to Nic. Tay was at work.

Nic looked up from her laptop where she was working on an essay for English. "He's going to take you traying? Awesome! You'd better hurry before they're all gone. Everyone wants one. The dining hall staff is probably on high alert for tray thieves already."

I jumped up. "What are we waiting for? Don't just sit there. Are you going to help me or what?"

Nic shrugged, shut her laptop, and grabbed her phone. "No worries. We have an inside connection in the dining hall. And fortunately for us, she just happens to be on shift when we need her."

"We can't ask Tay to steal a tray for us!"

Nic ignored me. She was already texting. She pressed send and looked up at me. "Who said anything about stealing? I prefer to think of it as borrowing. We'll return it later." Her phone buzzed. "Tay says she'll leave it in the alley. But we'd better hurry before someone else finds it."

"Aren't you going?" I asked Nic.

She grinned. "And ruin your romantic tray ride?"

But when we got to the alley a few minutes later, slinking around like cat burglars, there were two wet trays waiting for us. We grabbed them and dashed.

Back in Nic's room a few minutes later, we collapsed in giggles, clutching our prized trays. "I thought you said you weren't going?" I said when I finally caught my breath.

She winked. "I said I wasn't going *with you*. Pay attention to nuances, girl. They'll get you every time. Now. Go make yourself pretty for your man."

I'd barely finished refreshing my makeup when my phone buzzed with a text from Logan. *I'm at the front door.*

The dorm was locked at all times. You needed a key to get in. I texted him back. *Coming! Ha ha.* I grabbed my coat, gloves, and tray, slid the tray beneath my coat for stealth, and dashed to meet Logan. Just before I opened the front door to the dorm it struck me—maybe we should have stolen three trays. What was Logan going to do for a tray? Take turns?

My heart caught when I saw him, just like it always did. He was so incredibly hot, even bundled in a snowboarding jacket and black and gray beanie, the kind that flopped over the back of his head. I shouldn't have worried about the tray. Logan was carrying one.

He grabbed me and pulled me against him, kissing me with that fierce passion I lived for. His tongue was hot and talented in my mouth, giving me tingles all the way to my toes. When he pulled away, I was breathless.

He tapped my chest. "New bra? I don't like it. Too hard and plastic-y. Has a nice, hollow tap, though."

I laughed and pulled the tray out from beneath my coat. "Smart ass. I was being covert. The university will give you three to five hard labor if they catch you lifting one of these." I pointed at his. "Where did you get that?"

He shook his head and laughed. "The dining hall. Almost four years ago."

"You're supposed to return that after you use it."

He grinned. "I have every intention—when I graduate. This is a four-year loaner model."

"I see."

He took my gloved hand in his and led me out from beneath the covered front porch. "Isn't it gorgeous?" he said, but he was staring at me. "You look good enough to eat." He nuzzled my neck.

I laughed and pushed him away. "Wolf."

"Yeah," he said, pulling me along.

The streets were full of students playing in the white stuff.

"Where are we going?" I asked.

"Only to the best damn traying hill on campus." He led me to the large grass hill between the architecture building and the honors hall. It was covered with students sledding down on trays. The sound of laughter echoed off the buildings.

"If the university ever wises up and actually wants to catch tray thieves, this would be the place to look," I said.

"Yeah." He nodded. "If you see campus security coming—run! It's every man for himself." He kissed me again and pulled me to the top of the hill and tray run. At the top of the run, he pulled a small piece of snowboard wax and a lighter from his pocket and grinned evilly. "Give me your tray."

"What are you up to?"

"Take a look at everyone else as they slide down the hill. These things need a little help." He winked and used the lighter to melt the wax onto the bottom of my tray. Then he pulled a tri-shaped scraper from his pocket and scraped the excess off and buffed it. He sat the tray on the ground in front of me. "You're good to go. Hop on. But be careful. This thing's going to rocket."

I shook my head. "I'll wait for you."

"I'm ready to go. I waxed my board at home. Now get on."

He held my tray while I sat and wedged myself on it. "Hold on to the edge of the tray. These things have a way of scooting out from under you. Keep your feet up and aim straight for the bottom of the hill. On my count, push off. Three, two..." He slapped his tray on the hill next to mine. "One!" He gave me a push, jumped on his tray, and we were off.

His tray slid right and true down the hill, passing me almost immediately. He had the technique down. I wobbled and got sideways, falling off my tray less than halfway down. My tray slid away from me. Logan was already at the bottom. He ran up and retrieved my tray, then gave me a hand up, pulling me into his arms.

"I suck."

He shook his head and kissed me lightly as the snow fell on us. "First time's a bitch. You'll get the hang of it." He grabbed my hand and pulled me to the top again.

The second time, I got it. And it was like flying—the best thing ever. Better than sledding. Better than boarding. 'Cause I was with Logan. And about a thousand other students on the hill. But they hardly seemed to exist at all, except to add to the joy with their laughter and squeals. I screamed all the way down.

Logan beat me to the bottom of the hill. I tumbled off my tray into the snow just as I reached him, laughing. He caught my tray and grinned at me. "Well?"

"Again!"

We ran back to the top of the hill, hand in hand, carrying our trays, and went again and again. The seventh or eighth time down, I tumbled off my tray and rolled flat onto my back at the bottom of the hill, looking up into the falling snow as it caught in my eyelashes. Laughing, I opened my mouth to catch snowflakes and waved my arms in the snow, making a snow angel.

Logan rolled on top of me, poised above me, braced on his hands in the snow, studying me. "You're so beautiful, El. So beautiful." He kissed the tip of my icy nose.

I laughed, feeling a joy too deep to adequately describe. It was like music. He kissed my neck, burrowing beneath my scarf to bare skin. I sighed as he took me in his arms and really kissed me.

In Logan's arms, the world around me melted away. His mouth on mine was warm and wonderful in the cold, cold world. I wrapped my legs around his waist and kissed him back, oblivious to the snow falling on us and the snow angel beneath my back. Wanting him. Aching for him. I wrapped my arms around his neck and arched my hips up to meet his.

"I love you, El," he whispered in my ear.

This was the way life should be—full of love and laughter. As I opened my mouth to him and he kissed me again, I became dimly aware of shouting in the distance. Of a pause in the squeals and screams of delight of the tray-ers around us.

Suddenly there was a shout like a battle cry. And a series of screams. A snowball pounded Logan in the back, a direct hit. He started and pulled out of our kiss, breaking the spell.

"Hey!" He cursed beneath his breath as he rolled off me onto his stomach and looked uphill.

A crowd, like a battalion of soldiers armed with snowballs, lobbing them at an unseen opposing force, and as many tray-ers as they could, appeared over the crest of the hill between the interior design labs. All around us, tray-ers were arming themselves.

Logan took one look at the approaching horde and swore again, but this time he was smiling. "All-campus snowball fight. Shit." He grabbed a handful of snow and packed it into a ball.

I sat up. "All-campus snowball fight?"

He turned to look at me. "How good are you with a snowball?"

"I'm from Seattle. It hardly ever snows there. How good do you think I am?"

"Shit," he said again, but excitement shone in his eyes. "This could get ugly. *And* fun." He grinned. "We're going to have to make a run for it, El. I'll protect you with my life." He laughed like he was excited. "Grab your tray. I'll take you back to the dorm. We're going to have to run like hell to make it back. Are you game?"

"Do I have a choice?"

He grinned again. "Come on." He pulled me to my feet.

We were immediately bombarded with a round of snowballs.

"Early scout," Logan said, scanning the hill that was lit with streetlights, looking for the culprit. "We're going to have to shoot for a hole in their lines." Then he grinned as he spotted something.

I followed his line of sight. A guy leaned out from behind a tree lining the nearby sidewalk and wound up to throw. Logan fired his snowball and hit the guy in the shoulder. The thrower flinched as he was hit, dropped his snowball, and rubbed his shoulder as he ducked out of sight. Logan's prowess as a baseball player was evident.

"Impressive," I said. "You really got him."

"Yeah." He laughed as he leaned down and grabbed another handful of snow.

I followed his lead and made a snowball, too.

Then Logan grabbed my hand. "Run, El! And cover your head."

As we took off, snowballs rained down around us. The marauding mob got closer every minute and was between us and my dorm.

A snowball hit me in the thigh. "Ouch! That stung."

Logan didn't stop to let me brush it off. He fired back in the direction of the shot and hit another guy in the chest.

"You're accurate," I said, looking back. My breath came in clouds beneath the streetlight.

"Don't look back, El. And cover your head."

A snowball buzzed past my ear. I covered my head with my tray with one hand as Logan pulled me along with the other. He was fast, much faster than I was. I had a hard time keeping up as he charged us through enemy lines and the thick of the fighting.

The two fighting sides lobbed snowballs back and forth. Greeks fighting Geeds. People fighting whomever. Logan pulled me through the thick of it, shielding me with his body and tray, firing back at the worst offenders. His aim was deadly accurate, or would have been if he'd been throwing something with more punch, like a ball of ice.

He pulled me between the trees and up past the edge of Greek Row toward my dorm, which sat on the line between Greeks and Geeds.

As my door came into sight, Logan yelled, "Get your key out, El." He dropped my hand so I could reach into my pocket and still keep my head covered.

I managed to find my key just as we reached the slippery, icy front steps of my dorm. Logan took it from me, pulled me up the steps, slid the key into the door, and like a magician, whisked us into the safety of the foyer. A snowball flew in through the door just before it closed, smashing against the wall behind Logan and exploding to snow on us inside.

I was breathing hard.

Logan's eyes shone with excitement. "We did it!"

"My hero!" I laughed and put one hand over my heart.

Logan took the tray out of my other hand and dropped it and mine on the floor next to us. He bent at the knees to level our heights and pulled me into him so his crotch rubbed against mine until I could feel his excitement and an ache and a longing coursed through me. I wanted him, bad.

As I gulped for air, he kissed me. Deeply, holding the back of my head so there was no escaping his passion. I was so out of breath, I was lightheaded. And yet it was the most erotic thing, being kissed almost literally breathless. Every sensation was heightened. I moaned as I wrapped my arms around his neck. And then, just as I thought it was really possible I could faint, he pulled away, smiling, that look of exhilaration still lighting his eyes.

"Shit, El," he said, like a caress.

"Yeah." I stared into his eyes. He wanted to go out and join the fight. It was written on his face.

His phone buzzed. He pulled it out of his pocket. "Collin and Zave are on their way. They got wind of the fight." He was asking my permission.

"This snowball fight is strictly against university policy?" I asked.

"Yeah." He looked so adorable, my outlaw.

"Go, Butch Cassidy," I said.

He grinned. "I thought I was the Sundance Kid." He texted Collin back, leaned down, picked up our trays, and handed them to me. "Hold my tray for me."

"You don't need battle armor?"

His grin grew. I didn't even think that was possible. "You're right on the battle line. Stay in your room and keep the lights off. Keep away from the windows. This could get ugly." He gave me a quick kiss on the lips and was out the door before I could respond.

"Logan!" I called after him, but he took off at a run into the heart of the snowstorm and battle.

What had I just given him permission to do? And how right was Jason about Logan?

CHAPTER EIGHT

I followed the snowball battle in real time on Twitter. I mostly huddled against the wall away from the window with Bre on her bed, jumping up from time to time to peek out the window and watch the battle lines. The crowd surged one direction toward the dorms. Then back again toward Greek Row as the other side gained strength. The campus police finally broke it up in the early hours of the morning. Twitter was how I knew about the fistfights that broke out, the four windows in my dorm that were broken, and a rough number of arrests that were made. There was much more damage than that, but I didn't care about it, only that Logan got home safely. An hour in, as Bre and I watched the fight, a snowball hit our window so hard I was sure the window would shatter. I texted Logan frantically for an update, like was he still in one piece?

Around two, I finally got a text from him. *Home. Best all-campus snowball fight ever.*

I texted back. *No more black eyes?*

He replied. *Ha ha. These snowballs weren't as hard as pool balls. And I remembered to duck. But you should have seen some of the awesome kill shots I made.*

I texted him. *You can brag to me tomorrow.*

Will do. 'Night, Snow Angel.

I went to bed with a smile on my face.

The next morning the snow had already begun to melt and I had a big-ass bruise on my right thigh. The world was slushy and dripping as I hurried to chem lecture, late because the coffee line had been so slow in the dining hall. The carnage from the night before was evident everywhere I looked. The window of the room the floor above ours was patched with a piece of cardboard and duct tape. Now, in the slush, it was hard to imagine the wonder and beauty of last night.

In the lecture hall, Dex had saved me my usual seat. Byron had already started his stuttering lecture. I felt him watching me as I made my way past a row of knees to my place.

Dex was wearing headphones and had his iPod in his pocket, listening to music even though the lecture had begun. He didn't even look up when I entered, just pulled one earbud out and spoke to me while looking straight ahead. "Thought for a minute you were going to chicken out and I was going to have to iClick you in."

"I thought about it. Believe me." I felt harried and jangled and I hadn't even had my morning jolt of caffeine.

"How'd it go?"

"Tell you about it later."

Was it my imagination or was Byron staring at me the whole time he was talking? It creeped me out. The class buzzed with a low hum. Byron didn't exactly command attention. Until he outlined the new grading policy, including extra credit opportunities, and told everyone he'd recalculated their grades and they'd be posted online after class. And, by the way, everyone's grades were significantly higher, more in line with a typical chem class distribution. I swear Byron stared straight into the mass of five hundred of us right into my eyes like he had laser vision.

Dex popped out of his seat and began clapping. The rest of the class followed suit and gave Byron a standing ovation. All we needed was for someone to start singing, *Ding dong, the witch of chemistry is dead.* Byron turned a deep, bright, irrefutable red, like he was embarrassed to his core. But he wore a magnificently pleased look.

Dex leaned over and whispered in my ear, "This is your doing or I miss my guess. Good job." Then he put his fingers in his mouth and whistled so loudly I jumped.

After the lecture ended, I raced out of the auditorium so fast, Dex had to run to keep up with me. "Hold on! Where's the fire?" He was grinning. "What went on in that meeting with Byron? Whatever it was, me and about five hundred others owe you a debt of gratitude."

"Just remember that when I come to collect." I stepped in a slushy puddle and splashed muddy water up the leg of my jeans. I cursed beneath my breath.

"Don't tell me you really *did* sleep with him?" Dex sounded almost like he believed I had.

I decided in that instant that Dex was secret-worthy. He'd proven so far that he didn't have loose lips. "No, worse."

"Worse?" He sounded totally disbelieving. "Worse! There's something worse than prostituting yourself for chemistry?"

I winced and Dex backed off. That came a little too close to what Dr. Rogers had done to Logan.

"Sorry," Dex said.

"I'll tell you, but only if you promise not to tell any-one else, ever. I can't even tell Logan." I was still racing along, trying to put as much distance as possible be-tween me and that hideous chem building. I was begin-ning to think that place was a regular house of horrors.

"Come on. You know you can trust me." He made a look that was so innocent and puppy dog, I had to laugh.

"Cross your heart, hope to die?"

"Stick a needle in my eye. What are we? Five?"

I shot him a look that told him I was serious.

"Okay. Hit me with it. I promise on penalty of death not to tell."

We'd reached the mall that led to the SUB. I figured I had enough of a degree of separation from chem. I came to an abrupt stop and stared directly at Dex. "He told me he loves me and then he tried to kiss me."

"Yeah, horrible. Even prostitutes don't let the guys kiss them." He made a comical face. "What did you do? You said he tried. Did you duck out of the way? Obviously you didn't slap his face. Good move, by the way. He would have flunked us all for sure then."

I laughed. "Stop it! This is serious stuff, Dex. What am I going to do for the rest of the semester? He wants me to keep coming to our weekly session."

"Of course he does," Dex said. "Word of advice— don't close the door."

"Now you sound like Nic."

"You told Nic?"

"And Tay. They're sworn to secrecy, too. But for obvious reasons, Logan has no idea. And I don't want him to find out.

"I tried to tell Byron I have a boyfriend, but Dr. Homer interrupted and then I raced out of there."

Dex nodded like he understood. "You want me to prank Byron? I can get rid of him, too." He looked excited by the idea.

"No. No more pranks." I sighed. "Tay thinks I should carry on as usual with Byron. Bake him cookies and the like. Just maintain the open-door policy until he posts final grades and I get my A."

"And I get mine," Dex said.

"That's what I like about you, Dex. You're such a humanitarian, always thinking of others."

He laughed. "So true." He grinned. "I like Tay's plan."

"You would."

"Hey, come on, Ellie. I'm not going to leave you in a lurch. What you need is a plan and a wingman."

"And a new seat in lecture," I added. "Wingman?"

"Yep. And I have a plan—every week when you go in for your weekly help session, another student will show up within minutes—"

"Seconds," I said.

"Seconds, then, of when you arrive. That's your wingman. You'll never be alone with Byron. End of problem."

"Yeah, but how am I going to do that?" I stared at Dex.

"Easy. Leave it to me. I'll take care of it. Kirk and Joe owe us. I'll take my turn. Don't worry. You'll have a bodyguard at all times."

I pursed my lips, thinking the plan through. Finally, I smiled. "Genius. That could actually work."

"Yeah, to both," Dex said. "Never doubt me. As for lecture, a little evasive seat action is necessary. We'll mix it up. Sit in a different spot every time." He nodded and grinned evilly. "We'll see how well Byron can spot you in a crowd. A variation of Where's Waldo— Where's Ellie. Should be fun." He paused, looking deep in thought for a minute, then a grin spread across his face again.

"Uh-oh. Wipe that evil-genius look off your face. No pranking!"

Dex went all innocent looking at me. "Damn, I do love my seat, though. You know I'm a creature of habit, Ellie. I hate to give up my creature comforts."

I rolled my eyes.

He held up his hands like, *I give up.* "Anything for a friend and fellow conspirator."

I relaxed. "Good. Now that that's settled, don't you have to get to class?"

Dex shrugged. "No one will notice if I'm late. I sit in the back." He paused. "I need to talk to you about a couple of other things, though. A reporter from the daily paper called me up yesterday wanting to know what I knew about the prank."

I gasped.

Dex grabbed my arm. "Hold it together, Ellie. I was afraid you'd react like that, which is why I'm warning you. She didn't have anything on us. She was just fishing, calling up everyone in class."

"All five hundred of us?"

"Okay, maybe those who were the most likely suspects, those with the skill to carry it off." He looked proud of himself. "I didn't give anything away. And if she calls you, neither should you. Not that you're high on the suspect list." He laughed. "You know how to bluff. I know you can do it. Now that you've been warned, you'll be prepared. She's looking to trip someone up and scare them into revealing something."

I nodded. "Okay. Consider me warned. Is that it?" I didn't need any more bad news.

He hesitated.

"There's more?"

He looked pained. "This one is really out of my area of friend expertise. I don't really know how to say this."

"What?" I frowned, wondering why he was acting so weird.

He took a deep breath. "Do you have a thing for your boss?"

"What!" I stared at him. "You know I'm with Logan."

"Okay, that's what I thought. It's nothing."

"What's nothing?" My heart was pounding.

Dex shrugged. "Kirk said he saw someone who looked a lot like you at The College Grind yesterday morning looking intimate and involved with Jason. Making eyes at him."

I took a deep breath, suddenly afraid to confess to even a partial truth. I forced myself into lying mood and laughed like the whole thing was simply absurd. "A lot like me? Making eyes? You're trusting Kirk on this? Kirk?" I shook my head dismissively. "He's mistaken. I haven't been to The College Grind in a week." I made a note to be more careful.

Dex shrugged again. "Yeah, probably. That's Kirk."

I slipped into diversionary tactics. "So, tell me, what did you think of the snowball fight? I suppose you had a rapid-fire snowball machine?"

He grinned. "Legendary! I used my potato gun."

I was keeping secrets from everyone. Telling half-truths and lies at every turn and desperately afraid I'd be found out. How did my mom do it? Tell all those lies to her husbands and lovers? Keep them straight. I was constantly afraid of making a mistake, of letting something slip. Just a little over a month, five weeks, and I would be out of the nightmare of chem forever. That many fewer lies to keep track of.

I was on my way to work from studying at the science library when I walked past the career center and ran into Logan coming out. As always when I saw him, my heart did a flip. He was so hot—what did he see in me?

"El!" He pulled me into a hug, lifting me off the ground as he kissed me.

Logan knew how to kiss like no guy I'd ever known. Breaking a kiss down into its technical elements is not sexy. A kiss, after all, is the sum of all its elements. Like any art form, thinking about it too hard ruined the magic. Better to enjoy and appreciate. Or, in this case, melt and long for more.

Some guys have a knack, and Logan was the king of them. The right amount of pressure—urgent and hard, but not bruising. A way of stroking my lips with his tongue and entering my mouth that was so thrilling I got tight all over. The way he wrapped his arms around me, holding me like he never wanted to let go and the rest of the world didn't matter. Like his focus was only on me. That was sexy.

I felt the loss when he pulled away and smiled. "On your way to work?"

I nodded. "Glad to see you're in one piece after last night. And not incarcerated."

He laughed. "That was an epic fight. Collin and Zave have some great war stories.

"And you?"

"Mine are top secret. My lips are sealed."

"I see—what happens at a snowball fight stays at the snowball fight." I brushed his lips with another kiss. "What are you doing here?" I hitched my thumb at the career center.

He looked almost sheepish. "I'm a senior, El. I have to find a job if I don't want to move back in with Mom and Dad." He snorted.

I went cold and simply stared at him. Of course I knew he was a senior, but I'd never thought about him leaving, of him not being here for as long as I needed him to be. For as long as I was. Yes, it was selfish of me. Or maybe it was simply self-preservation, and with all the all things I'd had on my mind it just never really struck me that he was graduating in May. "In November?" I swallowed hard.

"November is not too soon to start. All the best software and high-tech companies are already taking applications for spring graduates and looking to set up interviews after Christmas."

"You've been applying?" I asked. I didn't mean to sound so much like he was carrying on a conspiracy.

"I have a few applications out." He shrugged. "It's no big deal. Hey, we'd better get going or we'll be late and Jason will have our heads. Or worse—dock our pay. And then how will I squire you around town in the style you deserve?" He grinned and took my hand as we started walking toward work.

We walked in happy silence.

At the top of the mall, Logan said, "How is having Byron as your prof? How did your meeting with him go?" His tone was casual, but the look on his face was fiercely protective and suspicious.

It was my turn to be evasive. "Fine. He wanted to talk about my grades. In class today, he announced the new grading system and the class gave him a standing ovation."

"A standing O, huh?" Logan said. "Bet he enjoyed that."

"He blushed like a ripe peach."

Logan nuzzled my neck. "Speaking of ripe peaches, I know who I'd like to give a standing O—a *long* standing O."

"Stop it. You'll make me blush."

"That was the idea." He paused and stopped walking abruptly. "El, is there something you're not telling me?"

Had I acted guilty? I tried to act casual to cover as I stared guilelessly back at him. "No, why?"

"I don't know. I just get the feeling you had something to do with Byron's new grading policy." It was hard to tell with Logan whether he was jealous or not.

I had a difficult time picturing any guy of reasonable looks being jealous of Byron. A guy like Logan, absurd! Unless he suspected me of flirting with Byron for a grade. I knew how he felt about that and wasn't going to go there.

I laughed a little too brightly to be completely convincing. "Nope. Not a thing."

He didn't look like he believed me. "Good." Then he grinned. "I'm thinking ahead to Saturday night. Our anniversary."

"Yeah?"

"Wear something hot."

I smiled as seductively as I knew how. "That goes without saying. I have the perfect turtleneck wool sweater."

He spun me around to face him, eyes twinkling. "You are such a tease, El."

CHAPTER NINE

"Logan told me to wear something hot." I examined myself in the full-length mirror that hung over the door in my room. I had literally spent hours getting ready for this date. A pile of rejected outfits sat on my bed.

Bre was already out with Dan. Nic had just left on her own hot date. That left Tay to hold my hand and reassure me of my hotness before she headed out with a group of girls from the dorm.

It was winter, so I'd chosen to wear my super-tight low-rider skinny jeans, knee-high stiletto boots, and a fuzzy sweater that bared my navel and revealed my bellybutton ring. I'd gotten my bellybutton pierced at the first Up All Night of the year, when I met Logan. I was plain, really, especially in comparison to my mom. But

at least she'd taught me to apply my makeup and how
to do perfect smoky eyes and a sultry evening look. I
didn't look half bad.

Tay was dancing to a tune playing on my iPod with
a glass of vodka and OJ in her hand. She paused and
looked me over. "You look great."

"What do you think he has planned?" I turned to
look at my butt in the mirror and see my backside. The
last thing I needed were baggy-butt jeans. This pair
had just come out of the wash and were nice and snug.

Tay rolled her eyes. "He asked you to wear something hot, what do you think he's planning? I don't expect you to come home tonight."

"That's not what I meant."

"Sure it is." She laughed. "Are you taking a coat?"

"And cover this up?" I shook my head. "It's a short
walk to the SUB."

She went to my desk, poured a shot of tequila, and
handed it to me. "Then you'll need an alcohol blanket,
honey."

"Thanks, Mom."

She took another drink of her vodka. "Slam it, baby."

As I downed my shot, my phone buzzed. I glanced at
it. "Logan's here."

She raised her glass to me. "Have fun."

I grabbed my keys. As I turned around, I saw Logan
in the door to my dorm room, looking hotter than any
guy had a right to.

As his gaze slid down me and lingered on my belly-button ring, every muscle I owned tightened with longing. "Wow, El." He was holding a single red rose.

"How do you get in here?" I said.

"Is that any kind of greeting?" His eyes danced. "I have powers of persuasion."

"Do you?"

"Yeah. I'll show you later."

Three steps and I was in his arms, wrapping my arms around his neck, pressing into him, his lips hot on mine.

"I guess I'll be going," Tay said, trying to squeeze past us with her drink in her hand.

Logan broke the kiss. "Taylor. Be careful with that in the hall." He nodded toward her drink. "No open containers."

"Logan. Look who's talking." Tay raised her glass to us. "Behave yourselves tonight."

"I thought you said to have fun?" I said.

She smiled, shrugged, and left.

I took the rose from Logan. "It's beautiful."

"Happy anniversary." He kissed me again.

I ran the backs of my fingers along his cheek. "Keep that up and we'll never leave my room."

"Would that be so bad?" His voice was sultry.

I smiled. "I'm looking forward to some magic."

"So am I." He took my hand. "I have a surprise for you. At my place." He took the flower and set it on my desk. "Let's go."

The SUB pulsed with music as we approached, hand in hand. Throngs of people were filing in. We joined the crowd, weaving our way inside.

"What do you want to do first?" he asked me.

"Dance."

"Dance?" His eyes sparkled. "I thought maybe another piercing."

I grinned back at him. "You this time?"

He laughed again.

"There is no piercing tonight, you tease. We'll just have to dance. I'm dying to see your moves."

We made our way through the crowd to the second-floor ballroom.

"The place we first met," he said as we reached the top of the stairs. "Bring back any memories?"

"Yeah, something about a pool ball comes to mind."

He slid his hot hand down my bare midriff and traced my bellybutton provocatively until I felt a clenching longing between my legs.

I gently touched his healing eye. "This is a nice, reminiscent touch."

He laughed. "I'd do anything for you, El. You know that."

I kissed him. "Let's dance."

As we made our way to the center of the ballroom dance floor, the bass of the music throbbed. The strobe lights pulsed. I smiled at Logan and danced for him, gyrating to the music, hands above my head, breaking into hip waves.

Logan put his hands on my hips, squeezing, holding them like he owned me, moving with me, and the game was on. I removed his hands from my hip and pole walked around him, sliding my arm around him, touching his cheek, looking into his eyes, daring him to keep up with me. Daring him not to get turned on. Treating him like he was a stripper pole I could wrap myself around and never let go of.

I stopped with my back to him and began body waving, sticking my butt into him. He pulsed with me, rubbing his hard crotch against me, turning me on. I broke into a booty shake. Slid into a sexy squat with my hands above my head. Logan grabbed my hands, pulled me to a stand and spun me into him. He put his hand at the base of my head and pulled me into a kiss, pressing me so tightly against me I ached with wanting him.

The song ended.

"Shit," Logan said, stroking my face. "You know how to move." His voice was ragged.

The lights came up. "Take ten, everyone." The DJ stepped down from his platform.

"Bad timing," I said.

"We'll have to make the best of it." Logan took my hand "Want something to drink? I'm parched."

I had the feeling he wasn't just thirsty. I nodded. "Sure."

He took my hand as we went to the drink bar. Nothing alcoholic here. Just mixers. If you cared enough, you could sneak your own liquor in. Logan got me a cola with a cherry in it.

"Wow! A mocktail," I said. "Impressive."

"Anything for my girl."

My heart did a little flop at that—*his* girl.

Logan got a pop for himself. We found a table to sit at. We were both still breathing hard, and it wasn't from exertion.

"Want to see what I can do with my tongue?" Logan pulled the cherry out of his pop by the stem.

"Are you propositioning me right here?"

He laughed. "No, just teasing you with a promise for later. Showing you how talented I am." He popped the cherry into his mouth, stem and all.

I watched as he made funny faces, like he was really working hard on something. Finally, he opened his mouth and stuck out his tongue, wiggling it in a way that made me laugh. He'd tied the stem into a knot.

He wiggled his tongue again.

"Is that for me?" I took the stem from him. "Such an anniversary gift."

"Now you can't say I never gave you anything. I have more tongue tricks to show you later—in private."

I set the stem on my napkin. "I'll treasure this always." I pulled the cherry out of my glass and held it over my mouth.

"You think you can do that trick?"

"I think I'd like to see a mouth-to-mouth stem tie." I made a show of balancing the cherry on my tongue. "Huh."

"You are too bad." He reached over, grabbed my head, covered my tongue with his mouth, and tried to steal my cherry.

I fought him, protecting it with my tongue. But Logan had a way of teasing me with his that made me surrender. He got the cherry. I had to keep up with him, moving to stay connected at the lips, probing with my tongue to feel what he was doing and tease him into tripping up. But finally, his tongue put a tied stem on mine. He pulled away and gave me a triumphant look as I pulled the tied stem out of my mouth.

"Wow, you are talented." I put the stem in the napkin with its twin.

Before he could answer, an announcement came over the loud speakers. "The next hypnosis show starts in five minutes on the first floor."

Logan popped out of his chair and grabbed my hand. "We have to see that show, El. It's the same guy as last year. He's epic. Really funny. You should see what he can make people do."

I raced to keep up with Logan as he led the way, dragging me along. He found us seats in the front just as the hypnotist took the stage.

"Welcome, everyone. I'm Bob Allen, hypnotist extraordinaire. The hypnotic quality of my voice is insured by Lloyd's of London. Just in the time I've been speaking, I can see some of you are already nodding. I have to get a less boring stage name."

I laughed with the crowd.

"This is an audience participation show," Bob said. "My first job is to find susceptible, willing victims. Not everyone is equally suggestible and I take only easiest, I mean, the most challenging candidates. I'm going to start talking. Just listen to the sound of my voice." He went into a comedic patter, pulled a pocket watch out, and began swinging it. "You're getting very sleepy."

Logan leaned in and whispered, "I'd love to be in the show. But he never picks me. El?"

I was already relaxed and happy, so calm. The sound of Bob's voice was like a pleasant lullaby. Bob worked his way through the crowd, tapping people to come on stage.

He stopped right in front of me. "What's your name, lovely lady?"

"Ellie."

Bob made an aside to the crowd. "You may have noticed—I go for the hot chicks if I can."

Logan, always the charmer, made a show of putting his arm around me.

"Whoa! Looks like I have a jealous boyfriend. The hot ones are always taken." Bob kneeled next to me. "Do you want to come on stage, Ellie?" He hitched a thumb at Logan. "He won't beat me up, will he? He looks tough, like a fighter."

"No, he won't. I can't."

"Come on, El, go!" Logan nudged me. "I want to see you up there. It'll be fun."

My heart was pounding. I didn't want to make a fool out of myself.

I hesitated.

"You want to, Ellie, I can see that. But you're afraid. I promise to be gentle." Bob's voice was so reassuring and calming, I relented and nodded.

Bob stood and took my hand to help me from the chair.

When Bob had all his victims, he ran us through another screening, weeding out people until only ten of us were left. Then he began talking and I began drifting, all my fears and worries vanished. The next thing I knew...

I'm driving down Stadium Way, going way too fast. Isn't the speed limit something absurdly slow, like twenty? I don't care. My window is open and the wind is streaming in. I'm having fun.

Suddenly, I hear a siren. Behind me I see lights. A cop! He signals to me. I pull over. He gets out of his car and comes over to me, big and intimidating, carrying something. He's going to give me a ticket. I know he is. I can't afford a ticket.

"Ma'am, are you aware you were doing fifty in a twenty zone? I'll need to see your license."

"I was? Officer, I'm so sorry." I turn on the charm and try to look vulnerable and helpless, really apologetic. "It's these shoes—see the heels?" I show him my sexy four-inch platform heels. "They make it hard to feel the accelerator. I'll take them off." I reach down and pull one off. "I'll drive home in bare feet. I promise not to drive in heels again." I bat my eyes at him. "Please, I can't afford a ticket. I didn't mean to speed."

The officer hesitates. He starts to put his ticket pad away. I smile at him.

He points to something. "Is that an open container?"

I turn to look at my cup holder. There's an open can of beer. "How did that get there?" I'm genuinely confused. And now I'm scared. How will I talk myself out of this one?

"We have an open-container law. I'm going to have to take you in. Please step out of the car."

"No! No, please!"

He takes me to jail. "You're allowed one phone call."

"But I have my cell phone—"

He takes it from me. I cry harder.

"Who are you going to call?"

"Logan, my boyfriend."

"The bruiser with the black eye? He's out of town. He can't come. Is there anyone else? Someone right here."

I put my face in my hands and sob. "My dad. Jason. I want my dad! Call Jason!"

"It's all right. It's okay. I won't lock you up." Suddenly I'm relaxed and happy, like I'm floating on a cloud.

Someone snapped his fingers right in front of my face. I blinked in the lights. It took me a second to realize where I was—on stage with Bob the Hypnotist.

"Thanks, all of you, for being such terrific sports. Give my participants a big hand!"

The audience roared with approval.

"That's our show for tonight. Thank you all for coming." Bob waved and left the stage.

Logan ran up and gave me a hug. "You were awesome, El."

I didn't feel awesome. I felt anxious and cold, panicky.

"El? Are you okay?" Logan took my arm.

A snatch of a memory came back to me—calling out for my dad, for Jason. I paled.

"El?"

I turned a wondering, dreading look on him. "I was in jail. He put me in jail. What did I say up there, Logan? What did I say?"

Logan took me by the arms. "It's okay. You were great." Logan explained the skit and how much the crowd loved me and felt for me. The way I'd cried had been so convincing. "Hell, half the guys in the audience wanted to comfort you."

"Who did I ask for?" The dread was so deep I cold barely speak.

"Me. But Bob told you I couldn't come bail you out. Then you asked for your dad. And Jason."

My heart stopped. My mouth went dry. The jig was up. I was sure it was. I waited for the recrimination. I waited for Logan to grasp that I'd been lying to him. I waited for the anger and his sense of betrayal.

Instead, he smiled and hugged me. "It's okay. You don't have a dad. You improvised and asked for your boss. I'm sure Jason would be flattered to know you think of him as a father figure."

CHAPTER TEN

I couldn't believe what Logan had just said—he didn't grasp the truth he'd just heard. I'd been given a second chance. I needed to talk to Jason. We needed to do something about this soon. We needed to come clean. I had to find a way to do it so I wouldn't lose Logan. I needed to think.

Logan pressed my head to his chest as the crowd thinned out around us. His arms felt so right around me. I never wanted to leave them and the reassuring thumping of his heart. I wanted it to always beat for me.

"I'm sorry, El." He kissed the top of my head. "I wouldn't have encouraged you if I'd known this was going to upset you. That's the last thing I wanted."

I had to buck up or I'd really blow things. "I'm fine. Just embarrassed I'm so suggestible. Did I really act outrageously?"

"You were completely adorable." He kissed the top of my head. "Do you want to dance again?"

I forced myself to smile as I looked up at him. "Don't you have a surprise for me at your place?"

"You want to go?"

"I've had enough excitement for one night."

He tipped my chin up to so he could look me in the eye. "The excitement hasn't even begun."

The drive to Logan's apartment took less than ten minutes. The snow had all melted and the roads were clear. He let us into a silent apartment and flipped on the lights.

"Where are Zave and Collin?" I asked as I walked to the console table by the door. I ran my finger along their betta fish's bowl, getting Spartacus to follow my finger.

"Out." The way he said it gave me shivers of pleasure.

"Zave hasn't killed Spartacus yet. He looks pretty happy. He's making a bubble nest."

"Yeah. And he likes you." Logan nestled up behind me. "Not as much as I do, though."

I spun around, into Logan's arms. "I like you, too."

"Do you?" He kissed the tip of my nose. "Wanna show me how much?" His lips were inches from mine.

I leaned into him and sucked his lower lip, then nibbled gently until he shuddered.

"Shit, El." He swept me into his arms and carried me to his bedroom, closing the door behind us with his foot.

In front of the bed, I slid out of his arms to my feet. I knew what I wanted. And I knew what I couldn't have. But I was going to get as close as I could come. I slid my hands beneath his shirt and ran them over the hard planes of his abs and chest. I slid his shirt up his chest, slowly, as tantalizingly as I could, tracing his skin with my fingertips until I pulled the shirt over his head and dropped it on the floor. "I want to see you," I whispered.

He leaned over, flipped the covers of the bed back and flicked a lighter, lighting a candle on the desk next to his bed. It flickered to life, casting a dancing glow on the picture of Logan in his high school baseball jersey.

"How romantic. You're prepared." I laced my voice with seduction and need.

"You have no idea," he said.

I wanted to drive him crazy with desire. I wanted to make him shudder and moan and feel the way I felt. I ran my tongue down the hollow of his neck, down the chiseled line between his pecs, down his very fine abs to the top of his jeans. As I unzipped them, he grabbed me.

"Not so fast." He kicked his shoes off and reached to unzip my boots.

I fell into a sit on the bed while he pulled them off for me. Then I fell onto my back and he fell into me. I wrapped my legs around his waist. He pressed his

mouth on mine and his hard crotch into my budding
wet one.

I wanted him. I wanted him to make love to me so
bad. But in the back of my mind, I was still calling for
dad. I still had a secret that could rip us apart. Until
Logan knew, until I knew he wouldn't leave me because
of it, I couldn't.

He was kissing my neck, sliding his hands beneath
my sweater. I held my arms over my head while he
slipped it off. I wore my lace front-hook bra and
matching thong panties. Yes, I was prepared, too. I
arched my back, pressing my breasts toward him, letting him know what I wanted.

He unhooked the bra as deftly as if he were a well-
practiced lover. My budded breasts burst into the cool
air of the bedroom and into Logan's hot mouth one at
time. As he sucked, he circled his tongue around them,
toying with me as the ache between my legs built. He
hadn't been kidding about being talented with his
tongue.

I ran my hands over his biceps as he let go of my
breast and traced a path of hot kisses down my abs. His
tongue found my bellybutton and circled it before
thrusting into it. My breathing was shallow and excited. I'd never known a bellybutton was so erogenous.

His mouth slid to the top of my jeans. I gasped as he
undid the top button and slid down the zipper. He slid
one finger down my lace panty and then pulled back. "I
have a present for you."

"Now?"

He just grinned and reached for a small package on the desk. He held it out to me, watching as I opened it.

"A bellybutton ring." I was touched as I looked at the jeweled ring. The jewel on the knob of it sparkled in the candlelight.

"It's hard to see in this light. It's green, a peridot, August's birthstone, for the birth of our relationship."

"It's beautiful." I hesitated. I still had another several months to go before I could swap out my original ring. "I'll save it and wear it as soon as I can." I started to put the lid back on the box.

"You can wear it now." He grabbed my hand and took the box from me. "Don't panic. I know you can't swap it all the way out for a while." He took the ring out of the box and unscrewed the jewel on the top. "Watch this." Pressing one hand reassuringly on my abs, he unscrewed my existing jewel with the other hand and screwed the new jewel on. "A perfect fit."

I leaned up on my elbows to look, unable to speak. It was such a sweet gift. "Amazing."

"Yeah." He kissed the top of the ring and then circled my bellybutton again with his tongue and slid down to my jeans. This time he didn't stop. He pulled my jeans off and then my panties. And then he parted my legs and worked his magic between them, sucking, thrusting with his tongue, leaving me gasping with pleasure and clutching the sheets.

He circled and sucked until waves of pleasure like I'd never felt before crashed over me and I called out his name again and again. Finally, he looked up at me and grinned that sexy grin that melted my heart every time.

He climbed up the bed, on top of me, pulling me to him and kissing me. I slid my hands into his jeans and tried to shimmy them off.

Finally, he released me, slid off the bed and out of his jeans and underwear, long and hard and ready. I fell to my knees in front of him and took him in my mouth, licking him and sucking him, returning the favor until he came, too.

When I was done, he fell back onto the bed. I climbed naked on top of him and lay there.

"You really know how to make a guy go weak in the knees."

I kissed him lightly. "You're not the only person with a talented tongue." I slid off him and snuggled in next to him. "But you really know how to knot a cherry. I'll give you that."

He laughed, kissed me back, and pulled the covers over us. As we lay there, gently stroking each other, he grew hard again. "El." His voice was ragged as he pressed between my legs. "I want to make love to you in the worst way."

I bit my lip.

"I won't force you," he said, stroking my shoulder as I looked away from him. "What's stopping you? Don't you trust me?"

I didn't trust *me*. I didn't trust fate. I didn't trust my lies to stay hidden. "I don't want to make a mistake."

"We'll be careful. We'll use double, triple protection." He ran his fingers through my hair.

"I'm living proof that mistakes happen, Logan." I swallowed hard. "Against the greatest odds. My mom is the world's crappiest mom, but I'll always be grateful she had me. I ruined her life, though. I don't ever want to face that decision."

He kissed my hair. I felt like crying.

"It's okay." His voice was soft and soothing. "And you are not a mistake, Ellie Martin. Don't ever think that. I love you."

My heart almost broke then and there. I turned to face him. "I love you, too, Logan. I know I'm the one who still owes *you* one, but promise me no matter what happens you'll remember that."

He looked puzzled. "Yeah. Sure."

"Logan?"

"Yeah?"

"Once I make love to you once, I won't ever want to stop. I'll want to make love with you a zillion times a day, in every place possible. I'll lose myself. I'll get reckless." I paused. "That's how mistakes happen." I took a deep breath. "I'm not ready. Yet."

He nibbled my neck. "Yet?" I almost felt him smiling. "That means there's hope."

Logan made me breakfast the next morning—frozen chocolate-chip waffles he toasted in the toaster. And hazelnut coffee from his K-Cup machine with foamed milk he made in a frother. He set my coffee, a jar of

peanut butter, and a bottle of real, one hundred percent maple syrup in front of me.

"What? No imitation maple syrup?" I teased. "What
kind of a place is this? And what is the peanut butter
for?"

"Your waffle." He grabbed his cup of coffee and
plate of waffles and sat down across from me. His hair
was tousled. His face had a sexy day's growth of stubble. "Try it, you'll like it." He grabbed the peanut butter and spread some on the end of my waffle, drizzled
some pure maple syrup over it, cut a bite, and stuck it
on my fork and held it out to me. "Open wide."

"I'm not a baby."

"Never said you were. But feeding you is kind of
cute."

"I am so not sure about this." I rolled my eyes and
took the bite he offered me, making a show of tasting it
like celebrity chef judges on The Food Network.

"Well?" He handed my fork back to me.

"Very peanutty, with a nice maple kick. You're an
excellent cook." I leaned over and kissed him, feeling
the prickle of his stubble on my mouth. Everything
about him turned me on.

"Yeah, I've worked really hard on my toasting skills.
Believe it or not, it is an art."

I bumped him playfully in the shoulder, trying to
think how to casually bring up the subject I had on my
mind. I poured more syrup on my waffle and handed
him the bottle. "How close are you and Jason?"

Logan set the syrup bottle down. "We're pretty
tight. Why?"

"No reason. Except...well..."

"Spit it out, El."

"I was wondering, you know, how much you two talk about personal things. Now that you and I are, you know, together. I mean, he's my boss." What a big, fat liar I was. My heart beat double time. I was digging myself in too deep. When Logan found out the truth, I hoped he forgot about this conversation.

Logan laughed. "Are you afraid I'm going to tell him what I did to you with my tongue and how you liked it and begged for more?"

"Shut up, Walker! I'm serious." I paused, thinking of my dad hearing that story I blushed.

"You are so cute." He squeezed my hand. "I won't tell him our private stuff. I never have."

I tried not to look as relieved as I felt. "None of it?"

"How tight-lipped do you want me to be?" His tone was still light, but he looked a little puzzled.

"I just think we should keep our personal and professional lives separate."

"You don't want me to talk to him about you at all?" He studied me closely, like he was getting wary and wondering what I was up to.

"Only to sing my praises and tell him what a great job I'm doing."

"Right. Looking for a raise?" He picked up his coffee.

"Oh, yeah."

He shook his head like I was really amusing. "Okay, I'll stay away from you as a topic of conversation. Satisfied?"

I nodded. "Hey, what are your plans today? I thought we could hang out."

Logan hesitated, which was very strange. "Studying. I have a ton of crap to do—a massive lab report and a homework set that will take me all day."

"We could study together."

Once again there was that hesitation. "I'd love to, but not today. I have to meet with my lab partner. We're doing the lab report together.

I nodded. "Logan?"

He looked at me.

"You're not keeping anything from me, are you?"

"El! Come on."

I frowned, getting the definite feeling he was hiding something from me. "You're okay, right?"

"Yeah, of course I am." He flashed me that sexy smile. "Now shut up and eat your waffles."

Zave came stumbling out of his room in his boxers. "I smell waffles. Are you cooking again, Logan?"

"Zave, buddy, put some pants on. There's a lady present." Logan teasingly put his hands over my eyes.

I pulled them away.

"If there's a girl here, that's the last thing I want to do." Zave spotted me. "Hey, Ellie. Don't mind Walker. He's just afraid you'll see how a real man is hung and his assets will pale by comparison."

Logan shook his head. "In your dreams, pencil dick."

"Ha ha, needle prick. There's a magnifying glass and a pair of tweezers in the bathroom. Make yourself happy." Zave shook his head. "Men with tiny pricks are so touchy."

He walked to the coffee machine and made a cup for himself before plopping down at the table next to me with his black coffee. "Hey, you were very funny last night at the hypnotist, Ellie. The best act there!" His gaze turned to Logan. "When Bob was making you cry, my roomie here looked like he wanted to jump out of the audience and take a swing at him." Zave laughed.

I froze and looked at Logan.

"I didn't. I wouldn't have," Logan said. "But he was pushing you too far."

"You cried very prettily," Zave said. "That's a compliment. Not many women do. Most get all red and puffy-eyed. Asking for Logan first when you were put in jail was very touching, too." He made a sappy gesture, clasping his hands in front of his heart. "Maybe not quite as much as when you wanted your daddy and then asked for Jason. You had a little boss-daddy confusion going on there."

I paled. "I don't remember."

Zave took a sip of his coffee. "What's the saying— girls want a guy like dear old dad? Logan will have to watch you around Jason."

Logan tensed and set his jaw. Zave had hit a nerve. "Shut up, Zave. Ignore him, El. He's still drunk." He turned to Zave. "Drink your coffee and go back to bed and sleep it off."

"Sorry, Ellie. Sorry, Walker. You're right—I'm a douchebag when I'm hung over."

"You're forgiven, Zave." I grabbed Logan's hand. "And for the record—you have absolutely nothing to worry about with me and Jason." I tried to sound teas-

ing and make light. "He is absolutely the last person I'd
ever go for. He's old enough to be my dad." See? I was
telling at least a partial truth.

Logan squeezed my hand back and laughed. "I don't
think he's *that* old, El. But good to know you don't
think he's hot."

I couldn't figure Logan out, and it made me insecure—a wonderful, romantic date on Saturday, and
then he's too busy for me on Sunday. I knew engineering majors had a ton of homework, but I couldn't help
feeling like he was blowing me off. Since Austin's betrayal, I had real trust issues. So maybe this was all in
my head. When I looked at my brand new peridot bellybutton jewel, I couldn't keep the smile off my face. I
was a flip-flopper—ecstatic one minute and doubting
the next. And I couldn't stop the pattern. Was Logan
up to something else? Would I see another girl moon-
ing over him in missed connections while he was having
coffee with someone like Amber?

And then there was that near miss at Up All Night
where I almost betrayed my dad and gave away our secret. I debated messaging him all day. But what would
that accomplish? He was at home with his wife and kid.
Why upset him? So I decided to keep it to myself and
bring it up on Tuesday at our coffee date. To keep my
mind off my insecurities, I dove into my studies. The
only problem was chemistry—it was easy now and
made sense. But it reminded me of Byron.

On Sunday night as I was getting ready for bed, I got a text from Dex: *Wear your black university sweatshirt to class tomorrow and put your hair in a ponytail.*

I texted him back. *Why are you suddenly so interested in my fashion choices?*

Humor me, he replied.

Fine.

What was Dex up to now?

I hadn't heard from Logan all day. Why wasn't he texting me? I broke down and texted him. *Get your studying done?*

And then I waited, totally insecure, seeing how eager he was to text me back.

He texted right back: *Still working on the report. Going to be a late night. There aren't enough hours in the day. My homework problem set for EE421 took me five hours. See you at work tomorrow.*

On Monday, I was my usual nearly-late-to-class self. I was hardly paying attention to anyone around me as I texted Dex to ask him where he was sitting. He immediately texted back his location. I looked up and around the auditorium, into a sea of black university sweatshirts. Over half the class was dressed like I was, and almost all the girls had their hair in ponytails.

I couldn't help myself. I broke out laughing. I found Dex and slid in next to him. "Black sweatshirts, really?"

"And ponytails. If you'll notice, I even got a few guys to put their hair up." He grinned. "Let's see Byron find you *now*."

"I said no pranks." But I was laughing.

"This isn't a prank. This is a show of school spirit. Nothing wrong with that."

"It's not even game day."

He grinned. "Sure it is—Where's Ellie game day."

Just then Byron came out of the instructor's door and walked to the podium.

"This should be fun," Dex whispered to me.

Byron looked into the auditorium and actually jumped, like he was startled to see that sea of school spirit. He looked almost scared, like he should be worried that something was up.

"This is more fun than I expected," Dex said.

When Byron spoke, his voice cracked and his gaze went directly to where I usually sat. He looked puzzled at first, and then obviously, like really obviously, disappointed.

Dex shook his head. "I should get an A just for running this successful experiment. You were definitely right—he's looking for you. We're going to have to mix it up next time."

I pursed my lips and made thin eyes at him. "You mean like wear our red university gear?"

"That's exactly it." He grinned. "And baseball caps."

"Dex, that's too mean."

"Come on, Ellie—where's the harm? It's not like we're doing anything destructive. Can I help it if Byron is pathologically nervous?"

"How did you even do this?" I said.

"I have my ways."

Then it dawned on me. Earlier in the semester he'd organized an email campaign to try to get rid of Dr. Rogers.

"You're using the list," I said.

He put a finger to his lips. "I'm trying to listen to your boyfriend's lecture, Ellie. Pay attention."

"Shut up!" I punched him playfully in the arm.

I showed up for work that afternoon with a six-pack of Red Bull for Logan. I'd used my dining hall account dollars to buy it in the market. It was sitting on my desk with a ribbon on it when he arrived.

He pointed to it. "Going to do some heavy drinking? Anticipating an all-nighter?"

"Not mine, yours. That's for you, late-night-study guy. Did you get any sleep last night?"

He grinned. "About two hours."

I handed the six-pack to him. "Then you really need this."

As he took it, he leaned across my desk like he wanted to kiss me. I shook my head almost imperceptibly and mouthed, *Not in the office.*

He frowned. "No one's looking."

But this was the office, and now that my boss was also my dad and knew it, I didn't want him seeing how into Logan I really was. Though in retrospect, the Red Bull might have given that away. According to our agreement, I was supposed to be seriously thinking about my relationship with Logan. And I was—I had decided I was hanging on to it for all I was worth.

Just then, Jason, who'd been out when I arrived, stepped into the office. I gave Logan a look that said, *See?*

He made a growling sound deep in his throat.

I laughed.

"Logan, there you are. I need to talk to you about some technical problems we're having in the family science building." His gaze landed on me like he wasn't happy to see Logan being so familiar with me.

Logan straightened up and smiled at Jason. "Hey, boss. Have a good weekend?"

Jason glanced at me with a concerned, fatherly look. "It was all right. I heard Ellie was a hit at the hypnosis show."

Uh-oh. Great, my dad had spies everywhere. Exactly what had he heard?

Jason's tone was teasing, but there was a new familiarity in it. It may have been my imagination, but I think Logan caught it.

"Yeah, she was a star," Logan said, with just a trace of a frown as his gaze bounced between Jason and me. "Who squealed?"

Jason smiled. "I never reveal my sources." His tone was light, but he flashed me a look that said we had things to discuss at our coffee date.

CHAPTER ELEVEN

On Tuesday I arrived first for my standing meeting at The College Grind with Jason. I ordered my coffee, grabbed a table in the corner, and watched for him like a spy waiting for her informant. He arrived right on time, waved to me, ordered, and took the chair across from me.

This time we dispensed with the fake greetings. No *Hey, what are you doing here*s for us.

"It's dangerous meeting here," I whispered to him. "My friend Kirk saw us last week and got the wrong impression."

"You set him straight?" Jason said.

I nodded.

"We should be fine, then. This is the most innocuous public place I can think of. I'm a regular. I always come here Tuesday mornings. Lyssa will think nothing of it if she hears."

"But always running into me? Isn't that a little too much coincidence?"

Jason seemed to consider the point. "Not now that it's your usual habit, too. You're a typical college kid— you drink a lot of coffee, right? And this is the most popular place on campus."

I smiled at him and nodded.

"I have a reputation for mentoring students. Let's just make you my latest victim." He grinned evilly.

I laughed. "So that's what I am?"

The barista called out his drink order. He popped up to get it. When he returned to his seat, he jumped right into conversation. "You nearly gave us away at the hypnosis show." He sounded sympathetic.

I was stunned. I thought he'd be mad. Jason really was a different kind of guy than I was used to. I nodded. "Yeah. Fortunately no one even thinks you're old enough to be my dad."

He looked stressed, but he smiled. "I get that a lot. People think I'm younger than I am. It's been hell on my career. No one thinks I'm old enough to be in charge."

I shook my head. "You know many women would kill for a problem like that?" I thought of my mom and her constant quest for youth. "So maybe I've inherited some good genes?"

He grinned as he took a sip of coffee. "Maybe. I hope so."

"That's not the whole problem. Even when they know how old you are, they think you're too young," I said. "You were a young dad."

"Yeah. And here I thought I was an old dad." He made a funny face.

We both laughed.

I turned serious. "I'm sorry I almost gave us away. No more hypnosis for me. I promise." I paused. "Lying to Logan is killing me. I keep feeling like I'm digging myself in deeper, that when he finds out, it's really going to hurt him. I know all the reasons, and they're good ones, but..."

"But we need an exit strategy," Jason finished for me. "I know. I feel crappy for keeping this from Lyssa, too. And I've been working on it, at least on the job front. I've been contacting other departments. I have a few leads on a position for you for next semester."

"That's good news. I guess." I loved where I worked. I loved the work and being near Logan and Jason.

"I know. I wish you could keep working for me, too." He set his coffee cup down. "What are you doing for Thanksgiving?"

I bit my lip. "Going home with Logan."

Jason frowned. "Walking into the lion's den?"

"Is his family that bad?" I asked.

"Worse, from what I've heard."

"I thought you're supposed to be my support system. Stop trying to scare me."

Jason smiled, but it was sad. "I wish I could have you over for Thanksgiving. I'd like to be able to acknowledge you. It's killing me not to." He paused, looking like he had something to say, but was hesitant and uncertain what my response would be. "I've thought about this constantly this past week—with your blessing, I'd like to tell Lyssa over Thanksgiving break."

My pulse leaped at the thought—my father wanted to acknowledge me. *Now.* I fought to keep my cool. "Yeah? Lyssa will miraculously be okay with me now? What's changed?"

He looked haggard. "Nothing. And everything. You're my kid. I'm lying to my wife. I hate that. I want us all to be a family. For that to happen, I have to man up.

"A family-oriented holiday that's a time to be thankful is a good time to bring up it up. You'll be out of town, which will give Lyssa a few days to deal with it while you aren't around."

I held his gaze. "You're taking a huge risk. What if she freaks out? What if she demands you fire me? Or never see me again?"

"I won't fire you. I won't cut you out of my life." His face was set, determined, and his tone firm.

I had to believe him. I wanted to believe him. My heart nearly broke. This man who I hardly knew was willing to risk everything to have me as his daughter. I'd missed an entire lifetime with him. I hated my mom for that. I'd been stuck with the parent who didn't want me, all because of her selfishness. And now my life was a complete mess. And even the joy of finding my dad was marred. My mom had a way of scarring me even when she wasn't around.

The stakes were so high. I swallowed hard. "Go ahead. Do it. If you want to."

He smiled. "I do."

"What about Logan?" I wanted to tell him, and yet I didn't want to at the same time.

"I've thought about that," Jason said. He took a deep breath. "I think you should wait until the semester's over. Logan's still emotionally raw and stressed about too many things right now." Jason looked genuinely worried about Logan. "Let's not add to it."

I wondered what Jason knew that I didn't. I had the feeling he was holding something back.

"He needs me right now, too," Jason said. "I don't want him to feel alienated from either of us. Or betrayed." He paused again. "We don't know how Logan will react. I don't want to put either of your jobs in jeopardy, either."

"Logan won't—" I cut myself off. I didn't really know what Logan would do. And that was what scared me. I'd asked for fatherly advice. Jason had seen Logan at his worst. He knew Logan better than I did in that regard. Now I'd have to trust him. Or maybe I was just rationalizing and putting off the inevitable because I was scared. "Okay. It's only a few more weeks. I'll tell him at the end of the semester. Before Christmas."

"Good." Jason looked relieved. More relieved than he should have been.

I swallowed hard. "You wanted to me to tell you something about myself that you don't know—I love Logan. And I can't bear to lose him. I mean, I *really* love him."

Jason covered my hand with his. "Oh, Ellie." He sighed like he was resigned and sad. "I already knew that."

After chem lab, I reluctantly went to see Byron, carrying a big plate of chocolate-chip cookies according to plan. Dex had promised to show up. If he didn't I was going to make him sorry. I'd gone over and over how I was supposed to act toward Byron after that profession of love. I thought if I acted normal, like it had never happened, maybe it would all go away.

Byron's eyes lit up when I knocked on his door and he saw the plate of cookies wrapped in plastic wrap with an orange bow on top.

"Happy early Thanksgiving!" I said to him as he stood behind his desk and I handed him the cookies.

He took them awkwardly, blushing, which made me uncomfortable all over again. "What's this for?"

"A thank-you for all the help."

"I didn't think you'd come." He sounded almost ridiculously happy as he set the cookies on his desk.

"Why wouldn't I? We're friends, aren't we?" I gave him my innocent look, wondering where Dex was and which method of murdering him would be most painful. "And I still need help in chemistry." I gave Byron my vulnerable, "poor, helpless me" smile. Yes, it was calculated to bring out his manly, protective instincts. I'd been using it all semester. It would be out of place to abandon it now when I was trying to act normal.

"Ellie—"

Just then, with impeccable timing, three guys and a girl from my chem class knocked on the door. "Professor Green? It's not your usual chem hours, but we're desperately in need of help."

I had to hold down my smile. Right then, I could have kissed Dex if he'd been there in person.

"This is a private session," Byron said.

"I don't mind," I said, a little too quickly. I reminded myself to play it cool. "We're all here for chem help. The more the merrier."

Byron looked defeated. "All right. Come in."

Wednesday dawned thick with fog, the kind of fog that doesn't look like it will ever burn off. I had nervously packed and repacked for the weekend with Logan's family. And then I panicked when I realized I should bring some kind of hostess gift. I had no time, and no way, to get to a decent store. In desperation, I made my roommate Bre go with me to the market in the dining hall to help me pick out a gift. After much deliberation and no solution, Tay came in to stock the shelves—she was on duty in the dining hall—and solved the dilemma.

"You said she likes to bake. And Logan says she only uses the best ingredients," Tay said. She grabbed a large jar of honey with a wood honey dipper attached with a ribbon with the university logo. "The university food science department is famous for three things: its ice cream, cheese, and this honey. Everyone needs baking honey for the holiday season."

I took the jar from her. "You are a genius. I'm going to miss you over break."

Tay rolled her eyes. "You're spending the weekend with Logan. You're not even going to think about me. But I am a great salesperson. I should get a bonus." She handed a jar to Bre. "Take one home to your mom. Maybe she'll buy you something nice on Black Friday."

"Good plan!" Bre took it from her.

"When are you heading out?" I asked Tay.

Her plans had been up in the air. She'd had trouble finding a ride that was willing to leave after she got off shift at five. Almost everyone else was taking off early. Jason had given the entire student staff the afternoon off with full pay, saying he could handle any problems that came up. No one was going to be in class anyway. The university was going into holiday shutdown mode.

"Six," she said. "I finally found an RA in Hill Hall that has to stay to close the dorm and has room in his car.

"Yeah," she said without enthusiasm. "He has a ten-year-old Ford Focus and four of us going back with him. I'll be lucky if there's room for my suitcase."

"I thought you had a chance with your grilled-cheese guy?" Bre said.

Tay rolled her eyes. "He left yesterday. Like Nic did."

"Better luck next time." Bre was actually being pretty sympathetic and not throwing the fact she had a boyfriend, and Tay didn't, around like she usually did.

"Yeah, I think I'm genetically doomed to be single."

Tay's supervisor walked by.

Tay sighed. "I'd better get back to work. It's going to be a hellacious day—we're serving crap leftovers. The cook is trying to clean out the refrigerator. Everyone who comes in complains. The only salvation is that the crowds are small and dwindling by the hour." She gave us each a hug. "Have a safe trip. Happy Thanksgiving!" Tay smiled at me. "And keep in touch. I want all the details."

Logan picked me up just after noon. The fog was still thick. As he loaded my bags in his trunk, I noticed his car was empty. "Where are Collin and Zave?"

"They have their own rides." Logan held up a gift bag. "What's this?"

"A hostess gift for your mom."

He smiled. "You didn't have to do that."

"Of course I did! I want to make a good impression."

He smiled and closed the trunk. "Don't worry—Mom will love you."

"You're awfully certain."

He pulled me into his arms. "Who wouldn't love you, El?" He kissed me in that way that made me want to sigh and pull him into me. That made me want to break down and make love with him, all the way.

I pulled away from him. "If you keep that up, we'll never get out of here."

He grinned.

"What are you doing with Spartacus for the break?" I asked.

"Zave took him home." Logan opened my car door for me.

"Opening my car door—what a gentleman."

"That's what you think now." He got a wolfish look in his eye.

"Hey! Stop trying to turn me on," I said, and kissed him lightly.

It took forever to get out of town. A steady stream of cars was making a mass exodus. The main road out was only one lane each direction. Visibility was poor and the going was slow. It was a five-hour trip to Seattle under normal circumstances. But today it looked like we were in for a marathon trip.

Logan turned on some tunes and rested his hand on my knee while he drove. "I wish you were wearing a skirt. I like the feel of your legs."

I tingled at the thought of his hot hand on my bare skin. "You're bad. Keep your thoughts on the road."

"On the road? Not possible." He laughed.

The fog was so thick the car in front of us was barely visible and the rest of the world was a gray-white cloud. I couldn't even see the road.

"This is going to be a long trip," I said.

"Hey! Are you insulting me?"

"I didn't mean the company!" I laughed and put my hand on his thigh. "I meant there's no view out the window to mark the passing of miles." I hesitated. "Then again, maybe that's a good thing. I'm nervous about meeting your family."

"Why? You've already met Dad. Mom is a pushover compared to him. And you'll like Caleb. Everyone does."

I might have imagined it, but I thought there was a touch of jealousy in his voice when he mentioned his brother. Or maybe it was irritation.

"Okay, I guess I can handle that many people," I said. "I'm fine in small, intimate groups."

He turned and stared at me.

"What?" I frowned.

"Thanksgiving at my house is never just a small, intimate affair. I told you—Mom always throws a big party."

He was right. He had told me. I had forgotten. "What? There will be more people? Like aunts and uncles? Cousins?" I quaked at the thought, but it also made me happy. Logan was going to introduce me to all of his family.

"And friends. Business associates." He turned his attention back to the road and hit the brakes as the string of cars in front of us slowed.

"Wait a minute—how many people are we talking about?"

"Fifty to sixty, depending on the year. Mom loves to entertain. Thanksgiving is her event. She loves being the one to kick off the holiday season."

So much for a small, intimate family dinner. The glow of being invited was beginning to wear off and more fear was setting in. No wonder Harlan had invited me so easily and with so little thought. He hadn't even seen the need to consult his wife. What was one more person to a gathering of that size? I was small. I didn't eat much. No one would even have to notice me. I was still wondering what Harlan's game was. There had to be a reason he'd extended the invitation. I could be lumped under miscellaneous guests and seated out of the way.

Logan shot me another look and shook his head. "Don't look so scared. This is going to be fun."

"Right. I'll keep telling myself that."

We lapsed into silence as Logan concentrated on the road and traffic.

"El?" Logan said at last.

"Yeah?"

"Have you noticed anything different about Jason lately?"

I froze. "What do you mean? Like what?"

"I don't know. He seems tense. Stressed." Logan frowned. "Distant."

I swallowed hard. That was my fault and I knew it. I'd asked Jason not to talk to Logan about me. I imagined that had put a strain in their relationship. I could imagine Jason backing off because he didn't want to hear too much.

"No," I said.

"Huh, that's funny. You two seem close these days." He sounded almost jealous.

It felt like my heart stopped for a second. When it started beating, it thudded way too loudly in my ears. What did Logan suspect?

I fixed my face in to a casual expression, trying to look like I hadn't really thought about it. "Close? Maybe closer than we were now that I've been in the office all semester."

Red headlights flashed in front of us in the fog. Logan hit the brakes again, cursed, and pounded the steering wheel. "Enough of this shit." He leaned next to his window, looked out, and pulled into the oncoming lane.

The fog was still so thick, I couldn't see a thing in the fields next to me. "Logan, no! You can't see." My heart raced.

Logan ignored me and hit the gas like he was angry. We surged forward.

I begged him. "Pull back in."

"Now that's what I like to hear a girl say."

"Logan, stop kidding." I grabbed his arm. "Get back in our lane."

"There's no one coming." He grinned and accelerated until we were going sixty miles an hour past the line of cars crawling along beside us. Five. Ten. Fifteen cars. Twenty.

"Logan! *Please.*"

When he finally slowed and signaled, no one wanted to let us back in. I covered my eyes. Logan laughed and his eyes were lit with excitement.

"Shit!" He became suddenly serious. He veered to the right and wedged his way in as the car behind us laid on their horn.

Seconds later, a semi truck cruised past us the other way, missing us by way too close a margin.

I was shaking. "Do you have a death wish?"

"Maybe."

"Logan!" My mouth fell open.

"Just kidding," he said. "We were completely safe. I could see better than you think. I have good reflexes."

"But no one wanted to let you in."

"I made them, didn't I?" He squeezed my leg. "I'd never put you in danger."

"I think you just did," I said.

"I was showing off for my girl." He spoke playfully.

"I wasn't impressed. *Don't* do it again."

We fell uncomfortably silent. I couldn't stand the weekend getting off to a bad start. "Kind of hard to play I spy with my little eye in this weather."

Logan looked at me out of the corner of his eye. "I'm sorry, El. You're right. I lost my temper back there and got impatient and took a chance I shouldn't have. I do that sometimes—take risky chances." He smiled at me. "That's why I need you, you ground me. And remind me to use caution when it's important. I wish I'd met you earlier. Before—"

I turned in my seat to stare at him, knowing exactly what he meant. He couldn't know how on target he was. "Yeah, me too." I stroked his cheek. "Me too."

Seven hours later, it was dark, but the fog had burned off. We sped west on I-90 toward Seattle, but stopped short on Mercer Island, meandering down a maze of suburban streets, down a private driveway, and came to a stop in front of a well-lit, gorgeous house on the water.

"Home sweet home." Logan shut off the engine.

I gaped at the house. A house, any house, even a crappy one, that sat on the waterfront on Lake Washington was expensive. This one must have been obscenely pricey.

"Ready?" Logan reached for his door handle.

"No. Will you take me home?"

"I just did." He laughed. "Come on, El. They don't bite." He hopped out of the car.

I reluctantly got out. He grabbed my hand and held it as we walked beneath the stars and the light pollution of the city to the front door. It was quiet and I could hear the lapping of the lake against the docks. But the peaceful sounds did nothing to quiet my nerves.

Logan squeezed my hand. "Lighten up. It'll be okay." As he reached to slide his key in the door, the door swung open.

A tall, striking, athletic-looking woman opened the door. I recognized her as his mother from her picture in Logan's room. She was smiling happily and proudly.

"Ma!" Logan dropped my hand and grabbed his mother in a bear hug, huddling around her.

"You finally made it. I was getting worried," she was saying as I stood off to the side, forgotten.

Before Logan could speak, he was attacked from behind by a guy I assumed was Caleb. Logan had to release his mother to fend off his brother. But his mom laughed as she watched them wrestle and struggle for supremacy, reprimanding them only when they threatened to knock over a vase on the entry table. "Enough horseplay, boys."

Caleb and Logan finally released each other. I got my first full-on look at Caleb. In person he was more magnetic than in his picture. I still thought Logan was way more attractive than Caleb, but Caleb was hot, too, and just a little bit more—an inch or two taller than Logan. Shoulders that much broader. Features that much more chiseled. And practically reeking with the confidence of a professional athlete.

Harlan stood off to the side, watching his sons and me. His expression was not one of joy like Logan's mom's. In fact, it may have just been me, but I thought he looked angry.

Caleb shot a glance at me and caused a chain reaction. Logan grabbed my hand and squeezed it possessively, pulling me closely next to him away from Caleb. "Everyone—this is Ellie, Elizabeth, Martin. El, you've met Dad. This is my mom—"

"Call me Sue." Her voice was smooth, but—maybe, again, it was my own insecurity—I thought I detected an unenthusiastic, not exactly warm undertone.

Logan didn't seem to notice it. "This is my baby brother Caleb." He seemed determined to one-up his brother.

Caleb was undeterred. He flashed me a smile I was certain never failed to charm girls out of their panties. "Nice to meet you, El."

Logan stiffened and squeezed my hand so tightly I thought it might turn blue. "Ellie."

Caleb ignored Logan. "What is a gorgeous girl like you doing with this guy?"

"Can it, Two." Logan's voice was icy hard.

Harlan looked on with interest. Was I the only one who hated the tension in the room?

"Two?" I said, and laughed, trying to lighten the mood and wondering if Logan was putting Caleb down again. "What kind of a nickname is that? Is it for number two son? Who's One?" I smiled at Logan. "That must be you."

Four pairs of eyes turned to me and stared at me like I'd made some kind of major mistake. Like calling Logan One was almost heresy.

Logan came to my defense. "Forgive her. She's not the baseball geek we are. Two is the catcher's number."

"Oh." I blushed, but I kept smiling. "What was your number?" I realized I didn't know. I'd never even asked or bothered to look it up in an old yearbook.

"I was the pitcher—number one, of course."

So I was right, even though it was for the wrong reason. But no one seemed to care or acknowledge that.

"That's only in the numbering system used to record defensive plays." Caleb snorted. "Stop bullshitting her. We affectionately call him Twenty-six. That was his jersey number. But he should have been Sixty-six."

I didn't get it, but it was obviously a putdown. I turned to Logan. His jaw ticked. "Players with numbers larger than sixty are usually cut from the team," he said, staring at his brother.

I had to bite my tongue to keep from making a snarky comeback. How dare Caleb poke at Logan's tender spot! He had to know what he was doing.

Caleb laughed. "Lighten up, Logan. I'm just teasing."

I took Logan's arm. "It was a long, tiring drive," I said, making excuses for him. "Foggy across half the state. We're both a little tense and tired."

It was the wrong thing to say. Logan stiffened, making it obvious he didn't need me to come to his defense.

Sue came to the rescue. "I held dinner. It's on the table. Let's not let it get cold."

CHAPTER TWELVE

The Walkers' house was built and situated just like you'd expect from a house on the water—it was long, all windows, with a stunning view of the water from every room and Seattle sparkling in the distance. Designed to catch and maximize the view. Every inch of the living area was expensively and tastefully decorated for Thanksgiving: glass pumpkins, ceramic turkeys, fall wreaths, and floral arrangements.

We sat at a spacious kitchen table in a room with curtain-less windows that showcased the view. Lake Washington calmly sparkled with lights from the houses around it. Sue and Harlan sat at the ends of the table. Caleb on one side, Logan and me across from him, with Logan nearest his dad and me next to Sue.

Conversation bounced around the table. The boys and Sue laughed and joked. I sat quietly by, answering politely when someone remembered to ask me a question. And Harlan contributed only minimally.

It wasn't until dessert that the focus shifted to me.

Sue set a plate of warm gingerbread and cream in front of me. "Tell us about your family, Ellie. What are they doing for Thanksgiving?"

Her question was so innocuous it was calculatedly dangerous. She knew exactly what she was asking. In fact, I was sure she knew the answer.

I smiled and looked directly at her. "Thank you. This looks delicious." I grabbed my fork. "My mom's on a cruise with her latest boyfriend."

"Any other family?" Sue set a plate in front of Logan and sat down.

"Not really. I'm an only child. I don't know my father." I almost stumbled on that lie, but it was the accepted story. "I don't even know who he is. That cuts out one side of the family." I laughed like it was a joke.

"Mom has never gotten along with her family. It has always been pretty much me and her and the stepdad of the moment. With her on a cruise, it's just me. Thank you so much for inviting me here for break. You're lifesavers."

Harlan answered for her. "We're glad to have you." His voice was seething with something unsaid. He turned to Logan. "What's this I hear about you testifying against Dr. Rogers?" The words burst out of his mouth with the force of having held them in for so long.

Logan froze with a bite of gingerbread on his fork. He set it down. "You heard right. It's the right thing to do." He stared his father down.

Harlan glared back at him. "I told you I have things under control—there's no need for you to get involved."

"I want to, Dad. It's the right thing to do." Logan's tone was surprisingly calm, but it was clear he wasn't going to back down.

Harlan pounded the table with his fist. I jumped.

"Damn it, boy! You will not drag this family's name through the mud. You won't make a public spectacle of us." Harlan's face turned rage red. He took a deep breath. "As long as I'm paying your bills, you'll do as I say. And I say you won't."

Logan's face was set and hard. He tossed his napkin on the table and pushed back. "Delicious dinner, Mom. I'm going to bring our bags in." Logan looked at me, sending me a signal to come with him.

"Yes, wonderful dinner. Thank you," I said to Sue, and rose from the table. "I'll help Logan."

Sue and Caleb looked unfazed, like these kinds of dinner explosions were more the norm than not. Sue looked a touch sad and resigned more than anything. "I put Ellie in the green guestroom, Logan. You can take her bags there." She wrapped her hands around her coffee cup.

Logan nodded and stormed out. I almost had to run to keep up with him. It was cold outside. I stood by the car and ran my hands up and down my arms as Logan opened the trunk.

"I'm sorry," I said.

He shrugged. "It's typical. Someday I'm going to be out from beneath his control. Someday soon." He sounded defiant and adamant.

"You can be out of his control now," I said. "We don't have to stay here. Let's get a hotel." The idea was highly appealing to me.

He shook his head and smiled sadly. "And hurt Mom? No. It'll blow over."

But I had the feeling he was lying. There was another fight brewing.

Logan took a deep breath and forced a smile. "You want to hear something funny? Mom put you in the room that's farthest from mine." He grinned and pulled me to him. "She must think you're a real threat to my chastity."

"Yes, I am just that kind of vixen." I grinned back at him. "Or you're a threat to mine."

"Yeah, that's it. Mom, the keeper of strange girls' virtue."

"Hey!" I shoved him playfully. "Did you just call me strange?"

He grinned. "You're strange in the cutest way possible." He brushed my lips with a light kiss. "She's going to have to try harder than that to keep me away from you."

Logan hadn't been exaggerating. The green guestroom was at the far end of the house on the opposite side from the family's bedrooms and was exactly that—very green. Green curtains, green walls, green bedspread and pillows. It was tastefully done, obviously by an interior decorator. The curtains were closed, so I couldn't see the view.

Logan set my bags down and pointed out my bathroom, which was fully stocked with fluffy towels and high-end guest toiletries.

"A private attached bathroom—wow! Nice." I looked around the room. "Maybe your mom was just making sure I'm comfortable."

Logan hugged me. "You are so naïve! We have three guestrooms. They all have private bathrooms. And she stuck you here in the north wing all by yourself at the end of the house."

"A wing all to myself—awesome!" I hugged him back, determined to make our first holiday together memorable and happy despite his family.

Sue strolled in. "Logan, did you show Ellie where everything is?"

Logan released me almost guiltily. "Yeah, Ma."

"Good." Her tone was pleasant and she was smiling, but when she looked at me her eyes shone with fear of a rival.

I'd seen that assessing, competitive look in my mom's eyes a zillion times before. It sent a shiver down me. I realized with a start that Logan's mom was in competition with me for him. She'd always been first lady in his life. And I was the interloper.

My first, natural response was to withdraw. I didn't compete with mothers. Why should I have to? And then I thought—why the hell not? I was sure his mother loved him, but I did, too. A mother's love was different than a girlfriend's. There was room for both of us in Logan's life. I took Logan's hand.

Sue ignored me. "Logan, I need your help getting the decorations and spare tables for tomorrow out of the attic. Caleb's already waiting."

"Sure, Ma." He turned to me. "It's a tradition. Two and I help mom while Dad relaxes and de-stresses with a glass of scotch. Caleb and I haul boxes around while Mom goes through her collection of Thanksgiving dishes, tablecloths, and centerpieces and makes the all-important decisions on this year's theme."

Sue shook her head. "Logan makes it sound like it's all last minute, like I haven't already planned every-thing out. You can't plan a party like this at the last second."

"But you can tweak it." There was an affectionate tease in Logan's voice. "And I mean tweak it big time."

"Are you implying that I can't make up my mind?" Sue's voice was happy and teasing, too, now that she had Logan's attention.

"Sounds like fun! I'd love to help," I said.

The subtle frost returned to Sue's eyes. "That's sweet of you, Ellie. But if you really want to help, you'll keep Harlan company and out of our hair. Decorating decisions and physical labor make him grumpy."

With Logan and Sue both staring at me, how could I refuse? "Sure," I said.

Sue's eyes shone with triumph.

Logan went off with his mom and Caleb. I found Harlan sitting in a plush leather recliner in the living room watching a game and sipping a glass of scotch.

"Sue wouldn't let you join them? You've been banned from their little threesome, too." Harlan muted the sound on the TV. "Ah, well, it's their thing. You must have hit a nerve."

Too? I was startled—he sounded bitter, and unhappy about being excluded.

"Have a seat." He motioned to the deep sofa. "Can I get you something to drink?"

I politely declined as I took a seat, wary of him, not liking him. "I think we're supposed to keep each other out of their hair."

"You mean Sue's?" He laughed. "A word of advice—it's not me you have to worry about interfering when it comes to Logan. Believe it or not, despite your unfortunate background, I kind of like you. At least you have spunk and guts. Unlike most of the girls Logan has dragged home."

There were others? That cut. That hurt. I wasn't special? I wasn't the first. He brought girls home all the time? My heart sagged. I masked my expression. "Gee, thanks. I've always aspired to being damned by faint praise."

His laugh would have been almost warm if it weren't for his caustic personality. "See what I mean? Not many people talk back to me."

I was about to say that Logan did, but Harlan didn't give me a chance.

"It's his mother who will be your undoing. She coddles the boys. Keeps them close. Wants them to adore her and be hers always."

"And you think it's better to keep them under your thumb?" I stared at him defiantly.

He swirled his scotch in his glass as he assessed me. "Is that what you think I was doing tonight at dinner?"

I shrugged, biting my tongue. I didn't need another enemy in this house.

"It's never wise to act based on incomplete information. You don't have the whole story, Ellie. You think I'm hard and harsh on Logan because I enjoy it." He snorted and took another sip of scotch, which seemed to loosen his tongue. "I'm ruthless in business. I expect a lot out of my boys. But I love my sons, both of them." He stared at me with a piercing, hard gaze.

"No matter what that bitch deserves, I don't want Logan to testify for his own good."

"But if he wants to, if he feels it's the right thing—"

"Wants to? Right thing?" He shook his head like I was talking nonsense. "You know who Logan was when I sent him to college?"

I didn't answer. I didn't think he expected one.

"A straight-A student with a promising baseball career ahead of him. A handsome kid who was almost too kind and sensitive for his own damned good. A fun, loving, well-adjusted son I was damned proud of."

"You never showed him. You pushed him!" The words burst out of me. "You pushed him too hard. He threw out his shoulder to impress you."

Harlan stared at me. "That was a tragic accident—a freak. No one could have predicted it. I'll never forgive myself..." He took a deep breath. "A kid like Logan needs pushing. He's not like his brother. Caleb could always hold his own. Logan needed a good shove."

I swallowed hard. I didn't believe him.

"You know what kind of boy I got back at the end of the year? A strung-out, out-of-control, drug-addicted, flunking-out mess of a kid."

That my father helped straighten out, I wanted to scream at Harlan. *That my father saved. Because you messed him up.* I was suddenly immensely proud of Jason. And glad he was mine.

"You blamed Logan for Dr. Rogers. You didn't believe him—"

"Of course I didn't believe him. You wouldn't have believed him, either. Not the guy he was then—lying, drunken, sleeping with anything in a skirt, making excuses for all his messes and taking no responsibility for them. If you knew half the things he did then, you'd probably have less faith in him than I did." He looked thoughtful. "You haven't seen him that way. Good for you. I hope you'll never have to." He downed the rest of his drink and set the empty glass on the end table beside his chair. "I hope no one has to again."

Harlan studied me. "No father should ever have to get the call that his son just tried to kill himself."

I gasped. I couldn't believe it.

"You don't know? Logan didn't tell you." Harlan snorted again. "Maybe I've miscalculated. Maybe you aren't as close as I thought."

I ignored his insult, pushed away the thought that he was quite possibly right. I was reeling from the revelation, making it hard to think clearly. "How?"

"You want me to betray my son's confidence?"

"You opened the box." I fought to keep my voice steady.

Harlan shrugged. "You'll find out sooner or later." He paused. "Logan wrapped his car around a tree. Slammed into it at over fifty miles an hour. Would have killed him. If he hadn't been so damned drunk. You know what they say about drunks walking away from accidents. Lucky for him."

I let out a sigh of relief. "I know about that. It was an accident." Logan had told me he'd wrecked his car.

Harlan shook his head. "I don't know what he told you, but it was no accident. He left a note. I still have it. Do you want to see it?"

"No!" I couldn't face Logan's suicidal thoughts. My horror must have shown on my face.

Harlan looked almost sympathetic. "I don't blame you. It's not pretty."

"You didn't believe Logan about Dr. Rogers until I confronted you." I had to fight to keep my voice from going shrill.

"Yes, that's partially true. Your son being raped is a horrible thing to face." Harlan looked far away for a second, lost in some terrible thought. "But a man can change. A reasonable man, when confronted with the facts, can change his opinion.

"I reread Logan's suicide note when I got home from Dad's Weekend. It was cryptic, but it was clear enough—what Dr. Roger's did to him was largely responsible for his depression. That coupled with the painkillers and alcohol." He set his jaw. "We have spent the last two years getting our boy back. I won't let him go through that hell again. I won't lose him. I will do everything in my power to stop him from testifying." His Adam's apple bobbed like he was fighting his emotions.

"I need your help, Ellie. I need you to talk Logan out of testifying."

I couldn't answer. I was too confused.

"A tip, Ellie—learn how to play the politics of life. Don't make an enemy of a potentially valuable ally."

Harlan, an ally? The thought was ridiculous.

"Why did you invite me here for Thanksgiving?" I asked him. Maybe I'd been wrong about his motives before. Maybe he didn't want to break us up, but I still didn't trust him.

"To show you what you're in for if you stay with Logan. And to test your mettle, see what you're made of. So, are you going to help me?"

Before I could reply, we were interrupted by a round of boisterous laughter as Caleb and Logan jostled a folding table around the corner.

"Mom changed her mind again." Logan rolled his eyes comically when he saw us. He looked like he'd been having fun. "Typical."

"She had us moving boxes around like slaves." Caleb hefted the table up. It was clear he was ribbing his mom, too.

Sue came around the corner behind them, beaming. "Are you two boys slandering me again?"

Logan's gaze bounced between Harlan and me like he was trying to assess how we were getting along. "What have you guys been up to?"

"Nothing much," Harlan said, unmuting the TV. "Just watching the game."

CHAPTER THIRTEEN

I didn't know what to think about what Harlan had told me. Logan—funny, sweet, gorgeous Logan—had tried to kill himself? It didn't seem possible. Why hadn't he told me? And how could I side against him with his father, no matter how much sense that made?

Logan and Caleb finished setting up the tables for Sue. Logan came to me where I was sitting on the sofa and grabbed my hand. "Mom's done working us for the night." He winked at her. "Get a sweatshirt, El. Let's go look at the lake and the stars." He pulled me to my feet.

"Just a sweatshirt?" I whispered to him. "Will that be warm enough?"

"I'll keep you warm, El," he whispered back.

His mom watched us with unhappy eyes.

I ran to the guestroom, grabbed my white sweat-shirt and met him in the hall. He carried his iPad.

"Are you going to thrill me with your vast knowledge of astronomy by reading from an app again?"

He grinned. "Absolutely. You have to give me some credit for being smart enough to buy the app."

I couldn't help smiling. "And knowing how to use it. I'm in."

He took my hand and led me out the back door, across the patio and grass and onto his family's private dock, taking me to the end of it, where the lake stretched big and dark in front of us.

"There's a lot of light pollution out here. This is the best we can do." He pulled me into a sit between his legs, wrapped his arms around me, and held the iPad in front of me so I could see as he brought up the app.

A moon shone over the lake, lighting it, my white sweatshirt, even my pale skin and Logan's hands, until they glowed pearlescent and magical. The lake lapped softly against the dock, gently bouncing us and making soft splashes that echoed off the water. The air held a tang of lake and rising mist as it formed over the lake.

For a moment, I got this crazy feeling that I had been here and done this before. And then I remembered the dream I'd had. It had been summer in the dream. I'd worn a white bikini, not a white sweatshirt. I shivered because it was still eerie, like fate was toying with me.

Logan wrapped me more tightly in his arms. "Cold?" His breath was hot in my ear.

I shook my head. "Happy." And still not able to rec-
oncile the Logan I knew with the description his father
had given me.

Logan pointed the iPad at the sky, aligning the
starwatching app with the stars above us, pointing out
the constellations. "Cassiopeia, Andromeda, Pisces." He
shook his head. "With so much light, you have to guess
at exactly where all the stars are and imagine the rest."

"Good thing we have the app," I teased, and snuggled against him.

Unlike the dream, no archer emerged to pierce my
heart. But he didn't need to. It already belonged to Logan.

"Logan?"

"Yeah?"

"Are you happy?" Since talking with Harlan, I'd
been unreasonably worried.

"Yeah. Why? Don't worry about that shit with my
dad earlier."

I nodded. "Okay."

I guess I didn't sound convincing.

He lowered the iPad until it rested on my legs.
"What did my dad say to you?"

"Nothing."

"El, come on. It's me. What did he say that has you
worried?"

I bit my lip. "Why didn't you tell me the full story
about your car accident?" I paused. "It wasn't an accident, was it?"

He held me so tightly in his arms, it was like he was trying to hold onto me forever. He pressed his face close to my ear. "No."

"You really—"

"Yes." He squeezed me tighter. "But it's not like I'm chronically depressed. It was a bad combination of the painkillers and alcohol and stress. I snapped. But I'm good now. It's not going to happen again. My doctor agrees. It was a freak thing. I know to avoid that combo now."

"Why didn't you tell me?"

"Because I don't like to remember. And I don't want you to see me that way." He pressed his cheek against mine and his voice got a hard edge. "Why did Dad tell you?"

"He didn't mean to. He thought I knew."

Logan didn't answer.

"How do you *want* me to see you?" I asked, stroking his hands.

"Like a hero," he whispered in my ear.

"Do I seem like a girl who needs a hero?" I stared at the lake and the twinkling lights across it, wishing they were shooting stars I could wish on and make everything come out right.

"No, definitely not. I just want you to see me as a hero." I could see his breath in the cold, humid night air, giving physical substance to his words.

My eyes misted up at the tender emotion in his voice. I swore I could feel his heart beating. I set the iPad on the dock next to us, pulled loose from Logan's arms, and spun around to sit in his lap, facing him with my legs around his waist. "I love you, Logan Walker."

He started to smile, but I kissed him before he could speak. Pressed myself into him, ran my hands through his hair, and squeezed him with my legs.

He slid his hands beneath my sweatshirt and T-shirt. His hands should have been cold, but they were hot, burning with desire against my skin. He pulled away from my kiss, stripped off his sweatshirt, rolled it into a ball, and put it on the dock as he extracted himself from my embrace. He moved like an athlete, graceful against the backdrop of the sky, mist, and stars, as he positioned himself over me on his knees and eased me back to rest against his sweatshirt like a pillow.

His bare arms glowed in the moonlight, only the edges of his tattoo remained a dark shadow of design where they peeked from beneath the sleeves of his T-shirt. As he straddled me, he kissed my nose and my lips, and then his lips were hot against my neck. The lake lapped against the dock, rocking us gently and slowly.

This was the dream. This was my dream coming true.

His kisses traveled down to this rise of my breasts. As he slid up my sweatshirt and shirt and unlatched my front-hook bra, my breasts budded in the cold night air, pointing toward the stars, aching for his touch. My breath caught as he bent and gently kissed them, as his mouth opened around them and his tongue circled them, licking until I moaned. Pleasure built between my legs with tight, pulsing intensity.

I needed his touch. I needed him. I forgot where I was and why I'd been upset. I arched up against him. He unzipped my jeans. Just as he slipped his fingers beneath the lace of my panties to the sweet spot that longed for him, I heard footsteps coming toward us from the house.

"Logan! Logan, are you still out here watching the stars? I'd like to see them, too." His mother, bundled in a jacket and hat, walked across the lawn toward us.

Logan rolled off me. I hurriedly hooked my bra, pulled my sweatshirt down and zipped my jeans as Logan grabbed his sweatshirt and slid it on.

By the time Sue reached us, we were both decent. She smiled at us like she knew exactly what she was interrupting. "What a lovely night for stargazing." She sat down next to Logan and put her arm on his shoulder. "What are we looking at?"

The lighting was dim, but I heard the smugness in her voice.

"Cassiopeia," I said, pointing toward the sky. "Chained to her throne. Good punishment for a mother who sacrificed her daughter Andromeda to a sea monster."

Yeah, I'd been reading over Logan's shoulder before. The app had all the details and mythology. Cassiopeia was also punished for boasting that she was more beautiful than all the Nereids. Guess Cassiopeia had a bit of both our moms in her.

Thanksgiving day was frenzied in the Walker household as Sue got ready for her evening party. Caterers and servers. Maids. I'd never seen anything like it. The house, already beautiful, was transformed into a Thanksgiving fantasy that looked like it belonged in a magazine.

Logan brought me breakfast in bed—gingerbread pancakes and syrup, ham, and an assortment of fruit, juice, and coffee. He warned me to stay out of the fray. "The kitchen. The dining room. The living room. Basically any room but this one are not safe to be in," he said with a laugh. "I should have warned you that breakfast is early. And you take it and dash to your room."

I was still in my pajamas. We cuddled on my bed while I sat and watched the parades on the TV in my bedroom until Sue found him and dragged him away. That was the last I saw of him all day. Sue kept him busy and away from me. I thought she was making a concerted effort to keep us apart.

I nervously waited for a text from Jason that he'd told Lyssa the truth about us. But my phone was silent except for a text from Logan apologizing for ignoring me and claiming his mom was a tyrant. I laughed at the absurdity of him having to text me when I was in his house. I kept thinking about Logan—what else didn't I know about him?

The guests began arriving at six for a seven o'clock meal. Logan picked me up at my bedroom door like we were on an official date. It was silly and sweet. He was dressed in slacks and a dress shirt and looked so good I wanted to stay in with him, not go out and face his parents' crowd.

I was pleased by his reaction and the way his pupils dilated like he was excited when he saw me. I'd taken my time and put a ton of effort into my appearance. I hated that I was preening like my mom did, but I wasn't going to be outdone at this party. I wore a short dress with a red lace bodice and three-quarter-length sleeves, a tight bright pink curve-hugging skirt and peplum, and nude heels. I figured if I was going to stand out as an outsider in this crowd, I might as well do it in vibrant color.

"You look hot." His eyes danced as he pulled me into his arms and kissed me, pressing me against his very hard crotch. And he seemed happy, almost euphoric. "Have I ever told you I love you urgently?"

"Urgently? That's new. Can love be urgent?" I smiled into his eyes.

"It is with me." His tone was sexy and low, totally serious as he ran his hands over the smooth knit fabric of my dress, caressing my ass.

How was it possible he could take my breath away with a phrase? I actually believed him. "I thought only passion could be urgent."

He grabbed my hips and pulled them into him. "That, too." He kissed my neck in a way that gave me goose bumps even though his breath was hot and his lips demanding.

"I'm allowed out of my room now, am I?"

"We aren't holding you prisoner."

I wiped my bright red lipstick off his mouth. "You could have fooled me." I paused, studying him. His mood was positively ebullient. Something didn't jibe—

how could helping his mom all day out him in such a good mood? "I can do as I please?"

"Absolutely."

"In that case, let's just stay in."

"I wish." He looked genuinely sorry. "But Mom will find us and there will be hell to pay." He took my hand. "Let's not ruin this fantastic day. Come out and meet the gang."

"You mean face the firing squad."

He shook his head and laughed like nothing could bring his mood down. "We aren't *that* bad."

He led me to the living room and the rounds of introduction after introduction began as new arrivals came in an almost steady stream. Caleb was dressed nearly identically to Logan. They were so close in age and looks that they could have been mistaken for twins.

But Caleb relished the spotlight, exuding warmth, drawing the girls to him with his with the magnetic combination of his looks and confidence as if it was his due. He worked the crowd as easily and effectively as he read signals on the baseball diamond. He was the prince of the party, the celebrity of note holding court with baseball stories and smiles.

Logan stood by me, understated, lurking in his brother's shadow, apparently content and unbothered by Caleb's bragging as he greeted guests and made small talk and introductions. Something was going on with Logan. But I couldn't figure out what it was. It wasn't that Logan was less charming than his younger brother. It was more that he preferred to be understated.

My head swam with names and faces, and my smile felt frozen on my face as I answered polite questions and was quickly abandoned in favor of more familiar faces and better connections. This dinner was as much a networking opportunity as it was social.

Logan introduced me to girls he'd known his whole life. Two in particular—Zo, short for Zoe, and Lacie—watched me with curiosity even after they drifted off to become part of Caleb's court. And then Kelsie, Logan's friend from school, arrived with her parents, looking blond and beautiful and seeking Logan with her eyes from across the room.

My heart fell. Why hadn't Logan warned me she'd be here? He'd claimed they were nothing more than friends, but I didn't miss the hero worship in her eyes when she spotted him. She'd been friendly and helpful the day I'd nearly drowned at the cliffs, but my mom's motto stuck in my mind: *Never trust another woman around your man.*

I should have listened to Mom's advice. I just hadn't thought she was talking about herself. I wouldn't make that mistake again.

Kelsie drifted over to us, flitting from greeting one person to another like a gorgeous blond butterfly until she reached us. "Logan!" She hugged him. "Quite the party."

"Mom's always are."

I held Logan's hand tighter, reminding him I was here and he was mine.

"You remember Ellie?" Logan said.

"How could I forget? It's good to see you again, El-lie. How are you enjoying life at our university?" Her tone was friendly, but it was obvious she was trying hard to make an effort and she couldn't keep her gaze from flitting back to Logan.

I also hadn't missed her use of the word "our" like I was the outsider and she had some kind of ownership over the school. And with the money it looked like her dad had, maybe she did.

"I'm loving it," I said with a smile.

"You're in that chem class, aren't you? Such a scandal." She gave Logan that hero look again, making it clear she was aware of his role in bringing Dr. Rogers down. I remembered what Logan said about wanting me to see him as a hero and suppressed a shudder. Kelsie was playing directly to him.

I thought it was cheeky of her to bring chem up, but Logan didn't seem to mind.

"I'm glad you have closure," she whispered to him as she touched his arm. "It gives me hope."

"You'll be okay, Kels," he said. "You're strong."

I felt their bond, the bond of shared experiences and the empathy of one victim to another. I didn't know much about her situation, just that she'd been date raped, too. I took her statement to mean her perpetrator had gotten away with what he'd done. But Logan's justice gave her hope. Their bond scared me with its strength and intimacy.

Before I had a chance to react, Amber Ranklin blew in wearing bright red lipstick and a tight nude slip dress with a wide-set, plunging neckline that left almost nothing to the imagination. Next to her I looked colorful, but prim. Her blond hair was swept up in an elegant bun. And it was more than just my imagination that her gaze swept the room looking for Logan. When she spotted him, she headed directly over. Unlike Kelsie, she didn't flit. She flew straight like an arrow looking for its target.

His eyes lit up when he saw her. It wasn't my imagination. Kelsie noticed it, too, judging from the quick frown that crossed her face. She didn't like Amber any more than I did, which put me even more on guard.

"Logan!" Amber gave him her widest smile and threw her arms open for a hug.

If he hesitated, it wasn't apparent to me. He dropped my hand and pulled her into a happy, affectionate hug. There was something going on between them. Something more than simple Thanksgiving cheer. I'd lived with a cheating mom long enough to recognize subterfuge and deception. And lust. Beneath her polished exterior, Amber was radiating with it for Logan. And Logan was riding a high I couldn't explain.

Just as I was about to clear my throat, he seemed to remember I was there. "Amber, you remember Ellie Martin? You met her at that infamous tailgate function a few weeks ago."

Amber turned a cool, blue-eyed gaze on me and extended her hand for me to shake, wearing a pleasant smile that held no warmth at all. "Yes, of course."

"Ellie is a regents' scholar," Logan said as he fawned all over a regent.

For the second time, Logan had managed to avoid the title of "girlfriend" when he introduced me to Amber. I felt the slap of it this second time, too. Because this time I was no fake girlfriend. That he'd remembered to say I was a regents' scholar this time only seemed to diminish me.

"That's wonderful," Amber said to me. "Congratulations. We're very proud of our regents' scholarship program."

She said all the right things, in the right tone of voice, wearing the right smile, and yet it felt like a put-down to me. She had avoided praising me, praising the program instead. I smiled. "Thank you." I wasn't going to elaborate.

Fortunately, I was saved any further contact with her by another family friend who spotted her and whisked her off to introduce to someone else.

The drinks flowed freely. By the time dinner was served, most everyone was in a festive, happy mood. Logan's high seemed even higher. Dinner was buffet style after Harlan made a show of carving a ceremonial slice off the roasted bird.

After dinner, the crowd split into factions by age. The under-twenty-five crowd staked out the game room with its bar, pool table, air hockey, ping pong table, and large-screen TV and video game selection as their territory, retiring there with their drinks.

Logan glanced at his watch. "Where the hell are Collin and Zave?"

"They're coming?" I asked.

"It's not a Thanksgiving party without them." Logan grabbed his phone to text them just as they strolled in the door.

"Finally done with the family festivities! Let the party begin." Collin strolled in carrying a gift bag, with Zave at his elbow. "I thought Grandma would never go home. Are we on for our annual pool tourney?" He spotted Caleb and slapped him on the back. "Caleb, my man! This year I am going to prove to you that being a major league baseball star does not make you a pool shark."

"Bring it on, Collin." Caleb slapped Collin on the back. "Zave." He shook Zave's hand. "Is that for me?" He nodded toward Collin's bag.

"No, sorry, man. This is for my man Logan." Collin pulled a black jock cup from his bag. "To protect the family jewels now that you have a girlfriend. Ellie will thank me later. The way Logan plays pool is positively dangerous."

Caleb laughed like he knew about the pool-ball incident that had given Logan a black eye just before I met him.

"That's the way *you* play, Collin." Logan reached for the cup. "Wasn't it your ball that gave *me* a black eye?"

Collin snatched the cup away and turned to Zave. "I don't know." He held the cup out, aligning it with Logan's crotch. "Now that we're here, it looks a little big."

Zave nodded. "You're right, Col. When in doubt, always go smaller. That's my motto."

Logan grabbed the cup from Collin. Unbothered, Collin pulled a pair of protective eye goggles from the bag and dangled them from his fingers, holding them out to Logan. "To protect those gorgeous brown eyes of yours."

Logan grabbed the goggles, too, and tossed them in a nearby wastebasket like he was shooting a basketball. "Shut up, Collin." Logan walked to a rack of pool cues hanging on the wall. "Prove your manhood at the pool table. Choose your cue and choose it carefully. I'm going to whip your ass."

"Not before I grab a beer. I don't play well stone-cold sober."

"You haven't had anything to drink today?" Logan said.

"Not enough." Collin and Zave helped themselves at the bar before selecting their cues.

As the guys chalked their cues, the girl named Zo grabbed my arm. "They're wild men when they play. Totally vicious. You won't want to be too near. Pool balls will fly."

Ignoring her, I turned to Logan. "The girls don't get to play?"

Logan brushed my lips with a kiss. "You saw my eye the night we met, El. Zo's right. Our annual game gets intense and involves a lot of insults."

"You mean insulting behavior," Zo said.

Logan laughed. "You want to stay and be my luck?" he said to me.

No, I want you to pay attention to me, I thought, feeling like I didn't belong in his world and trying hard not to pout or act like a petulant child.

"Sorry, Logan. I won't let you suck an innocent victim in. I'm going to take Ellie out into the safe zone, away from the smell of sweat and beer and the danger of being caught in the middle of your horseplay." Zo pulled me away. "Believe me, you don't want to play," she whispered in my ear, rolling her eyes. "It gets ugly and silly. It's better to just ignore it and them. Besides, we want to get to know the girl Logan has brought home."

On the way past the bar, she grabbed an open bottle of white wine and pulled me across the room to the cluster of sofas and chairs in front of the TV, which was playing a classic Christmas movie. She sat me down next to her on the sofa while Lacie stared openly at me and passed the bottle of wine around so Kelsie and Zo could refill their glasses.

Finally, I made a point of looking around. "What? Do I have a spot on my dress or something?"

Zo laughed. "Oops! We're too obvious. Sorry, Ellie. We're just trying to figure you out."

"I'm not that complicated," I said.

"Don't be so modest. Just being here with Logan makes you completely complicated and totally fascinating," Zo said.

"Really? Why?" I refused to be intimidated by these girls.

Lacie shrugged. "Because you're not his usual type."

I'd never thought about Logan having a type. And I guess I just assumed that if he had one, I was it. "What is his type?" I laughed like I didn't care what about the answer.

Zo nodded toward Kelsie.

I froze.

"Ignore her," Kelsie said, but the look in her eyes was hopeful. "We're just friends." She didn't sound completely thrilled.

"Now," Lacie said. "But you two were practically living together your sophomore year."

My mouth went dry. Logan had said Kelsie hadn't meant anything to him. He'd made it sound like they had just been friends.

"We were both going through some crazy crap," Kelsie said. "It was just a comfort thing for both of us." It was clear she didn't want to talk about it. "We're over it. We weren't really a thing." But she sounded a little wistful.

Maybe the other girls didn't know her story. I took pity on her and tried to redirect the conversation, for my own sake as well as hers. I refused to show weakness. "We all have exes. Logan isn't exactly my type either."

That piqued their curiosity. Three faces lit up, disbelieving. How could Logan not be someone's type?

"What is your type?"

I thought about it a second. "Lying, cheating douchebags."

That broke the ice. The other three girls laughed.

"Join the club," Zo said. "You're saying Logan isn't a douchebag?"

"You've all known him all your lives—you tell me."

Zo's eyes went wide with respect and surprise. But seriously, I was devious. I wanted to see the side of Logan he wouldn't tell me about.

"Are you serious?" Lacie stared at me.

I shrugged. "Sure. Warn me off now while I still have time to run."

Zo cocked one eyebrow and turned to Lacie. "She's right. We can dish her the dirt and then it's up to her. We *have* known him all our lives."

Lacie nodded her agreement. "Very smart, really. We should totally all have sources on any potential new boyfriend."

Whoops erupted from the pool table. Lacie looked in that direction and rolled her eyes. She turned back to me. "Well, where to start?"

"The beginning's always good," I said.

Lacie nodded. "Okay, fair enough. Unlike Caleb, who's always been a player, Logan used to be totally sweet, a serial monogamist in high school and before. All the girls wanted him. But he stayed true to his girlfriend of the moment."

"Very sad for the rest of us," Zo said. "Until after his freshman year in college. That baseball injury changed him." She grinned wickedly. "He fulfilled all of us that summer." She laughed. "You sure you want to hear this?"

"I asked, didn't I?" I said, thinking, *no I really didn't*. But I had to know.

Zo shrugged. "I slept with him at that big party Collin threw on the Fourth of July."

"Yes, you rotten bitch. You beat me to him." Lacie laughed now. "I didn't get my chance until August, practically the very last second before he went back to school. He took me to SeaFair. I'll never forget what we did after the hydro races. Best SeaFair ever for me."

I felt sicker by the minute. It seemed like I was the only girl in the room who hadn't actually slept with him. But I kept my smile, acting like it didn't bother me.

"But that's all *way* before he met you," Zo said to me. "We've all known guys who can be completely faithful once they find a girl who really turns them on. He hasn't touched any of us since. And he seems completely devoted to you."

Lacie nodded.

Kelsie frowned as she stared at the doorway. Zo followed her line of sight.

"What?" I said, and turned. Seeing who they were looking at my mouth went dry. Amber had arrived carrying two open longneck beers.

"I thought she wanted Caleb, especially after he went pro," Kelsie said softly.

Zo nodded. "She's always been a cougar with an eye for Logan."

I felt sicker and sicker as across the room from us Amber walked to the pool table and handed Logan a beer while he leaned against the wall, waiting his turn to shoot. They clinked bottlenecks like they were toasting something. She put her hand on Logan's shoulder and whispered something in his ear. He nodded. She laughed and squeezed his shoulder.

Caleb yelled to him. "It's your turn, big brother."

Laughing, Amber blew on Logan's pool cue and leaned against the table, watching him as he took his shot. The guys around the table erupted in groans, which I took to mean Logan had made a good shot.

"We're no threat to you," Zo said. "We were just hooking up with him. Having a little fun. Not that Logan isn't a catch, but you know." She paused and it was clear neither she nor the other girls liked Amber. "But I'd watch out for her. She's different. She wants him."

I felt pale. "Have she and Logan...?"

Zo nodded, looking like she was pained.

"You know for sure?" I had a hard time keeping my voice from shaking.

Zo gave me a sympathetic look. "I walked in on them here in this very house going at it during Sue's New Year's Eve party last year."

Lacie put her arm around my shoulder. "Don't let Amber upset you. Just keep an eye on her. We're on your side."

I had my phone with me in a tiny wristlet purse. It was sitting in my lap. The phone buzzed. I pulled it from the bag. Jason was calling. This must be important. I swallowed hard, but my mouth was dry.

"Excuse me," I said, getting to my feet. "I have to take this." Then I dashed out of the room, making a point not to look at Logan.

CHAPTER FOURTEEN

I caught the call just in time, making it to the guestroom and locking myself in. "Jason." I was breathless and my heart was pounding.

"Happy Thanksgiving, Ellie." He sounded upset.

Not good. So not good. "You too," I said. "Is that all you called to say?"

"No. Is Logan with you?"

"I'm alone," I said as my sense of dread grew stronger. "Did you tell her?"

Jason hesitated. "There's been a complication."

My mind froze. What kind of complication could there possibly be? "What?"

He sighed heavily into the phone. "I don't know how to tell you this, Ellie. I'm still stunned myself. I was going to tell Lyssa this evening after everyone left. But

this morning she stunned me with an announcement—
she's pregnant again. You're going to have another
half-sib."

I couldn't speak.

"I couldn't tell her after that, Ellie, though believe
me—I wanted to. I have to give her a few days of happiness and being in the spotlight. I couldn't take the
spotlight off this new baby so soon."

"No, I know," I said automatically. "Congratulations."

"Yeah," he said. "Mia's only six months old. This
wasn't planned. I'm still processing it." He tried to
laugh. "When it rains, it pours." He really did sound
stunned.

"Yeah," I said. "I know." And I did.

"We'll work it out. Nothing's changed. It's just de-
layed by a few days. That's all."

"Yeah."

"I can't talk. I have to go, Ellie. Just thought you
should know."

"Yeah. Thanks." I hung up and sat there staring at
the phone in my hands. It was all too much. Just way
too much. I didn't feel up to going back to the party. I
couldn't watch Amber flirt with Logan. I couldn't
leave. I didn't know what to do.

I don't know how long I sat there. In my dazed state
I lost track of time.

There was a knock on the door. "El? Are you in
there?"

"Go away," I told Logan.

"I'm not going away. What's wrong?"

I didn't answer. What could he do? I was safely locked in.

I heard his footsteps retreating and wiped a tear away. Minutes later, the push-in lock to the door popped up, the door swung open, and Logan let himself in.

My mouth fell open. "How did you?"

"I know where the key is." He held it up and closed the door behind him, locking it again.

I should have gotten up. Locked myself in the bathroom. But what was the point? He had the damned universal key. He sat down next to me and tried to put his arms around me.

I scooted away from him.

He backed off. "Zo said you got a call and left. What's up? Who was it? What's gotten you upset?"

My heart pounded. I couldn't tell him. Not now. So I did what I always did—I deflected the attention away from what I'd done. In this case, it wasn't hard to do at all.

"No one. Nothing. That was just an excuse to get away." I stared at him.

"What, El?"

"Am I the only girl here you haven't slept with?"

He gave me a half-smile. "It's not for lack of wanting to on my part." His voice cracked with emotion and desire. "We could remedy that any time." He reached for me.

I glared at him, warning him to back off. "Stop kidding. I'm serious."

He stared straight back at me. "So am I."

I ignored what he said. "You could have warned me. But you just let me walk in blind and stumble into a party full of your conquests." I held back a sob. I would not cry in front of him.

He swallowed hard and spoke quietly. "That's all in the past. I never lied to you. I told you I went through a rough patch where I was out of control and slept with a lot of girls."

I took a deep breath and stared at him. "A lot of girls. Not *these* girls. Your friends. Girls you see all the time."

He looked momentarily stricken. "This sounds bad, but none of them meant anything to me." A look of anger flashed across his face. "They shouldn't have told you. They're just causing trouble."

I shook my head. "You let me believe that you and Kelsie are just friends. Then I find out you two had a thing and practically lived together.

"You still didn't answer my question—if you knew she'd be here, why didn't you warn me?"

"Kels and her family rarely come. I didn't even know Mom still invited them. I was as surprised as you are she's here." His eyes begged me to understand.

His mom was behind that, too.

"I wasn't lying when I said she didn't mean anything to me. I don't expect you to understand, but after what Dr. Rogers did, I felt emasculated. Like I had to be in control again. And prove that I was a real man."

He sounded so broken, I couldn't push him any further. I had no idea what it was like to go through what he had. I would be the world's biggest bitch if I condemned him for it. But there was still Amber.

"Fair enough," I said.

He reached for my hand and held it tightly, lightly running his thumb over mine when I didn't pull away. "I love you, El. You have to believe me. You're special. You're more to me than just sex. That's why I wait."

The way he spoke made me ache inside. It was so heart-wrenchingly beautiful. I was almost distracted. Almost. I could have let things drop. Maybe I should have, but there was one more thing I needed to know. I looked him square in the eye. "What's going on between you and Amber? And don't you dare lie to me."

Logan stared at me for a long moment.

"I know you slept with her, too," I said.

"Yes."

"Is there still something there?"

He squeezed my hand, holding on so I couldn't pull away. "How can you even ask?"

"I have eyes. I see the way she looks at you. She wants you, Logan. And I don't like it. But there's something else going on. You two were simply too happy to see each other today, like you have some kind of inside joke going on. After living with my mom, I'm an expert at sniffing out relationship lies. Tell me the truth. If you lie I'll know and I'll walk right out of here and not look back." I was only partially bluffing.

Logan paled, but he kept his composure. "We're involved in a business deal. But you can't tell anyone else."

I stared at him, waiting for him to explain.

"Amber is an investment broker. She came to me, asking my advice on some technical matters in a company she was going to invest in, and presented me with an investment opportunity I couldn't turn down. I had some money my grandfather left me that wasn't tied up in my trust fund so I used that."

My heart hammered in my chest. "When?"

"Last summer. Before I met you. We just got good news today. We're one step closer to seeing our investment pay off. Don't you understand, El? When it does, I can tell Dad to go to hell."

I didn't want to know how much money he'd risked. "Get out of it."

"I can't. I'm in too deep and we're too close to the payoff."

I kept staring at him. "I don't like it."

"Amber won't come between us. I won't let her."

"Maybe not," I said, though I wasn't convinced. "But this obsession with proving yourself to your dad will. You can't spend the rest of your life trying to win his good opinion. You don't have to compete with Caleb. Harlan loves you. Both of you."

I'd said the wrong thing. Logan made narrow eyes at me and let go of my hand, looking at me like I was a traitor. "You don't know that. You don't know shit."

Right then I knew I could never convince him not to testify. I could never take Harlan's side, no matter how right it might be, on anything. "You're right," I said. "I don't know the whole story. I'm not in your shoes."

He looked only slightly relieved and less angry at me. Our families really were our hot buttons. Something dawned on me. "When you met Amber in the coffee shop, that was intentional. You were conducting business. You lied about that."

He didn't answer.

"And weekends, when you claimed you had too much homework and couldn't study with me—what was that? Web telecons? Video conferencing?"

He sighed and I knew I'd hit on the truth.

I knotted my hands in my lap. "This isn't going to work if we keep secrets from each other." But even as I spoke I knew what a hypocrite I was. I wondered again how I'd ever be able to tell him the truth about Jason being my dad without blowing us apart. I thought about telling him right then. But things were just too raw between us.

I put my hand on his thigh. "I'm sorry. Truce?"

He smiled, but it didn't reach his eyes as he covered my hand with his. "I'm sorry, too." He brushed my lips with a kiss and laced his fingers in mine. "We'd better get back to the party before Mom comes looking for us." He rolled his eyes comically.

I couldn't help smiling. "Sure. Is the tourney over?" I touched his eye. "You don't have a black eye yet?"

He grinned. "Zave and Collin know better than to get that wild here. Mom will kill them if they damage her pool table or her walls."

"Well then, let's go back so you can show them how it's done."

He pulled me to my feet.

"This time I insist on blowing on your cue for luck," I said as we walked to the door hand in hand.

"Sorry about that, too," Logan said. Then he grabbed me behind the head and pulled me into a kiss so passionate I forgave him.

The rest of the weekend was a blur of parties and shopping and date stuff. Logan took me to downtown Seattle. We rode the Wheel, the big Ferris wheel on the waterfront. He bought me flowers at the market. Neither of us talked about Thanksgiving or anything of real consequence. It was like we were avoiding all the major issues. We just enjoyed the time off and made jokes about his mom interrupting whenever we got a minute alone. All too soon, we were back at school and into the heat and stress of the last few weeks before finals.

Tay, Nic, Bre, and almost every girl in the dorm came back from break with an assortment of new sweaters and clothes bought at Black Friday specials. Tay was particularly happy—her heart-shaped grilled cheese dining-hall guy had been texting her over break and they were going out on Friday. Bre had had a minor fight with her boyfriend Dan, a misunderstanding over break that she complained about nonstop until they made up Monday night.

My wonderful mom got back from her cruise and decided she needed to text and email me day and night. I deleted them all without responding.

Tuesday morning I met Jason for coffee. He reassured me he would tell Lyssa about us. Soon. He asked casually about my long weekend with Logan's family. I told him I knew about Logan's suicide attempt. And the other girls.

Jason winced and nodded sympathetically. "Logan's impulsive, Ellie. I worry about him. He has to learn to restrain his urges and think before he acts."

"Maybe I'll be good for him. Sometimes I think too much," I said.

Jason stared at me. "Never try to change another person. It never works." He sounded resigned, almost sad. "Love them for who they are or leave them. If you can't live with the person they are, walk away."

I wondered if he was talking specifics. "What? I thought you didn't know how to parent teenagers," I whispered to him. "And now you've suddenly become the fount of fatherly wisdom?"

He smiled. "Be careful, Ellie."

I knew he was trying not to interfere too much, but his wariness was obvious.

I ran from coffee to chem lab. Bhat handed back the graded carbons for our most recent lab.

Dex looked through his eagerly and grinned. "One hundred percent—A, A, A!" He slugged me playfully in the arm. "What did you get?"

I rolled my eyes. "We're partners and we worked on these together. If I don't have the same scores as you do, I'm going to launch a formal complaint." When I opened looked at my lab report, red ink spilled over the page. Tons and tons of notes in the margins. I froze. A big red one hundred percent was at the top of the page.

Dex peered over my shoulder. "What the—"

The words swam before my eyes. The writing was definitely Byron's, not Bhat's. Love notes. There were love notes written all over my notebook, personal, longing love notes.

"Oh, shit," Dex said.

"Exactly."

"You could lodge a complaint with the dean. Claim sexual harassment," Dex said.

The report shook in my hands. I stuffed it in my backpack. "I can't. I have to think. This can't go on."

I skipped my afternoon chem help session with Byron. I just couldn't face him. Instead, I went back to my room and forced myself to read the notes he'd written throughout my lab report.

I love you, Ellie. You're out of my league, but our chemistry is undeniable.

What would a hot girl like you want with a nerd like me? You're a student and I'm your professor. If not for our chemistry, it would be impossible.

I can't stop thinking about you. About your smile. And the cute way you wrinkle your nose when you're thinking and trying to solve a problem. We could be like a covalent bond—sharing electrons.

I was not going to share electrons, whatever that meant, or anything other than cookies with Byron. *Ever.*

Will you go out with me? Say you will. I'll treat you nice. I have plenty of money. Call me. He listed his number.

There was more. Lots more. *You look so hot in your red sweater, the one with the dots. Wear it next time you come to my office so I'll know you saw my notes.*

Ew. I'd probably never be able to wear that sweater again. I felt guilty and horrible and icked out all at the same time. Why couldn't Byron be like a normal guy and see I was just being friendly? That the cookies were all I was going to give him in exchange for chem help. And that wasn't even strictly required.

Logan texted me, wanting to meet at the SUB coffeehouse lounge to study. I texted him back that I'd meet him there.

With finals and final projects looming, the lounge was packed. Everyone was bundled in sweatshirts. It took me a minute to spot Logan sitting by the windows. He was looking for me. I knew the minute he spotted me. His face lit up and he waved. He waited for me at the table with a hot mocha.

"You're a lifesaver," I said as I slid into the chair across from him and set my backpack down beside me. "It's icy out there. Does the wind ever stop blowing?"

He grinned. "In the winter? Dream on."

I wrapped my hands around my coffee and took a sip. "I am dreaming—of a white Christmas and finals and this semester being over, over, over!"

"Speaking of Christmas," he said.

I waited for him to continue, but his eyes just sparkled. "What about Christmas? Are you just dangling that out there to tease me?"

He grinned. "I might have a surprise up my sleeve."

"You are teasing me."

His grin deepened.

"You aren't going to tell me?"

"It wouldn't be a surprise then, would it?"

"You brought it up." I was still wondering and plotting what to get him. Really, it seemed like he had everything.

He laughed.

"Okay, subject change, then. What are you studying tonight?"

"A bunch of engineering crap." He held up a green engineering grid pad full of messy-looking equations.

"Nice," I said.

"You?"

"A bunch of management info crap." I winked at him. "I have a paper to write."

"Is Jason helping you with it?"

The question came out of nowhere. "What? No. Why do you ask?"

"You and he seem to be hanging pretty tight lately." His tone was a little too casual.

I shrugged. "You know Jason. He's a born mentor. He can't help himself when it comes to helicoptering around his students."

The way Logan studied me made me uncomfortable. "You've been having coffee with him regularly at The College Grind."

My heart skipped a beat, in the bad way. I thought about denying it, but what was the use. "Yes," I said. "How did you know? Have you been spying on me?"

He shrugged. "Word gets around." He paused. "Why didn't you tell me?"

"What's to tell? Look, it's no big deal. I have a free period and need a coffee to get me through the day so I started going to The College Grind. Jason takes his break at the same time. We ran into each other a few times and started joking about how it was becoming a habit and then it just did."

Logan's eyes narrowed. "What do you two talk about?"

I stared back at Logan and tried to make a joke. "Jealous? I never promised you coffee fidelity."

"I'm serious, El."

I took a deep breath. "Don't go all possessive stalker on me, Logan. We just talk."

"About us?" His gaze was steady. "After you asked me not to?"

"Of course not!" I tried to act indignant, but I wasn't sure I succeeded.

Logan frowned. "I'm just wondering what's going on. Jason's been preoccupied lately. Stressed. Distant. And yet you two are suddenly all buddy buddy." He kept staring at me. "Is something going on between you? Tell me the truth."

"If I tell you the truth will you drop it?" I said.

He nodded.

I hedged, making sure I told the truth, but only part of it. "He gives me advice about college stuff. I think he feels sorry for me because my mom is a crappy parent and I don't have anyone to turn to."

Logan held my gaze. "He's like that." He didn't sound completely convinced.

"How was your day?" I asked him, changing the subject.

"I had to talk to the police again to go over my statement." His voice was flat.

I wanted to tell him how brave he was. That he really was a hero. But at the same time Harlan's fears ran through my mind—could Logan handle the stress? Part of me wanted to ask Logan to call it off and forget about testifying, like his dad wanted. Part of me knew I couldn't. Testifying was the right thing to do. Logan would see me asking him not to as a betrayal.

I reached across the table and squeezed Logan's hand. "You're the bravest guy I know. Serious. I'll always be here for you. If you need to talk, or whatever."

He smiled back, but it was forced, like he was under a huge strain. "Thanks, El. But I don't want to think about it, let alone talk about it."

I nodded. "Study?"

He nodded. "Now we study."

I leaned over and unzipped my backpack. As I pulled my laptop out, my chem lab report fluttered out and landed at Logan's feet. I reached for it, nearly clunking heads with Logan. But I wasn't fast enough.

As Logan leaned down and picked it up, his eyes scanned the pages. "What the hell is all this red ink?" He frowned. "Are you still having trouble in chem?" He scanned the report and looked up at me. "What the fuck, El?"

CHAPTER FIFTEEN

Logan's voice and face were hard. "When were you going to tell me about this?"

I froze. "I—"

"You weren't, were you?" He slapped the report onto the table in front of him. "*We could share electrons. You look so hot in your red sweater. I love you.*" His voice rose with each word. "How long has this been going on? Is this why Byron wanted to meet with you?"

The girls at the table next to us turned and stared. A public lovers' fight was an event, college drama at its finest.

I'd never seen Logan angry at me like this. His cold look frightened me, like he was pulling away from me and I didn't know if I could reel him back.

"You told me having Byron as your prof was fine. Not a problem." His voice became suddenly low and controlled, and that was even more ominous.

"It is fine. It's...look, I have a plan. Everything's under control."

"You've been flirting with him." Again, the low voice. "Are you still baking him shit?"

"Well, not shit, but cookies." I nodded and tried to smile. "Yes."

Logan swore beneath his breath. "Baking for a guy is flirting with him, El, and you damn well know it. You're leading him on. It's looking for trouble. He could..." Logan took a breath to compose himself. "He's a *chem* prof, El."

I knew Logan's fears. I knew where he was coming from. He'd experienced the worst. But Byron wouldn't. "Logan, please. Byron is nothing like—"

"Dressing provocatively. Wearing your hot red sweater to private study sessions." His gaze was piercing and angry like I'd betrayed him.

"Hot red sweater?" I was astounded by the accusation. "No one but Byron would consider that sweater hot. It's so prim it belongs in a nunnery. I've been really careful not to give Byron the wrong idea—"

"You've been doing a damn shitty job of it."

I ignored Logan's comment. "The sessions aren't private. Dex sees to that. I'm never alone with Byron."

"Dex? What do you mean he's taken care of it?" Logan's eyes were hard.

I briefly explained Dex's protection system to him. "So someone always just 'coincidentally' shows up within minutes of me." I thought that would placate Logan, soothe him. "So, see, really, I'm not taking any chances. It's just until the semester's over and I have my grade and—"

"And then what? You let him down gently?"

I swallowed hard.

"You need to lodge a complaint with the university. Get that bastard out of the classroom." He raised his voice almost to a yell.

I could feel the silence settle around us. We were drawing attention and making people uncomfortable.

"No, that's extreme. I can't. This is Byron. He's harmless—"

Logan's gaze bored into me. "You went to Dex with this—why didn't you come to me, El? Shit, I'm your boyfriend. You're supposed to trust *me*." His voice had risen to a full yell now.

The buzz from the students studying around us totally died. In a few seconds, they'd start taking bets on whether we were going to break up or not. My heart pounded. My mouth went dry. I had to make Logan see I was only trying to protect and spare him. I was looking out for him. "You have so much going on. You're under too much stress. I didn't want to bother you—"

"And Dex doesn't? He has nothing going on at all. He has broad shoulders that can handle anything and is so smart he has all the answers. And I'm such a fucking weakling I can't protect my girlfriend?" He grabbed his laptop and notebooks and slammed them into his backpack.

I swore I heard every tooth of the zipper click in as he zipped his backpack shut, grabbed his coat, and slung his backpack over one shoulder.

"No, wait! No, of course not. Logan, please!" I hated the desperate note in my voice that exposed my breaking heart. "It's just—"

"I'm too fragile to trust. Damaged. Unable to cope."

"No—"

"You didn't want to hear my advice because it's so lame and goes against what you want to do, what you know is right?" He stood up as I frantically scrambled to put my laptop back in my backpack and reached for my coat.

"Screw it, El!" His voice was like quiet thunder, frightening in its intensity. He turned and pushed his way through a group of guys looking for a study table.

I shoved my chair back and stood. "Logan! Don't be like that. Don't walk out on me."

He had turned and didn't look back. It was stone silent in the lounge around me. I stood in a sea of curious, uneasy eyes and sympathetic looks, frozen.

One of the guys in the group Logan had pushed through looked at me. "Are you going to be using that table?"

I grabbed my coat, slid it on, and picked up my backpack, leaving my coffee behind. "It's yours. Enjoy." I held my chin high and pushed my way through the crowded lounge, breaking into a run when I hit the exit, chasing after Logan.

I pushed through the doors into the cold winter evening that matched my heart. Snow was beginning to fall. But Logan was gone. I put one hand over my mouth to hold my sobs in. I would not cry. I would not. But tears stung my eyes as I pulled my cell phone out of my pocket and desperately texted Logan. *I'm sorry.*

I held the phone as I walked back to the dorm, waiting. I waited and waited, but Logan was silent.

"Logan broke up with you? I can't believe it." Tay had her arm around me as I sat on my bed in my dorm room.

Bre and Nic hovered nearby, offering moral support and sympathetic ears.

My eyes were red and swollen. "The breaking-up part is ambiguous. Does *Screw it, El* mean we're done?" I snorted.

"Well, ambiguity is something," Nic said. "He left the door open, even if it's only a crack. You can still fix this. Once he calms down, you talk to him."

"He's not texting me back."

"Stupid asshole men. He'll calm down," Bre said, offering a platitude. "They always do."

"He loves you, Ellie!" Tay squeezed my shoulder. "He's just upset."

I sniffed. "Yeah, I knew he would be. That was why I didn't tell him." I dabbed at my eyes with the tissue. "Maybe I was wrong. Maybe if I'd told him..."

"You can't live in maybe land," Tay said. "You have to deal with what you have."

I nodded.

Our room was old with built-in floor-to-ceiling closet/cupboards that had two lower drawers. Bre went to hers, opened one of the drawers, and pulled out a giant-size chocolate bar and a bottle of vodka. "But for now, you need comfort. Chocolate and booze." She grabbed four red plastic cups and poured a round that she mixed with orange juice from our mini fridge. When we all had a glass and a hunk of chocolate, Bre raised her glass in toast. "To breakups and making up in style."

I chugged my drink, feeling the burn all the way down, hoping the buzz would do something to heal my heart. "You all agreed with my plan for dealing with Byron," I said.

Nic looked at me over her drink and shook her head. "I had my doubts."

"Yeah. Sorry. I'm not trying to pass on the blame. I did what I did. I just thought it was a good plan."

Tay nodded sympathetically. "Yeah, it was. I mean, it would have worked if Logan hadn't found out. That was the flaw."

I nodded. "That damn lab report. Why did Byron have to scribble love notes all over it?"

Nic looked at me sadly. "He's escalating, Ellie. That's probably what freaked Logan as much as any-thing. Given Logan's history...well, can you blame him?"

"Yeah," I said, swallowing hard. "Yeah." Nic was right.

"What are you going to do?" Bre asked. "If I were you, I'd ask my dad for advice. He's always level-headed." She shot me a sympathetic look.

They all knew about my mom and that I didn't have a dad. But they were wrong—I did have a dad. And Bre was right. I needed his advice. Sometimes there's no substitute for a parent. Not that I ever had a real one. But that was what I'd heard. Tomorrow after work, I'd see if Jason had a minute. I knew I could trust him to keep things secret. We were like our own society of secrets.

"And be careful about keeping secrets from Logan in the future," Tay said. "I think you have to trust him or you don't have a chance."

The dress code for chem class on Wednesday was anything black, which matched my mood perfectly. Though I thought maybe I should wear scarlet and stick out. Or wear that "hot" red sweater defiantly and just let Byron find me. That would be more courageous. Or maybe it would just send the wrong message again. I had to do something. Logan still hadn't texted me back and I was sinking further into the abyss of despair every hour.

"You're going to have to stop this dressing-alike thing," I told Dex. "I can handle myself."

"Hey, calm down. I'm sure you can," Dex said. "But this is so much fun."

I glared at him.

"What happened?" Dex asked.

"Logan found out about Byron's notes to me."

"Oh," Dex said, and let things drop.

I was nervous all day about work. I arrived early, before Logan. I jumped every time the door opened. At that rate I was going to have a heart attack before I was twenty. Finally, he came in. I looked up at him, certain he was going to blow me off and walk right past me.

To my surprise, he approached my desk. "We need to talk." His tone was still distant, but it had a hint of apology in it. At least he wasn't completely freezing me out. And he looked miserable, almost as miserable as I felt.

I couldn't tell if that was good or bad, in my favor or not.

I nodded.

"Later," he said. "Not right after work. I have some shit I have to do first."

"Sure."

"I'll call you."

"Great."

He nodded. "Now, what assignments do you have for me today?"

I handed him a printout. I had emailed him his assignments as soon as I'd arrived. So he could have avoided me if he'd wanted to. That gave me hope, too. I didn't mention it and neither did he. He simply took the paper I handed him and left.

Karen gave me a puzzled look.

"It's nothing," I said before she could ask. I didn't need her nosing into my business.

Karen left early. I caught Jason just before it was time for me to get off shift. "Do you have a few minutes? I need to talk. I could use your advice."

"Is this about Logan?" he asked.

I nodded. He would have had to be inhuman not to notice the icy atmosphere between us. "And more."

Jason nodded. "I always have time for you. Close the door."

I nodded, closed the door behind me, and took a seat in the guest chair in front of his desk. "I need some fatherly advice."

His eyes lit up like he was happy about getting to play dad. "Shoot."

I bit my lip, took a deep breath, and plunged in, telling him the whole story. His face grew grimmer with each detail I shared.

"So Logan saw my chemistry lab write-up," I said in conclusion. "And went ballistic on me."

Jason sighed. "This is some serious stuff. I see why it upset Logan, particularly given his history. I'm not happy about it myself. Do you still have the lab report?"

I nodded. "It's at my desk."

"I'd like to see it."

I ran and got it and set it in front of him. He scooped it in front of him and began reading. I sat quietly watching him, though I was so nervous I felt I could explode.

Jason looked directly at me. "You can't let this go. You have to put a stop to it. I can talk to the head of the chem department for you. Dr. Black is an acquaintance of mine."

"No," I said. "I don't want Byron to get in trouble because of me."

"Ellie—"

"Byron's harmless. Really, he is. I flirted with him, okay? I know it was wrong. I don't want him to get in trouble because of me. Isn't there anything I can do before going to the department head?"

"Don't take the blame, Ellie. Byron's a grown man. He's responsible for his own actions. Just because you baked him cookies and batted your eyes, doesn't mean he has to cross a line and start stalking you with love notes in your lab reports."

I nodded again, knowing he was right about that, too.

Jason sighed and ran his hand through his hair. "I'm still leery about this. But if you insist, you could confront Byron, tell him there's been a misunderstanding, that you don't reciprocate his feelings, and tell him to stop."

I nodded. I knew Jason was right.

"If he doesn't, we'll have to take this to a higher level." Jason picked up my lab report and rattled it in front of him.

"Okay."

"I'd feel better if someone went with you," Jason said. "It's always good to have a witness to verify what went on. And to play bodyguard. I'd be happy to go with you."

I tried to lighten the mood. "Don't even think about it. I can't have my dad go with me. That's lame."

He smiled softly. "Take Logan. That will show you trust him and allow him to protect you."

I stared at Jason. The idea was brilliant, but...

"Wait. Aren't you the one who warned me about Logan? You're not worried he'll take a swing at Byron? Does this mean you approve of Logan?"

Jason's smile grew. "The jury's still out. But I have more faith in him than you think. He's been through a lot. But he has a strong character. He needs the opportunity to let it shine. And since I seem unable to stop you two..."

I grinned back at Jason, feeling much better. "Okay. It's a deal. But what if Byron retaliates with my grade?"

"Then we'll take this to a higher level. If he's at all rational, he won't even think about it."

I nodded. "You are wise." I should have come to him in the first place.

Jason smiled back at me. "I have a bit more life experience than you do." He shook the lab report. "You need to hang on to this. It's our ace in the hole. Let's hope we don't need it."

I agreed. "I hope I won't lose it in my room."

"I can lock it in the file cabinet for you."

"That would be awesome."

Jason got up and filed it.

I stood to go. "Thank you for the advice. I really needed a dad to talk to." My voice broke and my eyes filled with tears of relief. I meant every word I said.

Jason took a step into me and tipped my chin up so I was looking him in the eye. "I know this sounds crazy, but when I held Mia for the first time, I looked into her scrunched, screaming face and fell in love with her. Knowing you're my daughter, too, when I look at you, I feel the same way."

He pulled me into a hug. I wrapped my arms around his waist and pressed my head against his chest, feeling the steady beat of my dad's heart reassuring me.

"It's going to be okay," he said. "I'll make sure it's okay."

A stream of light from the outer office came in through his door. I must not have latched it all the way when I came back in and now it had slid open. I heard laughter and voices in the hall outside the outer IT department offices.

"I love you, Ellie," Jason said.

"I love you, too." As I spoke those damning words, Jason's office door fell wide open.

Logan stood in it holding a single red rose, looking pale and stunned. Lyssa stood next to him, wearing a matching expression. I had a flashback to Doug and me catching Austin and Mom on the sofa. But it was like I was out of my body, looking back on Doug and me.

Logan's face clouded with rage and hurt.

Oh my God! I thought, and stepped between Logan and Jason even though Logan hadn't moved.

"What the fuck?" Logan threw the rose on the floor, turned, and raged off, brushing past Lyssa, who was still frozen in place.

"Logan! Logan, come back!" I ran after him, squeezing past Lyssa. I caught him at the door and grabbed his arm to stop him. "It's not what it looks like."

He stared at me with heat and anger in his eyes. "Then what the hell is it, El? Private coffee dates. Secret meetings. This new closeness between you. I just heard you say you love him with my own ears." His laugh was harsh and mirthless. "Do you tell that to all the guys?"

I took a deep breath and said the words I should have from the beginning. But timing is everything. And mine was way off. "Jason's my father!" I hadn't meant to nearly scream it.

Logan stepped back like I'd slapped him. His chest rose and fell quickly as he looked between Jason and me like he was searching for a similarity, anything to verify the truth. His eyes shone with the same betrayal as if Jason and I really were lovers. "I—"

"I know it's hard to believe, but it's true. I came to this school because I knew Jason was here. And he was the most likely candidate for my dad. We just found out recently that he really is."

Logan simply shook my hand off him. "Another secret you kept from me. Were you using me all along to get close to him?" His voice was so cold I almost didn't recognize it.

"No, no! When I met you I didn't even know you knew him." I took a deep breath and tried not to cry. "I knew you'd take it like this. I knew you'd feel this way. I was trying to find a way to tell you—"

"You couldn't trust me with the truth. Is there anything you can trust me with?"

"I tried to tell you. I just got in too deep."

He shook his head like he was confused. And I didn't blame him.

"I don't understand," he said.

"I can explain." I rested my hand gently on his arm.

He shook it off. "It's too late. I don't want to hear it. We're done, Ellie. Through." He walked out the door, leaving me trembling in place.

When I turned around, Lyssa was crying and looking at Jason like he'd betrayed her.

I'd ruined everything. *Everything.*

CHAPTER SIXTEEN

When I stepped back into the office, Lyssa turned to face me with tears streaming down her face. At her feet was the rose Logan had brought for me, looking bruised and beaten, looking like I felt. "Is it true?" she asked.

I nodded, more miserable than I could ever remember being, even after I caught Austin with Mom. "It is. I have the paternity report to prove it."

She turned back to Jason. "How long have you known? When were you going to tell me?"

"Not long." Jason looked miserable. "A couple of weeks."

"A couple of weeks!" Her screamed words were full of anguish.

"I made a mistake. I should have told you. I wanted to tell you—"

I came to his defense. "He did. But the timing was off. How do you tell someone news like this? Look what it just did to Logan and me."

She turned toward the door, looking like she was going to storm off, too. I couldn't let her leave. I had to fix this. I stepped into the door Logan had just left through. "Listen to me, *please*. This isn't Jason's fault. He didn't even know I existed until a few weeks ago."

"You mean all semester," Lyssa said.

I shook my head. "True, in the physical sense. But I mean as his daughter. Let me explain."

"I can't hear it! I can't hear it now." She was angry and upset, but she didn't move.

So I explained, giving her a brief version while Jason walked up behind her and put his arms around her. I expected her to shake him off, push him away, and scream out of the office. But she sagged against him, like she lived for his comfort.

"Who's your mother?" she asked when I finished.

I sighed. "A complete bitch. She's no threat to you, believe me."

Lyssa was still staring at me. "Her name?"

I laughed without mirth, really not wanting to give Lyssa Mom's first name because it was so similar to hers and I had no idea what significance the names had to Jason. "Melissa Carter, I think."

Lyssa's eyes went wide, like she was confused.

"Though it could have changed. Last I heard she was going through her third divorce. She may be back to Melissa Sawyer by now." I looked at Jason, silently begging him to forgive me. Then I went to my desk and grabbed my stuff. "I'll leave you two alone now. I'm sorry. For everything."

As I turned to leave, Jason bent, grabbed the rose, and handed it to me. "I'll be in touch."

I took it from him on autopilot, like it wasn't even me reaching for it. And then I left before either of them could protest. I slipped the rose in my backpack, out of sight. I found myself walking in the biting wind and not caring. I had nowhere to turn. Who could I tell without turning them against me? Without them accusing me of not trusting them?

Dex, I thought. *Dex will understand and not judge.*

My cell phone buzzed. I pulled it out of my pocket and, heart racing, answered it without looking to see who was calling, hoping it was Logan. I sounded way too eager when I picked up the call.

"Is this Ellie Martin?"

I didn't recognize the female voice. "Yeah?"

"Hi! I'm Jan, a reporter for the student paper? I'm looking into the Dr. Rogers scandal—the prank the day she was arrested, her arrest, her victims. You're in Chem 202, right?"

My heart pounded like it was going to burst out of my chest. Dex had warned me about this, but I was in no mood to deal with it. "Yes. But you're wasting your time talking to me. I just go to class. I don't know anything."

Jan laughed. "That's what everyone says. But you're Logan Walker's girlfriend, too, aren't you? My sources say he's come forward as one of the victims, the most high-profile victim. He has quite a story, that baseball injury his freshman year followed by being raped by his chem prof."

Oh, crap! I thought the victims were supposed to remain anonymous. This is going to kill Logan.

"I'd love to get together and chat. Hear your side of the story—how Logan's handling the pressure, that sort of thing—"

"I don't know who your sources are, but they have it all wrong. I'm not Logan's girlfriend. Not anymore. And I can't confirm he was one of her victims." My heart pounded, hoping she didn't see through my lie. Or was it a lie? I couldn't confirm it because I wouldn't betray Logan like that, no matter how hurt I was.

"My bad." Jan's tone switched to sympathetic, but I could tell she was on the scent of a story, a new angle to exploit. "But I know you were friends. Tell me about Logan, generally. Anything about him. I promise to leave your name out of it. I keep my sources confidential."

"Go to hell." I hung up and texted Logan a warning, hoping he hadn't blocked my number or something. Hoping he at least read the message.

A reporter named Jan just called me. Someone told her you're one of Dr. Rogers' victims. I didn't tell her anything.

I really needed to talk to Dex. I held my phone the entire way to his dorm, hoping Logan would respond. He didn't.

Dex was in his dorm room playing an online video game with his door opened. I knocked on it softly.

He held one finger up to me. "One sec. I just have to blast this bastard." He hit a few keys on his keyboard and broke into the gleeful laugh of a maniacal genius. "Take that, Burning Vengeance." When he looked up and saw me, his face molded into a look of sympathy and horror. "What did Logan do now?"

"I'm that easy to read?" I bit back a sob.

"Oh, shit. You're going to cry on me. I suck with crying girls. Let me set my status to offline." He did something on his laptop, got up from his bed, made his way through the mess of dirty clothes and pizza boxes in the overflowing wastebasket, and pulled me into the room, closing the door behind him.

I plopped onto his bed and a sob popped out. "Dex, I'm in so much trouble."

"Shit, what's up?" Dex grabbed a tissue box and handed it to me. "Where are all your girlfriends? Girlfriends are better at dealing with relationship shit than guys."

"This is relationship crap and more. Part of it involves you."

He frowned, puzzled. "Keep me out of this. If Logan is jealous of my animal magnetism, I can't help it."

"Be serious, Dex. I just got a call from that reporter you warned me about. She wanted to know if I knew anything about the prank and—"

"You didn't tell her anything?"

I shook my head. "No, of course not. She was more interested in me because she thought I was Logan's girlfriend." I burst into tears.

"Oh, boy. What do you mean by 'thought'?"

"We broke up. Just...before...she...called." I was making crying gulps between words. "Somehow she found out Logan was one of the victims. I don't know what to do. I texted him to warn him, but he hasn't responded. I know he won't talk to me. And he's out there all alone without even Jason to talk to—"

"Wait, wait a minute! Back up. I'm missing something. Why can't he tell Jason?"

"Because Jason's my dad. And I didn't tell Logan. And that's why he broke up with me. Part of it, anyway."

"Oh, shit," Dex said, looking stunned. "I didn't see that coming. Jason is your dad? How did that happen?"

"The usual way—my mom had sex with Jason. His sperm penetrated my mom's egg and nine months later I popped out." I tried to laugh, but it came out bitter.

"Yeah, I get that part," Dex said. "Have you been drinking?"

"No, I wish I had."

"I'm confused," Dex said. "Start at the beginning."

"It's a long story."

"I have all night."

I pulled a tissue out of the box, dabbed my eyes, and related the events of the last two days.

Dex interrupted when I got to the part about Byron and the fight Logan and I had over him. "Logan thinks I'm the hero." Dex's voice was pleased and full of tease.

"I like that. I *am* rather heroic when you think about it. And even when you don't."

He was trying to coax me out of my depression, but it wasn't working.

I let out another sob. "It gets better. There's more."

"There's more?" Dex awkwardly put his arm around me. "I'm listening."

When I was finished, Dex let out a low whistle. "Jason really *is* your dad? That is some serious shit. My little spy, I am totally proud of you. You are almost as devious and deceitful as I am. I knew there was a reason I picked you for my prank team. You have my admiration—getting a job with your probably dad was an awesome prank."

"Shut up," I said, even though I knew he was trying to cheer me up. "It wasn't a prank. I wanted to meet him and find out what he was like before I brought more parental problems on myself." I hiccoughed from crying so much and dabbed at my nose.

"Don't worry," Dex said. "Jason will fix things with his wife and you didn't rat out Logan or us, so you're good. Just stick to the story."

I sagged against the wall. "That's it? That's all your wisdom and advice?"

"You're going to have to get the rest, all the relationship junk, from your girlfriends. I'm no good at that. What experience do I have?"

"They'll be upset I didn't tell them about Jason being my dad."

"They're girls. They'll get over it. They eat drama for breakfast. They'll give you a hundred ways to eviscerate Logan and get back at him. And you'll feel all better."

I couldn't help smiling the tiniest bit. "You think?"

"Yeah."

I wondered what Logan was doing. Had he read my message? Was he worried? As depressed as I was? Would he talk to Collin or Zave? Or Kelsie?

"What do guys do after a fight with their girl-friend?" I asked Dex.

"They blow shit up."

I stared at Dex. "What?"

"Yeah, you should try it. It's fun. Very cathartic." He jumped up and grabbed his laptop. "Much better than wallowing like girls do. When you came in, I was playing League of Legends, LoL as we like to call it. It's an international game. But we're having a campus tournament. All the players are students here.

"My team is playing this team we've played several times earlier in the semester. They're good—strategic and diabolical. Especially Falcon26. That's his screen name. He's their star." Dex grinned at me. "But we're going to beat the suckers. Want to play? It will take your mind off things."

"I don't know anything about playing video games. Won't I bring you down?"

Dex shrugged. "It's only a game. It will make you feel better. I promise. Besides, we're short one player since Cramer decided he's too far behind on his studies to play."

I sighed.

"Get your laptop. The game's a free download. I'll get you set up."

And he did. "What do you want for a screen name? It can be anything. Just make something up."

"FrontGirl." The name just popped into my head, but it was the truth—I was Jason Front's girl, the Front girl. Which was the source of all my problems right now.

The idea of the game was to blow people up and win gold to buy things like potions and spells so you could take over the other team's tower.

Dex helped me pick a champion, a character that you play. I chose the Lady of Luminosity. She looked happy, all radiance and light, the complete opposite of me.

I sat next to Dex and stumbled my way around the game as Dex became completely engrossed. "Oh, crap. Here comes Falcon26 playing Jayce, Defender of Tomorrow. He's cunning and dangerous."

"He's handsome," I said.

"You *would* think so. Keep your mind on the game. Aren't you off men?" Dex rolled his eyes. "Watch out! He's at your back, ready to attack with his hammer."

I spun around. Players could send each other messages during the game. As I faced Falcon26, he stopped right in front of me.

"What is he doing?" Dex said.

A message popped up on my screen. *Hey, are you really a chick?*

I looked at Dex. "Duh. My screen name's Front*Girl*."

"We don't get many girls playing," Dex said. "He's probably just surprised. And wants to make sure you're not some dude with a bad sense of humor."

"You mean guys are usually behind these girl champions?"

Dex nodded.

I typed back a reply. *Yeah, what of it?*

Don't attack head on. Go back and buy more health potion first.

I showed the response to Dex. "Is he right?"

Dex frowned. "He sure is. Shit, Ellie. You may be my secret weapon. The real guy who plays Jayce has never shown any mercy before. Back your character off and do what he says while I think of a way to exploit his weakness." Dex turned back to his game, fighting off an enemy champion from the other team.

I replied. *Thanks. I owe you one.*

I went off to win gold and buy health potion at the market. I wished they had a love potion. Or maybe a make-things-right potion. When I returned to the heat of the battle with my potion, Falcon26 backed off and coached me again. For the entire game, he gave me almost more help than Dex did. When the game ended less than an hour later, we were victorious, largely thanks to Falcon26.

Falcon26 sent me a message. *Nice game, FrontGirl. I demand a rematch. Be my friend?*

"What does that mean?" I asked Dex.

"You have access to your friends' status and can see if they're online playing the game. It makes it easier to schedule matches or for impromptu games."

"What should I do?" I asked him.

"Friend him. I want to see how he coaches you if he ever makes good on his promise to play you again."

I shrugged and typed. *Sure.*

Dex showed me how to accept the friend request. "We won! You upset Falcon26 with your feminine charms. I've never seen him falter or show mercy before." Dex gave me a high-five.

"Yeah, I'm really hot when I'm drawn like the Lady of Luminosity." I pointed to the outrageously stacked character on my screen. She would probably have been like a 34GG cup size if she'd been real. With a twenty-two-inch waist.

"Next time pick a character with less clothes on. That will really rattle him." Dex paused like he was thinking. "I should pretend to be a girl next time. I don't know why I didn't think of it before."

I shook my head. "It won't work. You'd have to change your screen name. And you play too well to be a girl. You'd never carry it off."

"Is that a compliment?"

I shook my head. "Did I say that? I meant to say, do you really want a guy hitting on you, even during a video game? I don't think you have the flirting chops for it. There's skill involved in seduction." I looked at the time. It was getting late. "I'd better go."

Dex nodded. "I was right—playing helped. You feel better."

Not really. The game had only temporarily distracted me. But I nodded for Dex's benefit.

"Hey, you want to be on our team for the rest of the tournament? It's double elimination. We're going to play these guys again."

"Okay. Anytime you play them," I said. "Dex?"

"Yeah?"

"Can I ask a favor?" I grabbed my coat.

"Sure."

"Call off the chem class game of Where's Ellie."

He wrinkled his nose and opened his mouth to speak.

"I'm not finished. That's not the favor," I said. "Come with me when I tell Byron to stop writing me love notes?" My voice trembled. Logan was supposed to be the one who went with me and played hero.

Dex looked touched. "Sure. But only if Logan doesn't step back in before then."

I'd seen the look on Logan's face. He wasn't coming back. "We'll do it Tuesday during my regular study time with him."

Dex nodded again. "Sure thing, Ellie. Can I bring my potato gun, in case it gets ugly?" He winked to let me know he was joking.

"Just bring your wit and your brawn." I slipped my coat on and stood to leave. "That will be enough."

He flexed his bicep. "You got it." Dex grabbed his coat. "I'll walk you home."

I stumbled into bed and had the longest night of my life. Bre was spending the night with Dan, which was just as well. I wanted to be alone while I cried my heart out. I was back in that black hole where I'd gone after catching Mom and Austin together. But this was worse. I had thought I was in love with Austin, but I had been wrong. I'd only had a crush on him. The horror I felt was mostly due to Mom. But I loved Logan, with all my being. Losing him left a hole in me.

After Mom betrayed me, I had a purpose—find my bio dad. And a hope—that my dad would be worth finding, that I could be part of a family with him. And Jason had turned out to be a great guy. But had we just blown any chance of being a family? Why was there always a downside to happiness?

I tossed and turned. Cried. Cried some more. Ached with longing for Logan. I even worried that I wouldn't have any friends left when I finally came clean with them.

I didn't remember falling asleep, but I must have. I woke with Bre peering anxiously over me, still dressed in her clothes from the night before. "What happened? You look terrible."

"Bre?" I squinted at her. The sunlight coming through a crack in the curtains hurt my eyes.

"Oh, crap, that's a big-ass fight look. This can only be about Logan," she said. "Hold on." She went to the sink and ran me a glass of water, then grabbed me an ibuprofen. She handed them to me when I sat up. "You're going to need these." She hesitated. "Have you been crying *all* night?"

"As much of it as I remember." I swallowed the pill she'd handed me, draining the water along with it. She took the glass from me and set it by the sink.

"What time is it?" I glanced at the clock. I'd missed chemistry.

Someone knocked on the door. Bre went to answer it.

Tay popped in. "Is everything okay? Ellie didn't stop by for her morning coffee." And then she spotted me and mumbled something choice beneath her breath. "Are you sick? Do you want us to take you to Student Death? I'm sure they'll be happy to finish you off."

Bre shot her a look and mouthed Logan's name.

"Oh." Tay nodded.

"Look, I have something I have to tell all of you," I said, brushing the hair out of my eyes. Even after a whole glass of water, my mouth felt dry and my tongue thick. "Is Nic around? It would be easier to tell you all at once."

Tay nodded and ran off to get her. Minutes later they were back sitting in a row on Bre's bed. I launched into my story.

"Oh my God, Ellie! That is..." Bre shook her head.

"Awesome," Nic finished for her, giving her a dirty look that told her to shut up. "About your dad. Quite a tale, but you have a dad!" Her eyes lit up. "A good one."

Tay nodded her agreement. "Yeah!"

"Maybe," I said. "He might hate me now."

Bre joined in, shaking her head. "Not if he's the kind of guy you say he is."

"You guys aren't mad that I didn't tell you?" I couldn't believe it.

Nic shook her head. "No. Should we be? It's your business. What if you had been wrong and Jason wasn't your dad?" She shrugged. "He's entitled to his privacy, and you yours. You got caught in a trap, that's all."

"I only wish we could have been here to help you," Tay said. "I'm sorry you had to suffer alone."

My eyes welled with tears again. I'd misjudged them. "Thank you," I whispered.

"Yeah, and Logan should feel the same way." Bre was adamant.

Nic shook her head, warning Bre off. "He's in a different position than we are. I'm not going to judge him. I just wish his reaction didn't hurt you, Ellie."

"What should I do about Logan?" I asked, sounding pitiful and needy. "I should be there for him."

"Give him time," Tay said.

My phone buzzed on the dresser where I'd left it. I dove for it way too eagerly. A text from Jason. My heart fell. My hands shook. I made myself read it.

I'm sorry for the way things happened yesterday. Lyssa and I have talked. I explained things. I think things are going to be okay. It may take time before we'll feel like a real family, but I think we'll get there. Lyssa will come around. See you at work.

I started crying again. I handed the phone to Tay. She read the message to the group.

"Things are looking up already," she said in a voice too chipper to sound completely convincing.

I had to resist texting Logan again. It was clear he didn't want to hear from me. Everyone agreed he needed time. After Austin cheated on me, he texted me repeatedly. And I really hadn't wanted to talk to him. I

knew how he felt now, at least to a degree. I craved
forgiveness. I wanted Logan back so desperately I
could almost taste it. I hadn't done anything as hideous
as Austin had, but I knew Logan felt betrayed all the
same. And remembering how I'd felt, I also realized
that texting would only upset him.

When I opened my backpack to get ready for class,
it smelled like roses. The battered red rose from Logan
peeked out at me. I cried again. I should have thrown
that rose out, taken it to the garbage downstairs, out of
my sight. But I didn't. I couldn't. I handled it gently,
cupping it back together with my hand. I found a
thumbtack and hung it by a string upside down in the
corner of the room to dry. To haunt me.

I went to work that afternoon full of nerves, dreading it and wanting to see Logan in the worst way possible. Karen was quiet and sympathetic, kind and gentle
with me as she handed me the list of repairs for the
RTAs to handle. When I pulled up their schedules to
make assignments, Logan's name was missing from the
list of available techs. Before I could ask Karen why,
Jason came in from a meeting in another building.

"Ellie, can I see you in my office?" His tone was
kind.

I followed him in.

He shut the door and hung his coat on the rack,
looking like he'd gotten about as much sleep as I had.

"I'm sorry about yesterday. I've ruined everything."
I burst into tears again.

Jason pulled me into a hug, which was what had gotten us in trouble in the first place. "There's nothing to forgive. It's not your fault. We'll work it out."

He sounded so confident that I believed him.

"Are you going to be okay? Can you pull yourself together?"

I nodded.

"Good." He patted my arms and went around to sit in his desk chair. "Let's put the personal stuff aside for a minute. I have business to discuss with you. Sit."

I pulled up his guest chair.

"I just came back from a meeting at the admin building to discuss our situation."

My heart pounded like it was going to burst out of my chest. I was just about to lose my job, too.

"Hey, don't look so glum!" He smiled tightly. "It's good news. You can finish the semester here with me. After Christmas you're being transferred to the records department in the admin building. They have plenty of need for a good management info assistant. You'll like it there."

I let out a sigh of relief. "I like working here."

He nodded.

"You're not in any trouble?" I asked.

"I talked my way out of most of it."

"Most?"

His smile was still tight. "Don't worry about me."

I nodded and asked another question I was dreading. "Why isn't Logan on the list of RTAs?"

Jason looked me directly in the eye and smiled sympathetically and sadly. "He quit this morning."

I put my head in my hands. I'd done it, really done it. I'd ruined Logan's relationship with Jason just like I'd feared I would. And caused Logan to quit the job he loved, the job that had helped save him.

Jason didn't say anything, but I knew we were both worrying about the same thing—Logan.

CHAPTER SEVENTEEN

Logan didn't text me. He didn't call. When I Facebook
stalked him on Thursday, I discovered he'd unfriended
me. All I could see was his profile picture—him partying with a beer in one hand and his arm around Kelsie,
who was beaming. The picture was obviously recent,
like since our breakup recent. I swallowed hard to keep
from crying. He was turning to Kelsie for comfort
again. I tried, mostly unsuccessfully, to push images of
them together from my mind. He was back to his old
support system now that he had cut himself off from
Jason and me.

On Saturday night I stayed home to wallow alone in
my single-again misery. For kicks, I logged in to the
video game. Almost immediately Falcon26 contacted

me. *What's a beautiful girl like you doing playing video games on Saturday night?*

I replied: *How do you know I'm beautiful? That's just the way my character was drawn.*

Girls who play video games are hot, he said. *You still haven't answered my question.*

I hesitated and tossed caution aside. Even though he was a fellow student here, I had no intention of meeting this guy. Why not tell this video game geek the truth?

Bad breakup. I'm single.

His loss, Falcon26 said. *Want to play a game?*

Only if you help me.

Deal. What about you? What are you doing alone on Saturday night? Fair's fair, I thought.

Waiting for a girl like you.

Okay, so he was a sweet geek. Maybe my experience with Byron should have taught me a lesson. But I guess it hadn't. Besides, this was a fantasyland. No one expected reality here.

Haha, I replied. *Let's play. Be Jayce again. I like him. I could really use a handsome hero.*

But I'm the enemy, Falcon26 replied.

Yeah, isn't that the way it goes?

Mom texted me half a dozen times, begging me to spend Christmas with her. I deleted them all. The weekend went by and slid into Monday. Finally, I couldn't stand it. I texted Logan. *I'm sorry I hurt you. I didn't mean to. I should have told you about Jason. I should have told you about Byron. I should have trusted you. I'm really sorry I didn't. You should go back to*

*your RTA job with Jason. I'm transferring to another
job after the semester ends.*

My fingers trembled when I pressed send, and I still
wanted to cry. But I felt lighter, like a burden had lift-
ed. My experience with Austin had taught me about
forgiveness and making genuine apologies. All I could
do was apologize and take responsibility for my part.
Whether Logan forgave me or not was totally up to
him.

I held my phone in my hand, waiting for a response.
But the phone didn't buzz. Logan was silent. I ran to
the dining hall and grabbed a coffee. Tay had saved me
a cobblestone bar. I had it and my coffee for breakfast
as I ran to chemistry. To my relief, everyone was
dressed normally. Dex and I sat in our old favorite
seats. I set my coffee and cobblestone bar on the speaker in front of me.

Byron looked relieved when he went to the lecture
podium and saw the class wasn't dressed alike.

"This is no fun," Dex whispered to me.

"Chemistry isn't supposed to be."

He rolled his eyes.

Byron spotted me in the crowd and kept looking at
me during lecture. I knew what I had to do was the
right thing. Heartbreak sucks. But it's better to know
the truth than keep hoping for something that isn't
going to happen.

Logan didn't text me back. On Tuesday Dex went
with me to my chem study session with Byron.

Byron was sitting in his usual spot behind his messy
desk in his broom closet of an office. His eyes lit up

when he saw me and turned just as quickly to disappointment when he spotted Dex with me. Byron craned
his neck like he was trying to see if a whole crowd of
students would be joining us. He looked nervous about
that.

"It's just me and Dex today," I said.

Dex and I stepped into the office and closed the door
behind us. Dex was risking his grade coming with me.
He really was a true friend.

I took a deep breath and launched right in to what I
had to say before I lost my nerve. "The love notes in my
lab reports have to stop," I said.

Byron flamed so red the patches on his cheeks
looked ready to ignite. His gaze flicked to Dex.

"It's okay," I said. "Dex knows about it. I brought
him along as a witness."

"Is he your boyfriend?" Byron sounded angry and
jealous.

Dex elbowed me, obviously amused by the question.
I wanted to tell Dex to shut up, but I ignored him.

"No," I said. "He's my friend. Back to the love notes
and the missed-connection posting and wanting to ask
me out—I'm sorry, but I'm not interested. You're a
nice guy. A smart guy. And I know there's a girl out
there for you. I'm just not it. There's no chemistry between us." I tried to smile and sound light.

But the sad, defeated look on Byron's face didn't
make it easy.

"I'm sorry if I gave you the wrong impression by
baking you cookies. And I appreciate all the help you
gave me with the cobblestone bars and chemistry. But

writing personal notes on my lab report is crossing a professional line. It's unacceptable and has to stop.

"There's been enough scandal with this class." My voice broke as I thought about Logan. "We don't need any more. The university is in enough trouble already. They'll come down hard on anyone who even looks like they're violating the ethics code. For all our sakes, this ends here."

Byron looked scared now as well as heartbroken. "Are you going to turn me in?"

I shook my head. "Not if you stop now."

"Okay." Byron nodded and slumped in his chair.

"You have to promise to grade us fairly and not let this affect our grades," I said. I didn't mean to make a veiled threat, but it came out that way.

Byron nodded again. "Sure."

"Good," I said. "Thank you. And I promise not to tell anyone else about the notes. That's all I have. We'll be going." I nodded to Dex.

As we turned to leave, Byron called out to me. "After the semester? What about then? Maybe we could have coffee?"

I knew better than anyone that you can't just turn your feelings off. Logan was clearly sending me a signal that his feelings for me had died. I had to send the signal to Byron that I had *never* had any for him. I couldn't lead him on. "No thank you," I said.

Dex and I walked together in silence. When we were out of the chem building, Dex finally spoke. "Nice job. Seriously. I was proud of you in there. You did the right thing."

I had expected Dex to joke or poke fun. His words touched me. "Then why doesn't it feel better?"

"The perils of being a heartbreaker."

"And being a good baker," I said, trying to join in. "The way to a man's heart is through his stomach. I never grasped the power of it before."

"Then I'd better watch out for you," Dex said. "I've eaten a boatload of your cookies."

"Why does that sound dirty when you say it like that?" I said, punching him in the arm.

He laughed.

"I think you're immune to my charms. Too bad. I think I'd really like to torture you."

"Cruel woman," he said. "Let's get something to eat."

The week slipped by in a blur of studying and late nights. Then finals hit with a vengeance. I still didn't know what I was going to do about Christmas. My dorm was closing the day after finals ended. I could spend the holidays as a guest at the one dorm the university kept open for the foreign students who couldn't go home. Tay invited me to go home with her. I wasn't going to push Jason for an invitation. Lyssa still hadn't accepted me. I remembered Thanksgiving and thought about the surprise Logan had had for me for Christmas and I got depressed all over again.

I had finals all the way through Thursday of finals week. On Wednesday night, I was up at two a.m. still studying for my one p.m. MIS final when my phone buzzed. "Jason?"

"Ellie! I'm frantic. I need someone to watch Mia and I can't reach anyone." His voice cracked.

"What's wrong?"

"Lyssa's spotting. We think she's miscarrying. I'm at the emergency room with her and Mia, but I can't take Mia in with me—"

"I'll be there," I said. "Let me find a ride and I'll get there as soon as I can."

"Call the university ride-share service. They'll bring you."

I asked Nic instead. She drove me. I arrived at the hospital less than fifteen minutes later to find Jason frantic. Nic came in with me. Jason gave me his house key. We took Mia and her car seat and took her home. Nic dropped me off at Jason's. When I put Mia to bed, she went right to sleep. But I spent a restless night waiting for news about Lyssa.

Jason stumbled in about eight, looking worn out. "It's all right." He hugged me. "She hasn't lost the baby. The doctors say Lyssa needs bed rest, but they think the baby will make it. Thanks for being there for us."

I nodded. "That's what family does."

He saw my backpack lying in the entry. "Were you studying? Oh, crap. Don't tell me I made you miss a final?"

"Spoken like a real dad," I said. "Not until one."

He looked tiredly pleased. "Is the baby still asleep?"

"Yep, she's sleeping like—well, a baby." I smiled.

"I'll get her and take you back to the dorm."

I stopped him. "Let her sleep. We can wait until she wakes up. I have time. Want me to make you some breakfast? I'm a good cook."

He looked exhausted, but happy at my suggestion. "How can I refuse an offer like that?"

"Do you like eggs and cheese?"

"Love them. I think we have some good bread for toast, too. And some university honey."

So I made my dad breakfast and we sat down to eat together.

"Ellie, Lyssa's really grateful to you," Jason said when we were both full and sitting back enjoying our coffee.

I looked at him warily. "Serious? That's good."

"She wants to know what you're doing for Christmas."

I shrugged. "Tay invited me to go home with her."

"I didn't phrase that right. Lyssa wants me to ask you to spend Christmas with us. She and I, we both think it's about time we started acting like a family."

I stared at him, touched. "Really? One favor changed her mind about me?"

"No. Almost losing our baby reminded her how precious children are and how short life can be. You're my kid. She understands how important that is to me and all of us."

"Wow, that's heavy," I said.

"I can tell her you're staying with us, then?"

I nodded. "Yeah, if she'll let me help out so she can rest."

"It's a deal." Jason paused. "There's no chance you're going to see Melissa?"

I shook my head. Vehemently. "No. Absolutely not. She's been texting and emailing me. But no way." It was my turn to pause. I screwed up my courage. Now was as good a time to ask as any. "What happened between you and Mom? I mean, what happened that you made me? Why hasn't she ever talked about you?"

He looked away like he didn't want to talk about it. "You'll have to ask her why she's never mentioned me."

I prodded him anyway. I wanted to know. "You know the rest, though, like how it happened." I braced myself for the worst.

He got up and poured himself another cup of coffee. When he sat back down he looked resigned. "We went to high school together. Good friends. Or so I thought. I was a studious nerd back then. Not into partying. And she was the popular girl who all the guys went for."

I snorted. "Some things haven't changed. I can't believe you fell for her."

He looked bemused.

"Sorry," I said. "She just doesn't seem like your type, and that's a good thing. And you don't seem like hers."

"Yeah, that last was certainly true." He took a sip of coffee. "Your mom was gorgeous and charming."

His tone alarmed me. He sounded way too much like he was remembering fondly. I had to kill any good impression he had of her.

"She still is," I said. "And selfish and irresponsible and totally needy." I spat the words out. "Sorry," I said again. "I'll shut up and listen."

He shrugged, looking like he didn't want to talk about it in any detail. "I helped her with her math and science classes and we hung out to study. But I had a crush on her from the time I first met her in ninth grade.

"She had a boyfriend. Always had a boyfriend. She ran through them pretty quickly, but I never managed to catch her attention in between. She wasn't interested in me. I was just there to listen to her and pick her up between other guys. And, sadly, that was enough for me.

"Until my senior year. She got a boyfriend, Steve, and stuck with him the entire year. Steve was a jerk. I hated him. But Melissa was crazy about him.

"The summer between high school and college, they had a big fight and broke up. I, in my youthful foolishness, thought they'd broken up for good. I provided a shoulder for her to cry on. She called me, drunk, from a party she'd been at, and begged me for a ride home. She and Steve had just had a fight and ended things.

"I rushed in like a white knight. I should have squired her right home. But we made a stop and made you in the back of my car. She was drunk. I was ecstatic, crazy for her."

"Not an achingly beautiful love story," I said.

"You asked." He grinned, but it was forced and sad.

"You could make it sound more romantic."

"Sorry. I thought it was at the time. But they got back together a few days later. And she stopped talking to me. Just cut me out. I was torn up. For a while. I went off to college and that was that."

I nodded. "I waited almost twenty years and that's all there is to the story? Haven't you ever seen *The Princess Bride?* You need to spice things up to make a good story."

"Yeah," he said. "But they always skip the kissing scenes in that movie."

"Good point," I said. I paused. "No wonder you were so shocked by me."

"Yeah," he said. "But I'm glad you found me."

"Me too."

"Ellie," he said, "take it from someone who knows—the heartbreak does go away. You just need to give it time."

CHAPTER EIGHTEEN

I got my A in chemistry. Byron posted the grades the day after finals ended. Although I did well on the final and the labs, I didn't know whether I'd actually earned that A. I suspected I hadn't. But it had cost me every-thing—at least, I blamed that class for everything like it was the root of all evil. Yeah, I knew I lied to Logan. But sometimes I rationalized that if he hadn't been wounded by that class, he would have been stronger and my lie wouldn't have mattered. It would have just been a blip, a bump, a tiny misunderstanding. That I could have told him about Byron and he would have laughed about it and played hero. That everything would be totally different. But it wasn't.

I made the Dean's List and the President's Honor Roll. So did Logan. I saw his name on the university website and was relieved. He hadn't tailspun, at least not enough to blow his finals.

Christmas was bittersweet. If it hadn't been for breaking up with Logan, it would have been the best Christmas ever. I stayed with Jason and Lyssa for most of the break. Lyssa was confined to bed rest, so I took care of Mia and helped around the house with the cleaning and holiday baking. It snowed two days before Christmas and we had the most beautiful white Christmas ever. We hardly ever had white Christmases in Seattle. I remembered like one, ever.

Unlike Thanksgiving at Logan's, Christmas was a warm, intimate, family affair full of love and food and way too much hot chocolate with peppermint. Lyssa's parents came for Christmas Eve and Christmas Day. Her mother was the grandmotherly type. She adopted me right off as one of her own, even bringing me gifts and sock presents. She took over preparations for Christmas dinner and made me her assistant.

I would have liked to meet my bio grandparents, but it was their Christmas to spend with Jason's brother and his family. I had an uncle and an aunt and three cousins. Jason told them about me shortly after Lyssa found out about me. They were stunned, but accepting. Though I think they weren't happy about who my mother was. We made plans to get together with Jason's family in the spring. In the meantime, my new grandparents sent me a gold necklace with a single pearl pendant on it for Christmas.

Mia was so fun and adorable to play with. She cried when Jason and I took her to see Santa and have her picture taken. She got excited and worked up on Christmas Eve and Christmas Day, probably because everyone else was. Like most babies, she liked the wrapping better than her presents.

I gave Jason a mug that said World's Best Dad and a pound of coffee from The College Grind. It wasn't much, but he seemed really touched. Lyssa liked the earrings I bought her from a holiday craft bazaar in town. And Mia thought the wrapping paper on the stuffed toy I gave her was the best wrapping she received. It crinkled really nicely in her tiny hands and made her laugh.

Jason and Lyssa gave me pearl earrings to match the necklace from his parents and a Christmas sock full of small gifts, including a new bellybutton ring. I nearly cried when I saw it. I missed Logan so much.

January, the new semester, and my new job started out gloomy. Everything was dark without Logan. I kept wondering how long it would take to get over him.

The university held a reception for the President's Honor Roll recipients in January in the SUB ballroom. I went, hoping for a glimpse of Logan. He didn't show. President Lawrence gave a speech. When he shook my hand, he looked wary of me and made a joke about being careful at the buffet table. The university gave me a mug to commemorate my achievement.

Bre was busy with Dan, though they fought a lot. Which made Bre and me pretty compatible in the "misery loves miserable company" kind of way. Tay started dating her grilled-cheese guy. And Nic went through informal rush and was busy with her sorority. Dex was just Dex. We didn't have chemistry together any more, but we hung out and played LoL from time to time when he wanted to use me as his secret weapon. Falcon26 saw through Dex's strategy in the semifinals of the tournament, and although Falcon helped me, his team beat us. Dex was furious at being outwitted and outplayed.

I didn't date, though I was asked more than I ever had been before, maybe because I was either needy and helpless or too brightly wild. Maybe they saw an easy score as a rebound guy. But my heart wasn't in dating. No guy measured up to Logan. I was simply empty inside, emptier than I'd been after Austin.

I changed my bellybutton ring out for the one Lyssa and Jason gave me for Christmas and put the peridot stud in my jewelry box way in the back. And finally I took the dead, dried rose down from the corner and put it in a box in the back of my closet. To the outside world, it may have looked like I was healing, but I was really dead inside and longing for Logan all the time. Part of me wanted him to graduate and be gone so I could relax and not worry about running into him. Part of me was glad he was still close by and looked for him around every corner. That part worried that I'd never see him again once he went out into the work world.

After I refused to spend Christmas with Mom, she cut off all contact. Which was a relief and eerie at the same time. I kept expecting a sneak attack from her. My mom never lost. Ever.

I ran into Zave once at the SUB.

"Hey, Ellie!" He waved at me. "Long time no see. We miss your cookies. No one bakes for us any more."

I smiled at him, genuinely perked up by seeing him. "How's Spartacus? You haven't fed him to death yet, have you?"

He laughed. "Not yet. He's a tough fish. But lonely. He keeps making bubble nests like he's making a home for a lady fish. I hate to tell him he's doomed to bachelorhood."

"Buy him a lady fish," I said.

Zave shook his head. "I'm not ready for the responsibility of a whole fish family." He paused and his expression went serious. "I have to say this once and I'll deny it if you repeat it—Logan is being a complete shithead. Collin and I think he was crazy to break up with you. You're the best girl he's dated. It's his loss."

I choked up and could only nod. "So what have you been up to?"

Zave rolled his eyes and sighed. "Interviewing. Looking for work sucks. Who wants to be responsible? But my dad insists. He's not going to pay for another year of school so I'm out of options.

"Logan has been the king of interviewing. I've lost track of how many interview trips he's been on. I'm guessing he'll end up in California, though why he can't stay in Seattle, I don't know. Seattle is the hotbed of innovation. Collin and I are both determined to get jobs at home and room together. We can't understand why Logan wants to break up the gang. Imagine the parties we could throw if we didn't have studies to worry about? Epic!"

California. California. I couldn't get it out of my head. I'd never see Logan again. I barely heard what Zave was saying.

"Speaking of parties—Collin is already planning our graduation bash. It's going to be legendary!" Zave put his hand on my arm, startling me out of my shock. "Don't let Logan scare you away. You'll come as my guest. I insist. What do you say?"

I nodded automatically. I was such a desperate case, wanting to see Logan one last time before he left. I knew deep in my heart that as horrible as it would be, I was going to go to that party.

"Excellent! I'll add you to the guest list." He glanced at his watch. "Gotta run. Nice bumping into you again."

I nodded. "You too. Say hi to Collin for me."

Zave cocked an eyebrow. "Just Collin?"

"Spartacus, too."

He laughed. "You got it." He gave me a sympathetic look and dashed off.

I fell back into sadness. Logan was really leaving. I knew it was over, but...

I logged on to LoL. Falcon26 was online and asked if I wanted to play a game.

Sure, I responded. *I could use a diversion. I just ran into my ex's roommate. Sad. I need to blow something up.*

Blowing things up is good. Forget the shithead. He doesn't deserve you—Falcon26.

I played LoL regularly with Falcon26. We had a standing Friday night date. We played for half an hour to an hour and then went out to party in the real world.

With Falcon's coaching, I got better. But not good enough to compete with most of the guys. Mostly I enjoyed hanging out in a fantasy world and the funny, flirty comments from Falcon26. While we played, we talked about some personal stuff, like how my heart was broken and so was his. I told him things I wouldn't have told a lot of guys. But it didn't matter because I didn't plan on ever meeting him in person.

The girls and I spent an inordinate amount of time speculating on what the Falcon was really like and what he looked like. I was thinking a *Big Bang Theory*-type nerd. Tay was taking an art class. She drew her interpretation of him for fun—a pudgy, short nerdy guy with glasses and wings and a beaky nose. I hung it up in my room and we laughed about it.

"You know, you should really meet Falcon26," Tay said to me one night in early February. "You two seem to hit it off online. Wouldn't it be nice to, you know, get out in the real world with a real guy? Maybe he's hot, like Logan. He's funny like Logan is and you two hit it off like you did with him."

I shot her a look of disgust, a look that warned her off talking about Logan. "And ruin a perfectly good virtual relationship? You're crazy. Besides, how do we know Falcon26 *is* a real guy? He could be a fifty-year-old perv for all we know."

"Then why are you sharing your private life with him?" Tay asked. "Don't you even want to know what he looks like or who he is?"

I rolled my eyes and pointed to the picture she'd drawn of him. "You think he looks like that. Why are

you trying to set me up with him?" I sighed. "I prefer
my game version of him. Most of the time he looks like
a hot, built knight in shining armor, and that's the way
I like it. Reality won't live up to that. Reality will look
more like your picture of him."

"Yeah, but if he has wings like Tay's rendering, that
might be worth it. He could fly you around." Nic
winked at me.

"Shut up. He's made no move to ask me out. Which
is what our relationship is built on."

"Yeah, but you can tell he likes you," Nic said. "He's
probably just shy and awkward around girls. He just
needs a little encouragement." She lowered her voice
into the seductive range. "You could make a real man
out of him."

"Oh, that's just what I need—to go out on an awkward date with a socially inept guy like Byron." I shuddered.

Nic had to poke some more. "He could *be* Byron."

"Shut up again. He's not Byron. He hasn't said we
have a covalent bond we need to explore our anything
tacky like that. Falcon is charming." I didn't know why
I was defending Falcon. But I was glad Byron had
dropped out of sight.

"Great! He's a *charming* fifty-year-old perv," Nic
said with a sparkle in her eyes.

"I'm just saying, this sitting around with no guy is-
n't a good thing," Tay said. But she was so happy that
she thought relationships were fabulous and every girl
should have one.

Just wait until she hit the inevitable speed bump.

"Not meeting him." I stuck my fingers in my ears. "And not listening to any more about it."

So I was a non-dater. Until early March, when this guy from my business ethics class asked me out. He was kind of cute and kind of funny. We'd worked on a couple of projects together. He wanted to take me to dinner and a movie and I thought, why not? He wasn't Logan, but I couldn't spend my life alone forever. Tay and Nic were ecstatic.

But I had to cancel my standing game with Falcon26 and I was reluctant about it. I could have blown him off and just let him log in and see my status was offline, but that seemed kind of cruel. It wasn't like I was cheating on him, but I didn't want to leave him hanging, waiting for me to log on. It was just respectful to let him know.

So I checked in earlier in the week and caught him when he was online.

He immediately sent me a message. *FrontGirl what are you doing here on a Wednesday? Did you know I was missing you? Want to play a game? I can scare up a team.*

After getting that message, I felt like a jerk, kind of like Byron all over again. But we were only online video rivals and friends. *Not tonight. Just wanted to catch you. Have to cancel our Friday night game. I have a hot date in the real world. Take some towers for me.*

I waited for a minute and sighed, feeling let down when he didn't reply right away. I was just about to log off when a message from him popped up.

I'm losing you to the real world. Shit.

I was stunned by his bluntness. Maybe Bre, Nic, and Tay were right. Maybe the Falcon really did like me. And maybe I did want to meet him. The thought surprised me.

Then make a move to meet me in the real world, I replied, and signed out before he could say anything else.

My date with the business ethics guy was fun, if not mind-blowingly great. He wanted to hang out again. And I thought I would.

Falcon26 kept trying to message me when I was online and asking me to play. I ignored him. It was time I came back to the real world and found a real hero. But I finally relented because I kind of missed him. And I decided that honesty was the best policy. I had to tell him I was done playing video games. I'd never been that into it. It had just been something to do to forget the real world. And now the real world was calling.

So I got online and he immediately messaged me.

FrontGirl, I'm screwing up all my courage. There's an Up All Night on Saturday. Meet me there. On the second floor in front of the ballroom. You'll recognize me. I'll be the guy with my heart in my hand.

I didn't reply. I couldn't. I showed the message to Bre, Tay, and Nic. "What do you think he means by having his heart in his hand?"

Nic shuddered. "All I can say is I hope he's not an anatomy student."

"Or a butcher," Tay said.

"I think it's figurative," Bre said.

We all stared at her.

"What?" Bre stared at us like we were crazy.

"Yeah, I hope so," I said.

"What are you going to do?" Nic had an evil look in her eye. "I think you should go. He's given you the perfect out. You go. You see what he means by having his heart in his hand. If he's a creeper, you back out and run like hell." She laughed. "It's completely safe. He has no idea who you are."

"Yeah!" Tay said. "We'll come with."

"I don't know," I said, but I was intrigued. "I kind of like not knowing who he is. That way he's anyone I want him to be."

"It's an adventure! It'll be fun." Tay was really getting into it now. "You have to do it."

"We'll see," I said. But I was considering it. The thing was, sometimes Falcon reminded me of Logan. And I kind of liked imagining he was. Kind of like picturing him as the Logan I wanted, not the Logan who'd broken my heart and shut me out. Despite what I'd said about living in the real world, a big part of me wanted to keep the fantasy alive.

CHAPTER NINETEEN

All right, it was dumb. It was stupid. I flipped and I flopped. But finally the girls convinced me I had to go and meet Falcon. That sometimes a fantasy wasn't all you needed. Sometimes you needed truth and reality.

"How do I dress for this stupid meeting?" I asked. "What if he stands me up? Stood up by a video gaming nerd—how could my ego stand it?"

"You dress hot. Scorching," Nic said. "So he'll want you no matter what. And if he stands you up, you'll have options. Like guys fighting to get to meet you. We'll help."

Which is how I found myself dressed in tight low-rider jeans, heels, and a cute, tight, low-cut blouse. My makeup was sultry and my hair fell loose.

"You look just like one of your game characters!" Nic nodded approvingly.

I rolled my eyes. "Right. Tell me again why I'm doing this?"

"Because you're back among the living and putting yourself out there." Tay handed me a set of dangly bracelets. "Wear these."

I slid them on and Nic handed me a jello shot. "For fortification. Nothing ever looks as bad when you're buzzed."

I set the shot down. "I'm not going to be blinded by alcohol goggles when I meet Falcon. I want to see him in all his nerdy glory."

"You are so pessimistic!" Nic raised her shot. "Let the adventure begin." She, Tay, and Bre downed a shot in my honor.

They propelled me all the way to the SUB, past the budding crocuses that were just coming up in the flowerbeds, optimistically spring-like. Into the building and to the bottom of the stairs, where we paused.

"Okay, this is the plan," I said. "I am going to have to face Falcon alone. You three can walk behind me for moral support. If we catch a glimpse of him and he's a creeper, we go to plan one, ditch him, and enjoy the rest of the entertainment."

"You mean troll for guys," Nic said.

"Exactly," Tay said for me. "She's dressed for it."

I ignored them. "If he's hot, or even decent, you all back off and blend into the crowd, leaving us alone. Agreed?"

They nodded.

I took a deep breath. "Let's do this." Somehow I made my feet move up the stairs. This was such a stupid idea. I kept flashing back to meeting Logan at that first Up All Night event. How far I'd fallen. I kept pushing him from my mind. The stairs curved halfway up at a landing. I paused again. The girls encouraged me to keep going. I was so stupid nervous it was crazy.

As I came up the stairs, I saw a red heart-shaped balloon with the words *My Heart* printed on it in neat engineering block letters floating on a ribbon in a pair of strong hands, being held between a guy's legs. I couldn't see the guy's face, but his strong thighs looked promising.

The girls gasped when they saw the balloon.

"He's a romantic!" Tay said. "This *is* promising."

I made myself keep moving, telling myself I could do this. His knees came into view as we climbed the stairs. Then his chest. And finally his face. He was totally hot. The hottest guy I'd ever seen, and he was watching the people coming up the stairs, watching for me with an expectant, hopeful look.

"Logan," I whispered, and froze.

The girls saw him an instant after I did.

"Go!" Tay gave me a shove.

Logan spotted me. I panicked. As I turned to run, I got a glimpse of him rising to his feet. "No! I can't believe this. I can't do it. He's not expecting *me*. I—"

"Of course he is, fool girl." Nic grabbed my arm. "You don't think Logan recognized you from your screen name? He knows who he's meeting."

I brushed her off and tried to run past her, trying to thread my way between her and Tay and Bre and the rest of the crowd coming up the stairs.

"Ellie! Wait! El!" Logan called after me.

"Excuse me. Excuse me! Coming through." I tried to push my way past the crowd, swimming in the wrong direction, going upstream against the current.

But Logan was fast. "El!" He caught me at the bottom of the steps, wrapping his arms around my waist from behind, the balloon still in his hand, floating in front of me. "You forgot something." He pressed the ribbon of the balloon into my hand. "This belongs to you. It has since I met you."

Tears danced in my eyes. I tried to swallow them back, but they came anyway. "You shut me out. You cut me off. You lied to me and pretended to be someone else. Someone I could talk to. Someone I told about you. I was telling you about you." I tried to pry myself free.

"El, please. Listen to me. You still owe me one. I'm calling it in now—just hear me out."

I took a deep breath. When it came right down to it, I owed him my life. "Stupid, stupid debts of honor," I said through my tears. "Why did I ever make them?"

"You'll listen?"

I nodded. Bre, Tay, and Nic had disappeared, probably staying on the second floor to give us space.

"El, come on," he whispered in my ear, his voice breaking with emotion as he cradled his height around me. "I thought you suspected Falcon was me. I thought it was our way of testing the waters and coming back together."

"Why? There are over eight thousand guys here. How would I know Falcon was you?"

"Falcon's my high school mascot. And twenty-six is my baseball jersey number, El. You know that. Caleb is two and I'm twenty-six." He paused.

"Damn," I said. He was right. I'd just never made the connection. I cursed myself for falling for Logan a second time even without seeing him. Falling for his sweetness and his personality. Falling for the hero he could be. I wondered if I was doomed to love him no matter what form he presented himself in.

"I need to talk to you in private," he said.

I nodded. I *had* agreed. "Where do you have in mind?"

"My place." It wasn't a question. "My car's in the lot down the street."

I nodded again, resigned. And because this was Logan and I couldn't run away no matter how scared I was or how much sense it made. "Okay."

"If I let you go, you promise not to run?" There was the barest hint of tease in his voice.

"Promise."

He grabbed my hand and pulled me out of the SUB to his car. We rode to his place in awkward silence. I had no idea how to break the ice. I kept marveling that he was Falcon26 and berating myself for not seeing it. Neither of us spoke as we entered his apartment. I was still carrying the balloon. Inside, I let it loose to hover in the air, symbolic, his heart unleashed.

The lights were on, but it was quiet. A bouquet of roses sat on the table next to a bottle of wine chilling in a bucket of ice.

"Zave and Collin are out for the night," Logan said.

I turned and stared at him. "You planned this." It was an accusation, not a question.

"Yeah, of course." He looked nervous, more nervous than I could remember seeing him. "I took a chance you'd come. You never answered. If you didn't know it was me, why didn't you give me an answer?"

"Because of you," I said without elaborating. "And because Falcon26 could have been anybody. You should see the way Tay drew him."

"Nerdy?"

"Yeah." I crossed my arms, keeping my distance from him though I ached to touch him. I walked to the living room and sat on the couch. "You can't win me back with flowers and wine. I'm not that shallow. You walked out on me. Ignored me. Yeah, I know I should have trusted you. But you should have been happy for me—I found my dad. The dad I've wanted my whole life. You don't know what it was like growing up with my mom—"

He paled, looking even more uncomfortable. "El, I have something to tell you, but you have to remember your promise to hear me out."

My heart practically stopped. "What?"

"You promised, remember?"

I was sitting in the middle of the sofa, but he managed to slide in next to me so close I could feel his body heat as his thigh brushed mine. I knotted my hands in my lap to keep from touching him.

"You'll listen to everything I have to say and then if you want to go, I'll take you home."

"I promised, okay?" I chewed on the inside of my lip and waited for him to continue.

"Okay, here goes—you're right. I was a complete douchebag for storming out like I did. I was hurt and upset and shocked. And jealous because I needed both of you—you and Jason. And I felt betrayed by both of you. You were mine and Jason was my mentor and now he's your dad and I couldn't talk to him about you. And, hell, what had I told him? And how could you have kept it all from me? What a dupe I was.

"I felt weak, like you couldn't trust me with the tough stuff in your life. Like I had so much shit going on that you didn't think I could be there for you."

"No, that's not true," I said. "I started lying and I got in too deep. I came to school looking for Jason. I got the job with him on purpose. I met you and fell for you, but I was afraid any relationship would interfere with what I was here to do. And then it turned out you worked for him. And I couldn't tell you until I knew for sure Jason was my dad and that I wanted to let Jason know I was his daughter.

"The lies and the half-truths spiraled out of control from there." I sniffed, fighting back tears. "And, okay, I admit, I didn't want to burden you with more junk. And I didn't know how to tell you in a way that you wouldn't feel betrayed." I stared in my lap.

He covered my hands with his. "I love you, El. I tried to stay away from you. I tried to forget you. But I couldn't. I tried to be your hero—"

"In a video game?" I shook my head and sniffed again. "By pretending to be someone else so you could spy on me?"

"No. In real life." He hesitated. "This is where you're going to freak out—I've been talking to your mom."

I felt faint. The room spun and I thought I might throw up. I tried to stand, but he wrapped his arms around me and held me in place.

"Listen to me, El. Let me explain. It's been killing me staying away from you. And seeing you hurting. When you started seeing other guys, I lost it. I had to act.

"When I came home that night I found out Jason was your dad, I had a letter from your mom."

"No!" I stared at him, waiting for full comprehension to sink in. "How could she know about you?" And then it hit me—the memory of Logan punching Schwartz out before the football game. "Schwartz! Damn him."

I took a deep breath. Schwartz, I bet he went running to my mommy. I even bet he slept with her. If she wanted him to. And she probably did.

"What did dear old mommy say?" A big part of me really didn't want to know.

Logan pressed his face against mine. "She wanted—wants—you back. And my help doing it. She was desperate to reconnect and beg for your forgiveness."

I snorted. "Right."

"I have the letter. I can show you." He took a deep breath.

"Don't bother. I'm sure she's very convincing." And then a new fear hit and my heart raced out of control. "Jason?"

Logan shook his head. "She has no idea. She doesn't know he's here or the real reason you chose this school.

"And then I got an idea. A crazy idea that I could lead her off your scent for a while. Feed her false information. Act like her ally and give you time to get to know your dad before she finds out and comes screaming in to ruin things. That's what you're worried about, right?"

I looked up at him, astounded. "Yes, but—"

"I couldn't tell you, El. You wouldn't go for it. And I realized something else—my relationship with Jason had changed now that he was your dad. Everything made sense—the way he didn't want to hear about my relationship with you. How he tried to steer the conversation away from personal details. How upset he got about my fight and how fast I drove and how I lose my patience.

"He likes me as a person, but as a boyfriend for his daughter, I'm not like bring-home-to-mom material." Logan spoke matter-of-factly, but there was a subtle undertone of hurt in his voice. "In fact, I suck."

"No, Logan—"

"Don't lie to me, El." He squeezed me. "We're past all that now and we both know the truth."

I hung my head.

"I didn't want to come between you and your dad. You needed time together to bond and figure things out. I was a complication in an already complicated situation. I'm damaged goods and I've done a lot of bad crap. But I stayed away and kept your mom off your back until I couldn't stand being away from you any more. Until I couldn't lose you for good. Until you blew me off for another guy.

"I graduate in a few months and then I'm gone, out of here. I'm selfish, but I couldn't blow my last chance with you. El? You're really quiet. What are you thinking?"

I was trying to take it all in—Logan hurting me to protect me. Logan keeping my mom at bay. "What do you think of Mom?"

He stared at me like he was measuring what he should say. Finally, he sighed. "She's beautiful, seductive, and deceitful, a lot like you."

I almost laughed through my tears, but his description of her caught me short. "You've met her." I fought back a surge of anger. "How did she arrange it?"

"It's not like you think," he said. "She ambushed me at SeaTac. I was on an interview trip. She caught me while I was in line for security."

I almost asked him how she knew he'd be there, but I stopped myself short again. I had to trust him. She was devious and frighteningly clever when she put her mind to something. "Did she hit on you?"

He didn't say anything.

"She did!" I swore beneath my breath, hoping and praying I'd heard the last of Logan's revelations.

"I'm immune to her charm. To everyone's but yours." He pressed his forehead to mine. "I'm desperate for you, El. *Desperate.*"

I reacted to the ragged edge in his voice. My whole body went tight with longing and desire. I'd missed him. So much.

"El?"

I was taking deep breaths, trying not to freak out. Trying to hang on to the remains of my self-control and not think about my mom and what her plans would be. About how she could ruin everything.

"Melissa's determined to come to campus and confront you. I can't hold her off forever. But I'll protect you. I swear it."

I nodded, feeling the heat from his fingers as he cupped my head. Wanting him. Wanting to cry and give way to emotions I couldn't name.

"I love you." His tone was low and seductive, pleading. "Take me back, El. We'll work things out."

I could barely speak. "No more secrets?"

"No more secrets." His lips brushed mine with a soft kiss, just the barest hint of lips touching, so tender it nearly broke my heart.

"I love you, too." I was lost in him. I returned his kiss, my lips moist and tender on his. When I parted my lips and his tongue darted in, my entire body tightened with wanting him.

I pulled away and slid into his lap with my legs straddling him, pushing him back against the sofa as I slid my hands beneath his shirt and pushed it up. His eyes went wide.

I couldn't stop myself from touching him. I ran my hands along the hard planes of his chest and slid his shirt over his head. He tossed it over the arm of the sofa as I took in the sight of him, hungry for him.

I bent down and slid my tongue into his navel, thrusting and circling before sliding it up his abs and chest and sucking on his nipples until he moaned. He pulled my shirt over my head and unhooked my bra, tossing them both to join his shirt on the floor.

"I've missed you, Logan." I bent to kiss him.

"Not as much as I've missed you, El." He cupped my butt, grabbed me around the waist, and stood as I wrapped my legs around him and kissed him. Passion like I'd never felt before welled inside me.

He carried me to the bedroom and kicked the door shut as I coiled around him, trying to meld myself into him, aching for him, every muscle tight with building need. My heart raced as he pulled back the covers and laid me on my back on the bed. As he braced over me, I knew what I wanted to do, what I was going to do. For the first time in my life, even fear was powerless to stop me. Logan Walker was the one.

"You're so beautiful." His voice was low and seductive. His eyes dilated in the dark.

As he reached for the zipper of my jeans, I blinked back tears of happiness. His fingers skimmed my bare skin and played around the edges of my bellybutton ring, scorching with their heat, teasing near the edges of my panties as I grew flushed and tight and wet. I wanted him so badly. I wanted him to want me badly, too. He unzipped my jeans slowly, tantalizing me with his restraint. Impatient, I kicked my heels off and shimmied out of my jeans before he'd finished unzipping them. I was determined to act before reason and logic and fear took over.

Our gazes locked. He grinned. "Eager?"

"Desperate." I felt flushed and tight in a way I'd never been before. I unzipped him and slid my hands inside the soft denim of his jeans, beneath his boxers to his bare skin. "These have to go." I slid them off and arched up to kiss him and press my tightly budded breasts against his bare chest.

He let out a ragged breath and slid his hands beneath my panties, finding the pulsing heat between my legs that flamed at his touch, and stroked me until I let out a gasp of pleasure.

He stared at me with heat shining in his eyes. "I want to make love to you, El. I want you so damned bad. I'll wear a double layer of condoms, triple even. And foam. Whatever you want."

I met his gaze and slid his hard dick between my legs and sighed as I rubbed against him. "Yes."

His stare turned to astonishment. He hesitated. "Yes?" His voice was excited and incredulous at the same time, like he couldn't believe his good luck.

"Yes."

"Yes to one condom or two?"

I traced his chest with the tip of my fingernail until goose bumps rose on his arms. I was on the pill, had been for years for other reasons, but I didn't tell him that. I still needed the reassurance of more. "One. Two defeats the purpose."

He rolled off me and reached into a drawer in his desk as I salivated over the sight of his naked backside. A guy should not be allowed to be so hot. Logan was way too easy on the eyes, and way too hard on my heart.

He pulled out a plastic bag and dumped the contents on the bed around me.

Boxes of condoms, tubes of foam, and an assortment of lubricants tumbled out. I stared at them in disbelief and then at him. "Confident you were going to get lucky tonight? Did you buy out the entire stock at the drugstore? I'd pay good money to see the look on the clerk's face when you bought all this."

He laughed and shook his head. "Then you'd be seeing a shitload of clerks. I bought this one tube, one box of condoms at a time. Every time I thought of you and wanted you and hoped."

"That's so sweet." I was really touched.

He tore open a box of condoms and spilled them onto the bed. "Ribbed, plain, lubricated, scented, spermicidal?"

I leaned over and kissed him as I picked one up without looking at it. "This one." I ripped the wrapper open and pulled the condom out. I cupped Logan's cheek and kissed him deeper as he eased me back on the bed again.

When he was braced over me, I grabbed his hard dick, perched the condom on the end and tried to roll it on. It should have been easy to do, but it took more skill than I had. I cursed myself for being inexperienced. "Guess I should have practiced on a banana."

"A banana isn't nearly hard enough. Practice on me." He covered my hand with his and expertly placed the condom. "You're cute, El, and damned sexy."

I eyed his dick, suddenly apprehensive at its size.

"Like what you see?" he asked.

"You're huge."

He smiled like I'd paid him the highest compliment and kissed me lightly. "Don't be scared. I'll be gentle." He grabbed a tube of lubricant and, still balancing over me, took off the lid, squirted some on his fingers, and rubbed it on me using gentle, seductive strokes. "This will help."

I was already tight and tingly, perched on the edge. I gasped as a warming sensation filled the cleft between my legs. "Traitor. That's warming gel."

He grinned and positioned himself between my legs, rubbing against me until I wanted release with Logan deep inside me.

"Now. Make love to me *now*, Logan."

He covered my mouth with his kiss and pushed just inside me. I gasped into his kiss, willing my body to let him in even as it resisted him. I wrapped my legs around his waist and pulled him deeper into me, feeling him opening me wide. To everything—love, lust, ache, need, pain. I felt his hesitation, conscious he was restraining himself and trying not to hurt me, trying to hang on. The slow progress only heightened my need and the pain.

He stroked my hair. "Are you okay?"

"Thrust deeper, Logan. Harder. Take me the way you want to." My voice broke and tears slid down my cheeks.

"You're so tight, El," he murmured. "I can't hold on long. You're pushing me to the edge."

"Push us both over," I whispered and ran my hands through his hair.

He let go of his restraint. I bit my lip to keep from crying out. He thrust deeper and deeper until he broke through a barrier of pain and virginity.

I was tight all around him. I tensed and he moaned. I realized in my inexperience that I could squeeze him and he liked it. I squeezed again and released and he thrust and the pleasure overrode the pain. I arched against him, blooming for him.

He thrust and thrust until the pleasure was so strong it needed release. And then waves of pleasure like I'd never felt before rocked through me. I cried out.

Logan thrust once more. "El!" He collapsed on me, gently, holding his full weight off me.

Neither of us spoke. I throbbed, feeling his bulk inside me. I was happy and sore, and though my body wanted to slim back to its virgin size, I didn't want him to pull out.

He held me for a moment and reached between us to hold the condom and pull out.

"Don't. Not yet," I said.

"I have to, El. Believe me, I'd like to stay inside you until I go small and grow large again. And then make love to you again. But if you don't want to chance an accident, I have to pull out."

I reluctantly nodded and let him go. He pulled me into the crook of his arm and tugged the covers up over us. "Are you okay?" He kissed the top of my head.

"I'm perfect." I stroked his chest. "And sore."

He laughed. "I love you, El."

"I love you, too."

He kissed me lightly and I knew I'd been right. Now that I'd made love with him, I'd want to do it again and again. And if I wasn't careful, I'd get reckless and make a mistake.

"Everything okay?" Logan asked.

"It's perfect. I was just thinking."

"About what?"

I almost said "the future." But that's a sure way to scare a guy off. Where was this all heading? There was still so much to face—my mom and the trial. I hoped we could weather it. I really did. Because I couldn't bear to lose Logan again. I pushed those anxious thoughts away. We'd make it somehow. I *knew* we would.

"You," I said. "I was thinking about you."

Don't miss the conclusion of Ellie and Logan's love story—*Reckless Together.*

Ellie's mom arrives to cause trouble. And, boy does she know how.

Reckless Together available early 2014

ABOUT THE AUTHOR

Gina Robinson lives in the Pacific Northwest with her husband and children. She was not a prankster in college, although she knows a good many people who were. They will remain nameless to protect the guilty.

She married her college sweetheart and has never forgotten that wonderful feeling of falling in love.

Most days she writes while wearing slippers, flip-flops, or tennis shoes, depending on the season. But she loves a great, sexy heel and has a closet full for special occasions.

Connect with Gina online at www.ginarobinson.com

www.ingramcontent.com/pod-product-compliance
Lightning Source LLC
Chambersburg PA
CBHW070738180626
46818CB00007B/2903